MW00879621

THE KINGDOM : I

# ALLIANCE

TYLER SVEC

Alliance

---



---



---

Cover Art courtesy of shutterstock.com
Cover Design by Tyler Svec
Interior Design by Tyler Svec

---

ISBN #9798850424671

# ALLIANCE

TYLER SVEC

# Foreword

It was twenty years ago that I started dabbling in writing. Nothing interesting, but it became a secret hobby of mine. It didn't take long for me to realize I was horrible at writing short stories. Often I would spend weeks, or a month or two writing longer stories and then as quickly as I finished them I would throw them in the trash and start a new one.

This story is the first story I started twenty years ago, but it has gone through many different forms and undergone many changes and rewrites from that of the original form so many years ago. Only elements of the original story remain.

The movie called *Dinotopia* was my initial inspiration to begin writing in the first place. Ever since seeing that movie, the idea of flying on huge creatures in some fantasy land had always been interesting to me. For years I worked and reworked on the idea, but still after many years the story was incomplete and lacking a bigger vision.

Years later, *The Chronicles of Narnia* became the inspiring force to complete the vision. The story was reworked into its second form, where there was a cabin that would lead the main character to another world and the adventure would begin as this person tried to adapt to living in another world.

The third version came a few years after that, bearing many elements of the original books but adding more to the world than had been originally been created. That version was ultimately published in 2011 under the title *Rise*.

Although *Rise* was much better than the previous versions, I now have a chance to republish the book over ten years later, and it has become the version that you are about to read.

Some of the beginning of this book is identical to that of the 2011 version. But as always happens with any re-write, it has been changed and added to.

Nonetheless, I am glad to say that a few scenes of this trilogy are from the original book written in 2001. I hope you enjoy reading this book, as much as I've enjoyed working on it all these years.

Tyler Svec

# 1

**ROY VAN DOREN** looked out on the beautiful mountainside as he drove through the lush, green landscape. He glanced in the rear-view mirror, seeing the boxes and packages piled high in the back of his old pickup truck. Today was a day to remember.

"You sure you have to go so far away?" his older brother, Geoffrey, had asked him as he was loading his things.

"Yes, I do," Roy had answered. "It's not that far."

"And five hundred miles is a small distance?"

"I know you might not understand, but I have to leave. I have to get out."

"I understand. I just don't approve," Geoffrey replied. "Mom and Dad had their faults, and I know their dysfunction affected too many things, but it seems like you're running from the only family you have left."

"That's not what I'm doing, okay?" Roy defended. "I just found a nice cabin and want to move there. Is that a crime?"

"No, it's not," Geoffrey replied. "We're the only family either of us have left . . . so come visit every now and then, alright?"

"I will," Roy had said as he climbed in his old red truck.

Three days later, those words still echoed in his mind, reminding him that he was now officially on his own. Nothing compared to smelling that long-awaited independence.

He loved his parents, but there was something that told him that he needed to get away, and he was well on his way to doing that. He had bought a small cabin in the middle of the Appalachian Mountains, nestled in an opening between several hills, with one of the most beautiful views that he had ever laid eyes on.

From the moment he had first seen the cabin, he had fallen in love with it, and it seemed nothing could keep him from getting it. The cabin itself had been abandoned for years and was in terrible shape; he had payed next to nothing for it. It might take some fixing, but he was good with his hands and would have it looking like a jewel in no time.

He cracked his window open and was greeted by the cool morning air. He took a deep breath, glad that he hadn't moved to the city like Geoffrey had a few years earlier. As a small charter pilot, Geoffrey had made a good life for himself and made a very nice living besides. Roy knew he would probably never come close to being as well off as his brother, but that didn't matter to him.

All his life he had watched his dad work without stopping, and Roy had been beside his dad as he passed away on that dark, cold morning. He would never forget hearing his dad had say, *"I wish I'd spent more time with you guys."* Roy found it ironic as he and Geoffrey had always come in second when presented with anything concerning making more money. However, his dad's sorrowful words had hit home in Roy's heart, and he had vowed that he was going to live his life differently.

He didn't exactly know how he was going to live differently, but he knew that if he put his mind to it, anything was possible.

He flipped the radio on, listening to the slow, sad, country songs. The music drowned out this thoughts and pushed the memories from his mind.

He focused on the twisting, pothole-filled road as he drove on.

He had only been up to look at the cabin one time before, and part of him wondered what it would look like this time. The picture he had seen when he was there was far different from the one the realtor had shown him in the file, but aside from it all, it was the same old, beat up cabin.

It was a nice cabin with a fantastic view, but there had been no explanation as to *why* it had been abandoned. The cabin inside looked as if someone had just picked up and left one day. The floor was dusty and dirty, and even some of the dishes were still in the sink.

He drove on, long into the night, struggling to push away the intruding thoughts of slumber. The radio sang another sad song, slowly lulling him into a light sleep.

His eyes closed, and his hands fell from the wheel as his truck went straight instead of navigating the turn. He was snapped awake and was brought back to the present as his truck crashed through the guardrail that had been put there to protect the vehicles from the one-hundred-foot drop that was immediately off to the side of the road.

He careened over it, and the back end of his truck was thrown up into the air, tipping the truck vertically as Roy looked down the face of the one-hundred-foot drop. The momentum carried his truck over the edge of the mountain, sending him racing towards the incline.

Roy closed his eyes and didn't think he'd ever open them again as he plummeted toward the mountainside. His truck crashed into the ground and was sent end over end, flipping and rolling violently down the mountain. His belongings were scattered and broken as the boxes were thrown out of the back of his truck.

The airbags on his truck deployed, and Roy was caught by his seat-belt as his truck rolled and flipped. The sound of crunching metal and breaking glass rang in his ears as the back end of his truck slammed to a stop into a tall oak tree. The tree had heavily damaged the back end of his truck.

He now sat unconscious in the driver's seat. The airbags had deflated, and the noise of the horn filled the valley far below the road. Smoke rose from under the hood of his truck, and a few bare wires dropped sparks onto the ground.

The sparks fell to the ground and ignited the pool of gasoline that had collected under his truck. The flames grew larger and began to lick at the outside of his truck, burning hotter and hotter. Roy was awakened by the smell of the smoke. He looked out his passenger side window and saw nothing but flames.

Completely awake now, he threw off his seat-belt and threw the door open. He jumped out of the truck, falling on the ground, and then quickly scrambling back to his feet and took off running. He only made it about ten feet away before his truck exploded.

The force of the explosion knocked him off his feet and sent him flailing to the ground as his truck was destroyed by an explosion that filled the night sky. He looked back at his truck as it burned. The flames and black, thick smoke billowed from the truck, rising to the dark night sky above.

He wondered how he would ever be able to get to his cabin now, and wondering whether any of his belongings has survived the crash. He limped up the hillside in the darkness, searching for anything that could be salvaged. His foot hit something on the ground, making him look down.

In the middle of a well worn path there was a lone, small, flashlight. Roy pondered the placement of the flashlight; it wasn't something he had had in his truck. He turned it on and shone it around the darkness, thankful for the light that someone had apparently lost.

*Someone's trash is someone else's treasure,* Roy thought.

He walked up the hillside, gathering some of his clothes and possessions that had been scattered and not broken during the crash and began walking back down the mountain. He shone his flashlight on the ground, lighting up his path, and then moved it to the left quickly and stopped. A gold flicker came up out of the brush.

He walked off the foot path that had been worn down during the years and then put his stuff on the ground, and continued walking up to the strange object. He knelt down to pick up the object and studied it carefully.

It was about a foot long, three inches wide, and a brilliant gold color. There were carvings that ran along the entire object. *I wonder what it's worth,* Roy thought. After a moment, he decided it was probably just gold plated and worthless, so he threw it back on the ground. He turned and made his way back to the path, grabbing his things as he went.

He kept walking and didn't notice a man drop out of a tree behind him and stand in the darkness watching Roy. The man walked over to where the gold object was and picked it up. He clipped it to his belt, and walked away into the darkness.

Roy walked down the hill the rest of the way, past his smoldering truck, picking up anything else that wasn't broken. He shone the light around him in the darkness, trying to get a picture of just where he was. He didn't recognize any of it but hoped he might see something familiar as he set off into the forest.

He walked through the lush forest that was deeply shaded and wandered along. It was thicker and darker than any he had ever seen, and it became more mysterious as the time wore on.

The forest became more and more silent, but Roy somehow found that comforting. A few animals here and there scurried in front of him, lost in the darkness.

He finally came out into a clearing and smiled to himself when his flashlight illuminated his cabin sitting peacefully in the middle of the valley. He hurried up to the front porch and breathed a sigh of relief. He'd made it.

He put the key in and turned the knob. The door noisily squeaked and groaned as it opened, welcoming Roy to the dark, cold cabin. He shone his flashlight around. Dust and cobwebs covered everything, as would be expected of a building that had been deserted for years.

He walked in and turned on a light switch that was just inside the door. The cabin might look like a disaster to most people, and any other time he would agree, but right now it was the best thing he had ever seen.

He gathered his few belongings and took them to one of the bedrooms on the main floor. There was an old bed and a dresser, but nothing else. The silence was strange to Roy, but to an extent he didn't mind. He had heard enough yelling and fighting in his childhood home.

Roy got all of his things put where he wanted them and then proceeded to build a fire in the fireplace at the center of the small living room. He uncovered all the furniture and slowly began to clean up the dusty space. An hour later, completely exhausted, he sat down in a chair next to the fire and closed his eyes and smiled. He had done it.

He was finally on his own; he was free of his family. It was a great feeling to finally be out on his own. He may not know quite what he was doing yet, but he would. This was the best day of his life.

He fell asleep by the fire, which slowly burned down until eventually it was reduced to a pile of coals.

The door slowly opened but didn't wake Roy. A fairly tall man with short brown hair stepped into the cabin. The man looked around the edge of the door, and saw Roy, and therefore did his best to not wake him. He came in the rest of the way and closed the door, gently clipping the gold cylinder to his belt again, knowing that it wasn't needed yet.

The man looked around at the cabin and noticed it was cleaner than it had been earlier in the day. The living room had been cleaned, while most of the cabin was still a mess. The man held out his hand and waved it through the air, and the downstairs was instantly cleaned, spotless.

He smiled and moved towards the staircase and climbed it, hoping the stairs wouldn't squeak as he did. He grabbed the handle of the door at the top of the stairs and pushed it open. The floor only squeaked lightly as the man walked inside the room and closed the door behind him.

Meanwhile, Roy was sound asleep, lost in his dreams as he sat next to the fire.

* * * *

The sounds of the birds chirping in the forest around the cabin were the first thing that came to Roy's ear. The morning air wound its way through the cracked window to the side of the fireplace. He stretched and groaned with a smile as he stood. He paused for a moment, feeling his leg, which no longer hurt as it had the night before.

He ran his hand along the mantle of the fireplace and began walking through the room to the kitchen to fix himself some breakfast. He stopped dead in his tracks as he looked at the kitchen in confusion.

The kitchen, as well as the rest of the house, was spotless. There was not one speck of dust or cobweb to be found in the entire cabin. He turned on the light, which showed everything was so spotless and shiny, he could see himself in all the appliances. He scratched his head in confusion as he slowly turned around in a small circle, looking at the cabin.

# ALLIANCE

*Must have been my imagination that this place was even dirty,* Roy thought with a smile. He turned toward the door to go outside and get some firewood from the stack that was on the left side of the house.

He walked along the cabin and then went around the corner to the woodpile that was stacked against the wall and stared at what was in the driveway. His old, beat-up truck sat in the driveway as if nothing had happened to it the night before.

He ran to the truck, opened the driver's side door, and looked inside. What was going on? His truck had been destroyed in the explosion the night before; how could this be possible? He pulled back the floor mat and looked at his name which he had scratched into the floor of his truck with a jackknife, confirming it was his.

He shut the door of the truck and moved to the back, which was nearly overflowing with all of his belongings that he hadn't been able to get last night. He stared in awe as he rummaged through some of his things, not finding any of it broken or even damaged. He shook his head and then closed his eyes. He opened them once more, hoping for the sake of sanity that his truck wouldn't be there. But when he opened his eyes it was still there.

He turned towards the woodpile, walked quickly to it, and started to grab a few pieces of wood. He stopped mid-motion, noticing his keys on the ground as though they had been dropped there by accident. He tried to make sense of everything as he shoved them deep into his pocket, and then focused in on a set of footprints next to where the keys were found.

The footprints were clear and seemed to be fairly new; they turned around the corner the way he had come. He grabbed a few more pieces of wood and followed the footprints around the corner of the cabin and up along the side until they stopped at the door. He opened the door and walked inside, putting the wood next to the fireplace and then going back to close the door.

He looked around the cabin and stopped at the staircase. For some strange reason, the footprints disappeared and then reappeared at the stairs, which were a good ten feet from the door. He walked over to the stairs, noticing that they weren't clean like the rest of the house. The footprints went up the stairs to the door at the top. He walked up and ran his hand along the rail, getting dust and cobwebs all over it.

He reached the top where the door was cracked open. He pushed it open farther, seeing that the footprints made their way inside. He walked inside, leaving the door wide open, and grabbed a baseball bat next to the landing on the stairs. He hoped he wouldn't have to use it, but he would if he had to.

He walked into the barren room, looking around and suddenly losing all feeling that he need the baseball bat. It was a fair-sized room with a high ceiling. The room was dead silent except for his own breathing, which was calm and steady.

He put the baseball bat down in one of the corners, walking along the edge of the room and running a hand along the wall. He came to a window and looked out, staring into a land he didn't recognize. The window was only three feet by three feet, but outside was a lush green forest. The trees and shrubs grew right up near the window, which showed no fog as the downstairs window had.

He turned and ran back toward the stairs, running outside to see what the weather was like. He opened the door immediately met by the same foggy air that had greeted him the first time. He slowly walked back up the stairs and into the room. He looked out the window again seeing the lush, green, fog-free forest, as he had before. He unlocked the window and gave in a jerk, opening it, and stuck his head out of the window.

The sky was clear and blue. Roy took in a big breath of the fresh mountain air. The forest was greener and far more beautiful than anything he had ever seen before. The air was light and easy to breath and seemed to welcome him. He pulled his head back in the room, closed the window, and then grabbed his head, trying to bring himself back to the real world.

*No wonder this house was abandoned,* Roy started to think, realizing that this was too weird to explain to anyone. He rubbed his neck and looked at the floor. The footsteps went right up the middle of the room to the far wall where they disappeared.

He paused in thought once he realized they seemed to go right through the wall. He reached out a finger and moved it toward the wall, relieved when his finger touched the wall and didn't go through it. *Thank goodness, I'm not going crazy,* Roy thought, taking one more step forward. He didn't hear the small click as he stepped on one of the floorboards.

A tremendous bang filled the room as the staircase door swung itself shut. Roy whirled around and ran toward the door trying to pull it open but found the door stuck. He tried to turn the knob but couldn't. Instead he only succeeded in rubbing his hand raw. He turned back around wondering what he was going to do now that he was locked in the upstairs of his own house.

He turned around and shut his eyes as he sat down on the hard floor and laid his head up against the wall. He rolled his eyes, wondering what was happening now. He glanced across the room to where the footprints led and saw a door in the wall where there hadn't been one before.

The door was large and made entirely of wood with a fancy golden handle on it. He stood up and brushed the dust off him as he made his way over to the strange door. He studied the door looking for any sign that all of this might be a trick. The door seemed to have built itself into the wall, showing no signs that it had been previously put there.

He reached for the handle, half expecting the door to blow up or not even be there when his hand reached it. He paused, thinking about all the strange things that had happened.

Finally, with much reluctance, he grabbed the handle and turned it. The door easily swung open. Before him, just outside the door, was a land unlike any he had ever seen. Green trees and lush forests lay before his eyes. A light breeze blew through the trees, and the sky was blue and clear, giving him a sense of peace and security that he didn't expect to feel.

Birds chirped in the forest all around him. He took a step out of the door and into the green forest that waited for him. It was full of life and ready to be explored. He turned and looked at the forest, which reached far above him. Wild flowers and plants grew on the forest floor; small animals scurried along the ground. Roy breathed in the strangely refreshing air, feeling energized and restored.

He looked back to where the door and his cabin had been and realized it wasn't there anymore. *What's going on here?* Roy asked himself, walking to the clearing where his cabin and the door should have been. He frantically brushed aside the sticks and leaves, wondering where it had gone.

*This is just great,* Roy lamented. He had only stepped out five feet from the door, and now the door wasn't even there! There had to be an explanation. He searched the area for several minutes and pondered his predicament for another few minutes until finally he let his eyes rest on the small worn footpath that wound its way through the hills. He breathed deeply, a new energy coming to him. He stood and considered his options one more time. Concluding there was no better option at the moment, he started down the path in front of him.

# 2

**ROY LAZILY WALKED** through the rolling mountainside, trying to make the best of this unusual situation. The path meandered through the maze of trees, appearing at times to have no clear direction as to where it was going.

The sun was right above him, yet he didn't get uncomfortably hot. The sky only seemed to become clearer. The air was clear and refreshing as he drew in a nice deep breath of the crisp mountain air, not remembering a time when he had breathed air so fresh.

Even the breeze seemed to become more refreshing as it passed through the forest. He couldn't help but let a smile stretch across his face. He didn't know why he was feeling this good, but at the moment he didn't care. He felt an unexplained desire to keep pressing forward.

This place seemed to be perfect.

He walked for hours not having a clue where he was going, and to an extent not caring. Still as much as he was enjoying himself, as one hour turned into another, he did find it strange that he hadn't seen any roads or any signs that a person or two might be nearby. The land was as silent as a tomb. Yet the farther he went the more he enjoyed it, smiling from ear to ear as he eagerly explored this new land.

The path eventually turned down a steep embankment, and he followed the path, practically sliding down the embankment because of how steep it was. He regained his footing when he came to a small landing twenty or thirty feet below. The path turned and continued on its way to his right. He started following the path again but stopped when he spotted a large opening in the side of the hill.

He walked up to the opening in the hill, soon realizing that it was an old cave. He ran his hand along the rock to either side of it, taking notice of the carvings in the rock along the side. They were carvings of things he didn't recognize, and he quickly began wondering what they meant.

He stopped mid-motion as he heard talking from inside the cave. He froze, not sure what to do. Should he run? Should he see if they were friendly? If they weren't, what would they do to him? He sighed heavily wondering what else this day had in store as he listened to what the voices were saying to each other.

"You ready for this?" one of the voices asked; the voice was fairly deep.

"Oh yeah, let's blow this sucker and have some fun," the other voice replied. This voice was a little higher in pitch.

"Not until you say the magic words," the deep voice told the other one. Roy looked into the darkness, straining his eyes, hoping to see the people in the cave.

"All right. I'll say the magic words as long as we both fire our bows as soon as I say them."

"Deal, and then we run like we're being chased by twenty thousand Hentar," the deep voice replied with a laugh as the other voice joined in. Roy just shook his head, not having a clue what they were talking about or what they were doing.

"Ready?" the higher pitched voice asked. "Let's boogity!" the sound of arrows being loosed from a bow reached Roy's ears as two guys came running around the corner, screaming as explosions ripped through the cave and filled it with fire.

"Run!" the higher pitched voice yelled at Roy, who was standing there dumbfounded. They all screamed and ran, jumping out of the cave and down another embankment as the explosions consumed the entire cave and sent fire shooting out the cave entrance. They all crashed on the ground and rolled further down the embankment, finally coming to a stop as they slid down the hill.

"Oops," the deeper voice replied as the top of the cave exploded and sent chunks of rock and fire flying through the air, many of them hurtling in their direction. They covered themselves as the rocks crashed into the ground and trees around them. When finally the smoke cleared, the two men started laughing.

"Yeehaw!" the higher voice said, high-fiving the other one and slapping Roy on the back.

"Now that was fun; let's do the other one!" the deeper voice said to the other person. Roy just tried to imagine how crazy these people were if this is what they did for fun.

"No, Cyrus, we can't do that. We told Abby she could do that one herself," the man with the higher voice replied. If he had been standing, he would've been about six feet tall with longer brown hair. The guy with the deeper voice, Cyrus, was a little shorter, standing about five foot nine with longer black hair that came down to his neck.

"How'd you like that, buddy old boy?" Cyrus asked, slapping Roy on the back. Roy just sat there speechless for a moment.

"Who are you?" Roy asked; they just started laughing again.

"Forgive us," the man with the higher voice said. "My name's Alexander Reno, and this is my brother, Cyrus. We have a sister around here somewhere."

"Man, that was fun," Cyrus stated, looking up to the cave opening where a small pillar of smoke was still rising.

"You have a weird sense of what's fun," Roy replied as they started laughing again.

"You're darn right we have a strange sense of what's fun; but hey, life's never boring." They both looked around. "Where did Abby get to?"

Another cry was heard in the forest as a woman came jumping over the edge of the hill as another explosion came from a cave directly behind them. Alexander and Cyrus pumped their fists and cheered as she landed on the ground near them, the mouth of the cave engulfed in flames, sending rock and smoke through the air. The smoke cleared, and the woman came over and high-fived them and celebrated.

"Good job, sis!" Alexander exclaimed as she sat down on the ground next to them. "Good to see you came out alive."

"Any more caves we can do this to?" Abby asked.

"Not around here," Cyrus answered.

"Why did you guys do that?" Roy asked, completely lost.

"For fun," Alexander answered. "And that was definitely fun."

"Oh, yeah. You know it," the woman replied. She was a slim, attractive woman standing close to six feet tall with long brown hair. She appeared as though she was going to speak but then stopped in mid-sentence when she looked at Roy. "Who is this?" she asked the others.

"That's a very good question," Alexander said turning to face Roy. "Sorry we scared the crap out of you, but we should probably learn your name."

"My name's Roy Van Doren," Roy told them; they screwed up their face at his last name, and Roy couldn't help but wonder what was going to happen next.

"Van Doren?" Alexander pondered, thinking aloud. "I can't say I've heard of that name before. Are you from around here?"

# ALLIANCE

"Well, that depends on where *here* is," Roy started, a little nervous about talking to complete strangers. "If *here* is the Appalachian Mountains in Vermont, then I know where I am."

"Are you drunk or something?" the woman asked.

"Abby! Talk about an opening line. What kind of a question is that?" Cyrus asked, shaking his head.

"Sorry! But have you ever heard of the Appalachian Mountains, let alone Vermont?" Abby argued; Alexander and Cyrus looked defeated.

"Well, no. I haven't heard of them, but that doesn't mean he's drunk," Alexander replied turning to Roy. "Sorry...anyway, this is our sister, Abigail; we call her Abby. She's always been known to say off-the-wall things like that."

"I'm almost afraid to ask why," Roy stated. Cyrus smiled.

"They're twins and it's my theory that they both have a few screws loose. However, in the case of Abby, ever since she was a little girl she's had a little problem with the filter between her head and her mouth. The problem being that she doesn't use it. She gets her own punishment for it though; she usually gets herself into all sorts of trouble,"

"Don't let my brothers fool you," Abby replied. "I don't bite that much. And I certainly *try* to be civil, even if I fail."

"Pleasure to meet you," Roy greeted, holding a hand out for her to shake. She shook it warmly, acting more like a lady than she had up to that point. "So what were you guys doing exactly?"

"We were . . . uh . . . just doing a little bit of archaeology," Abby replied. They all chuckled.

"Archaeology. Right!" Cyrus exclaimed. Roy just couldn't help but smile at this strange group of people.

"You are the first archaeologists I've run into that use dynamite," Roy replied; they instantly stopped laughing and just smiled awkwardly as they gave him blank looks.

"Just what exactly is dynamite?" Abby asked.

"You don't know what dynamite is?" Roy asked. They shook their heads no, making him more confused than ever. "Well, if you didn't use dynamite, how did you make those explosions?"

"How did we make those explosions? What rock have you been living under?" Abby asked. She turned to the others. "Idiot!"

"Abigail Vivian Reno! Stop calling this guy . . . Roy, an idiot," Alexander exclaimed. Cyrus turned to Roy.

"Middle name; she's in trouble," Cyrus replied. Roy smiled weakly.

"He doesn't even know how we made the explosions," Abby argued.

"That's why we tell him, and then he knows," Alexander said turning back to Roy, who was shaking his head; he really was in the nut house. "We have these special arrows for our bows that explode when they hit something other than people. They're called Tantine Arrows."

"You expect me to believe that?" Roy asked. "That's just not possible." Cyrus was going to argue and speak up, but Abby stopped him with a hand.

"Allow me," Abby said grabbing Alexander's bow and fitting an arrow, Roy couldn't help but cringe as she payed no attention to where she was aiming. She fired the arrow, sending Roy into a panic as the arrow flew just over his head and behind them. It struck a tree and exploded, obliterating the trunk of the massive tree. They all ran and took cover as splinters of wood went flying.

"Roy, we'd better get out of here," Alexander said, yanking him off the ground. They took off running through the forest as the large tree began to fall toward them. They scrambled up the hill and out of the way with inches to spare as the tree crashed into the valley and sent sticks and branches flying everywhere.

"I admit, that was not my brightest moment," Abby said when the dust had settled. “But no one can deny that was really cool!”

“Abby, I think you've had a little too much fun today,” Alexander replied, taking the bow from her. Roy just sat in awe, not knowing what to say; finally after a moment, he spoke.

“Where am I?” Roy asked, almost afraid to know. At this point he knew it wasn't possible to be any place he would recognize.

“You, my friend, are in the region of Evar, and, let me guess, you've never heard of that either?” Cyrus said. Roy just nodded. “Man, I'm a genius.”

“Who told you that?” Abby asked, getting a round of laughter out of them all. “Well, I guess if you're not drunk and you don't know where you are, that must mean you're new around these parts. So consider this your official welcome.”

“Thank you,” Roy said, not sure how to take Abby, but so far not liking her too much.

“Hey! You know what? He might be one of those off-worlders,” Alexander said.

“Off-worlder?” Roy asked.

“Yeah, a number of years ago, there was a guy by the name of John Dubby who claimed he had been checking out an upstairs room in his cabin and somehow showed up here,” Cyrus replied.

“What happened to him?” Roy asked.

“He lived a normal life here, and eventually people just forgot that he was even an off-worlder,” Abby replied.

“I've always heard of off-worlders, but I've never gotten to meet one,” Alexander said, standing and helping Roy up.

“You mean there's been more?” Roy asked.

“Yeah, over the past two thousand years there's been a few of your kind. Not many, but a few,” Cyrus answered. They all started walking back up the hill they had come down and found the path they had started on.

"So what happens now? I mean, apparently I don't know squat about this place," Roy pointed out; they all nodded in agreement and then looked at each other with looks of confusion on their faces.

"For now, I guess just tag along with us; we've got to get back home before the sun sets or else our parents are going to kill us," Alexander said motioning for Roy to start walking with them through the forest. "Once we get home we'll ask Mom and Dad what to do with you."

He just nodded and went along with what they told him as they walked, talking and laughing through the forest. The mood had changed since he had arrived to one that was even lighter and more cheerful, or uplifting, than when he had first stepped into this strange world.

They walked in silence for a while, allowing Roy time to study each of the three people he was with a little closer. He fell in behind Alexander and Abby, walking next to Cyrus just listening to them banter. For being related, they sure seemed to get along well in this strange land.

He looked at Abby as she turned to talk to him as she had several times before. He tried to ignore her for the most part. The other two seemed a little more level headed than she was. Abby was a little different from the rest of them, making him wonder if they were really a family.

Cyrus and Alexander did their best to make Roy feel comfortable in a land that was all new to him. It was a little strange for Roy as they talked about things he had never heard about, but he tried his best to pick up on it as he got farther and farther away from where he had first come to the this.

They walked for a good half hour through the woods until they came to a large hill that rose high in front of them. Here the path split and went in two different directions. One went right up the hill while the other one seemed to go around the hill and wandered off to the left.

There was an old wooden sign sticking in the ground with two planks of wood crudely nailed to it. The sign was old and worn as each wood plank pointed in two different directions following the different paths that lay ahead of them. The one that pointed up the hill had 'G*rondish Valley'* written in black ink on the wooden plank while the other one had '*Eden'* written on it.

"I wonder which way we should go?" Cyrus asked sarcastically.

"See that we live in Eden, I figure we should go that way," Abby replied.

"I always knew you were my brightest student," Alexander commented with a slight laugh as Abby smacked him in the side.

"I'm your only student," Abby told him.

"Well, that automatically makes you the brightest," Alexander replied.

They turned down the path that meandered to the left toward Eden and started walking again through the ever peaceful forest that surrounded them. The birds sang, and the squirrels scurried along the ground, running just a few feet in front of them. The sun slowly sank in the sky, creating a beautiful sunset.

The light grew dim as they talked with each other until a noise was heard from behind them. They all turned to see a man with a horse and cart coming up the trail. They got off to the side of the road, making way for the man who stopped right next to them.

"Can I give you folks a lift anywhere?" the man atop the cart asked with a warm smile. They told the man where they needed to go, and they climbed on the back of his cart; after several hours of walking they were grateful for the ride.

Roy was taken aback by the attitude of the stranger who had offered to give them a ride. He knew back in the real world you would be hard pressed to find someone to help you out as this man had so generously offered. He found this place nice and peaceful and unlike anything he would ever experience back at home.

The longer he stayed here and talked with the people that he had met, the more he was beginning to not want to go back. He smiled, looking around at his newfound friends.

With the exception of Abby, he had taken to liking everyone he had met. He looked at Abby as she and Alexander talked and laughed. He wasn't quite sure how to read her yet, but there was one thing he had figured out for certain . . . she was a lunatic.

He shook his head knowing that if he ever wanted to settle down with a family, there would be no way on earth that he would ever want his wife to be anything like Abby was. They were as different as night and day. He watched the landscape go by wishing this moment, this feeling, could last forever.

They rode on for a few more minutes until they came out into a clearing in the forest. The clearing was completely bare, resembling more of a desert than the forest landscape that surrounded them. A house appeared on the horizon, smaller at first but then growing into a full-blown house size the closer they got.

A rough wooden fence surrounded the house, running against the trees that were a good quarter mile in the distance on each side of the house. Alexander motioned for the man to stop, and they climbed off and onto the dark, desert-like ground. The house was fixed up with some flowers that grew just outside the main fence.

"Thanks for the ride, my friend," Alexander told the man on top of the cart. The man smiled.

"It's no bother at all," the man replied waving at them as he pulled away and was soon against lost into the brush and forest that they had come out of.

"So what do I do now?" Roy asked, not sure if it was polite for him to just walk in with them.

# ALLIANCE

"I imagine you can stay with us for the night, and then we'll have to take you to the capital tomorrow and get you registered and all that lovely junk," Cyrus said as they walked through the opening in the fence. The ground was hard and they easily kicked up dust as they made their way to the house.

A few small lanterns were lit at the front of the house. Their light flickered in the darkness as they walked up to the front door. They proceeded to go inside with Abby leading the way. Inside, the house was larger than it appeared from the outside, opening up into a huge living room that resembled the layout of his own.

They all entered into the house, Abby being the first and Alexander being the last. Roy came through the door, not knowing what to do as two people, probably their parents, came down the stairs to greet them. They looked over each of the kids and scowled at them and then showed a lighter face when they saw Roy.

"You guys are late," their mom said, not looking all too thrilled.

"We tried to be on time," Abby explained. "but you know, we got stopped when the freak arrived."

"Abigail!" Alexander scolded.

"All right. I guess *freak* was a little harsh," Abby admitted.

"You think?" Cyrus replied.

"You three weren't by any chance blowing caves and seeking thrills today were you?" their dad asked.

"Of course not, Dad. What would make you think we would do a thing like that?" Abby asked, trying to act innocent and clearly not convincing her father.

"Well, it's a little obvious when you've got the bows in your hands," their mom replied pointing to the bow in Abby's hand. Abby just smiled dumbly.

"Oops," Abby replied; her dad shook his head and half chuckled.

"Oops is right," her dad replied holding out his hand to Abby. She handed over the bow. "I still don't understand where you get these arrows, because they are illegal. Plus, whenever you're late, you've been blowing caves. How many times do we have to tell you not to do that?"

"One more apparently," Alexander said, getting smiles and chuckles out of all of them. Their mom and dad moved down the line until they came to Roy and then stopped.

"So who is this, and what cave did you blast him out of?" their dad asked. Roy just smiled.

"This is Roy Van Doren," Cyrus replied. "We're not really sure where he's from; we think he's an off-worlder. I don't think we blasted him out of any cave."

"No, I think I would've remembered that," Roy replied, trying to keep things light.

"An off-worlder, eh?" their dad asked. They all nodded as Roy grew more nervous by the second, wondering what was going to happen now. "Well, Roy, I welcome you to our home. I'm Victor, and this is my wife, Norah. I take it you already met the kids."

"Yeah, I guess you could say that," Roy said, shaking both their hands shyly as they all made their way over to the fireplace and sat down. "I don't mean to impose, but what am I supposed to do now?"

"I'm not entirely sure," Victor answered, sitting back and thinking for a moment. "I've never met an off-worlder before; I've only ever heard of them, but the best I can figure is that someone will have to take you to Sayatta. It's the Capital city, currently. You can stay with us for the night."

"Thank you, Mr. Reno," Roy said. They had no idea how thankful he was to finally have figured something out.

"Please, just call me Victor; you'll probably have to be 'adopted' by us in order to skip through a bunch of questions and paper work, which can be such a hassle. How old are you?"

"Eighteen, almost nineteen," Roy answered.

"Well, what a coincidence," Norah concluded. Roy just gave them a look of slight confusion. "What I mean is that the kids are that age, save Cyrus who is a few years older, and they'll all be joining the Hentar Academy in a few days. I don't see why you couldn't do that same." Roy tried to understand what she had been talking about, but came up short.

"Sounds like a plan," Roy concluded. Not like he had anything better to do.

"Can we offer you anything to eat or drink?" Norah asked him with a warm smile, seeming to have the same selfless attitude as the man who had offered them a ride.

"That would be great, thank you," Roy answered as he sat down with them at the table and chairs that were just to the side of the stairs. He breathed a sigh of relief, comforted that at least the people he was with appeared to like him. "So what is this Hentar Academy anyway?"

"Man, are you a complete idiot?" Abby asked. Alexander's jaw dropped open.

"Abigail!" her mother scolded as she and Victor came toward them, each with two bowls of hot soup.

"She's been like this all day," Alexander said. Victor and Norah handed them bowls of soup before sitting down at either end of the table.

"Abby, just because he's not from around here doesn't mean he's an idiot," Victor pointed out, holding up a hand to silence Abby, who was ready to argue about it. "I'm sure there's just as much that we don't understand about his world."

"Yeah, right," Abby said. Roy had to fight the urge to laugh.

"Abigail!" her mother scolded again as Roy held up a hand to speak.

"It's okay, Mrs. Reno. To be honest, I find her quite amusing," Roy stated, getting a comical look from Abby.

"You're finding something amusing here?" Abby asked. He couldn't help but laugh.

"Yes, I am," he declared. "You're definitely not afraid to speak your mind."

"Thank you," Abby replied.

"That's not necessarily a good thing," Roy pointed out.

*"'That's not necessarily a good thing,'"* Abby mocked with her mouth full of soup. "What's that supposed to mean?"

"I'm saying that people who don't think before they speak have a tendency to get themselves into trouble," Roy answered.

"I had no idea," Abby replied, her words once again dripping with sarcasm. "Are you saying I don't think?"

"That's not what I said-"

"Yes, you did. You probably think I'm one of those bubble-headed idiots from the far territory of Rogna or something like that."

"I've never even heard of Rogna," Roy pointed out as he and Abby kept on arguing and didn't even notice that everyone else was trying not to laugh at them.

"Looks like tonight we get dinner and a show!" Cyrus stated laughing. Victor just looked across the table at Norah who smiled and winked before motioning that it was his turn to stop the argument. He raised his hand up to stop them, but it didn't even faze Abby or Roy for a second. He brought his hand down hard on the table. Instantly they both turned and looked at Victor and flashed innocent smiles.

"Are you two done?" Norah asked them.

"Not really," Abby answered.

"I sure hope you are," Alexander said, pointing to their bowls of soup.

"Better eat before your soup gets cold." Abby and Roy smiled innocently as they both picked up the rather unusual spoon and started to eat. A look of confusion came across Alexander's face as he stopped eating.

"Abby, where exactly is Rogna?" Alexander asked. Abby, who had just put a spoonful of hot soup in her mouth, burst into laughter. In the process, the soup in her mouth was sprayed onto Roy's face. Roy just sat there with soup running down his face, unable to stifle a laugh and a smile. Abby was laughing hysterically.

"Can't say I expected that," Roy finally replied, finding more humor in the situation than he wanted to.

"You can say that again," Norah said, handing him a towel to wipe off with.

"You know," Roy started as he wiped off his face, "they say giving is better than receiving. However in this situation I don't think either one is a winner." They chuckled at Roy, who couldn't hide a smile and pointed at Abby, who was laughing so hard tears were rolling down her cheeks.

"Abby, do you mind if I ask just what was so funny?" Victor asked. Abby finally stopped laughing but appeared to be struggling at it.

"Rogna doesn't exist," Abby finally managed before losing it again. "I made the whole thing up!" Roy smiled.

"You may have gotten me this time, Abby, but next time this foreigner won't be fooled so easily," Roy told her, finishing the last of his soup.

"However, I daresay that if there was a Rogna with bubble-headed idiots, Abby would fit right in, eh?" Cyrus said as they all laughed.

"Cyrus, as funny as that was, it was a little mean," Norah told him.

"It's funny though, I'll give you that," Victor said, laughing and turning to face Norah, who just gave him a look. Victor immediately stopped laughing and turned back to the kids.

"Well," Norah told them, "You kids should probably get to bed if you're going to travel to Sayatta and back tomorrow to get Roy registered. You're going to have a full day." They all cleared the table and then headed upstairs. Roy was put in Alexander's room for the night.

He took a spot on the floor and went to sleep wondering if he would wake up in his cabin. He wasn't getting his hopes up but as long as tomorrow was more straight forward than today, he would be all right. Finally, he drifted asleep.

# 3

**THE SOUND OF BIRDS** chirping outside the window was the first thing that Roy heard the next morning as he rolled onto his back. He opened his eyes with a glimmer of hope that he might wake up in his own cabin. His eyes focused and brought to him the ceiling above that was not his own, quickly dousing all those hopes.

He stretched and moaned as he lay on the hardwood floor. To one side of him was a wall, and to the other side was Alexander's bed. Alexander had offered to take the floor the night before, but Roy had insisted that he would, saying that he could sleep anywhere.

Roy lay on the floor looking at the unfamiliar surroundings that were all around him, noticing the unusual amount of woodwork that had been put into all the furniture. He smiled knowing that he was the first in his family to ever see anything like this and was suddenly filled with a curiosity and a hunger to learn more about this new world.

Roy looked up again and instantly went into panic mode. Alexander had woken up and had proceeded to get out of bed. Roy didn't have time to say anything as Alexander's feet met his stomach. Roy groaned in pain as Alexander noticed what had happened.

Alexander quickly moved forward but lost his balance, thumping into the wall and then tripped as he backed up and fell once again onto Roy.

Roy groaned, pinned to the ground with Alexander on top of him, too dazed to even try to do anything. Alexander finally got up, holding his head, which had been the first thing to hit against the wall.

“Sleep good?” Alexander asked, flashing an innocent smile. Roy groaned and sat up.

“Oh, yeah, I just love being impaled by someone's foot first thing in the morning.”

“Then you're in the right place,” Alexander replied. “Sorry about that. I'm not used to having someone else in the room with me.”

“I'm alive, so you're forgiven,” Roy told him as they both climbed up off the floor and headed for the door. “So what's for breakfast?”

Even as he finished the question, the door that they were standing in front of was flung open. It hit both of them in the head, making them stumble backwards, tripping and falling on the floor. Abby peeked her head in and around the door, spotting the two of them on the floor.

“Good morning, sleepy heads,” Abby greeted them, a little too peppy for Roy at the moment. “Why are you on the floor?”

“We like the view,” Roy answered, pointing at the ceiling.

“That's odd,” Abby stated. “Anyway, Mom wanted me to tell you that Cyrus isn't coming with us today; he's got to stay and help harvest the Gonshoesas.”

“Glad we don't have to do that,” Alexander replied. “With Cyrus out of the picture are we skipping out on registering for the Hentar Academy?”

“That's my plan. Breakfast is ready when you want it,” Abby told them. “That is if you ever get tired of looking at the ceiling.” She closed the door, leaving them sitting on the floor. Roy looked at Alexander and half smiled as they stood up.

“Do you mind if I say that your sister is one of the strangest people I've ever met?”

"Not at all," Alexander answered with a smile. "I already think that . . . and I've lived with her my whole life."

"So what is the Hentar Academy, and why don't either of you want to go there?" Roy asked. He had only started to feel as if he shouldn't go to the Hentar Academy a couple minutes before he had fallen asleep, but even so the feeling seemed to be growing. He was relieved to find he wasn't the only one feeling that way.

"Well, I guess you should know," Alexander started. "The Hentar Academy is a special school owned by the Alliance, which is our form of government, the leaders as it were. It's very hard to get into; they choose only the best to become the high up officials called Hentar Knights."

"Hentar Knights?"

"Yeah, they're kind of the elite police. They take commands from only one person, and that's the king himself. That's what *almost* every kid our age dreams of becoming," Alexander explained.

"But you don't?" Roy asked back.

"No. Abby and I have a feeling that there's something else behind the Alliance, something dark and evil. The title 'Hentarian' doesn't sound good to us."

"What is it that you think is wrong with the Alliance? I mean, they're in charge, aren't they?"

"Yes, they're in charge, but there's just something inside Abby and me saying that there's something else, and we shouldn't fall into the same traps that everyone else has . . . I don't know how else to say it."

"Is there anything else out there?" Roy asked, curious.

"There are several others, but they're all affiliated with the Alliance. If there's any other options besides those, I don't know. Abby and I are hoping to look for some other options when we take you to register today. Roy, there is one thing you must do," Alexander started. "Abby and I can't choose for you what you want to do. If you want to come with us, that's fine; if you want to join the Alliance, that's fine too."

Roy sat in silence for a minute. "I want to come with you. I really don't know what else to do at this point, and you guys have been good enough to me already. So count me in."

"Welcome to the club," Alexander said, shaking his hand and smiling. "It's a small club, but if we're lucky, we'll find what we're looking for."

They both got up and changed before making their way downstairs. Everyone else was already out of bed. Abby sat at the table eating her breakfast and stealing a glance at Roy when he wasn't looking. Cyrus and Victor made their way outside into the calm morning, leaving only Abby and Norah to eat with them.

They sat down, and Roy couldn't help but smile and hold back a chuckle as he sat across from Abby again. He picked up the fork and slowly began eating his plate of food that was already waiting for him.

"You're not going to spit any of that food in my face, are you?" Roy asked.

"No, I only do that the first time a new person eats with us," Abby answered with a smile and a wink.

"You boys sleep good last night?" Norah asked, sitting down at her spot at the head of the table.

"Yeah. I slept like a log, a little sore, though. Mostly due to the fact that I was stepped on by Alexander when I woke up."

"Nice way to treat our guest," Norah scolded.

"Nothing permanent or on purpose, mom," Alexander replied.

"Too bad," Abby commented. Expecting everyone to give her a hard time, she held up a hand. "I'm just kidding. However, on another note, I heard some pretty interesting noises coming from Alexander's room last night."

"What was it?" Roy asked, wondering if yet another dig at him was headed his way.

"I could be wrong, but I think it was you snoring," Abby answered.

"No, it couldn't be," Roy said. "I don't snore."

"Yes, you do! Besides, if you're asleep, you can't know whether you snore or not. If you really don't snore than you must have a propeller up your nose."

"I suppose that's a possibility," Roy concluded, getting a laugh out of all of them. They talked and laughed as they ate the breakfast that had been prepared for them before they got ready to leave for the day. They packed a bag of food and then stepped outside. The others started walking while Roy looked around and stood expectantly.

"Are we waiting for something in particular?"

"Uh . . . aren't we going to get in a car?"

"A car?" Abby asked. She looked at Alexander. "Have you heard of a car before?"

"No. Can't say I have. I've heard of a Cariby . . . but we don't have one of those."

"We were just going to walk."

"Walking, right! Got it!" Roy said.

They started back into the woods following the path that they had been on yesterday. Despite everything that had happened to him he was actually enjoying this new strange world he found himself in. Even though he apparently had a lot to still learn, for the moment he was able to easily forget his past and focus on life here and not worry about getting back to the cabin.

He had never really been accepted by anybody, especially strangers. Now, though he had two people who had taken him in without a moment's thought and apparently didn't have any opposition to him staying for a while. Roy knew that people in his world would never act like they had here, which was unfortunate because Roy knew there were people back home that just needed a friend.

Morning faded as they walked further than Roy had ever walked in his life. The lush green forest was far overhead, and overall, it didn't feel as though they were in any kind of hurry. They heard a slight stir behind them and glanced at a small wagon with only two wheels coming toward them. A creature that Roy didn't recognize was pulling the cart.

They stepped off to the side of the trail that wound through the woods and waited for the man to pass by them before continuing any farther. To Roy's surprise, the man atop the cart pulled back on the reins and spoke a strange word. The creature pulling the cart instantly came to a stop.

"Would you by chance need a lift anywhere?" the man asked. The man, if he had been standing, would have been of middle height with longer brown hair. He had blue eyes that almost seemed to pop right off his face, and he appeared to be in his forties, with a few wrinkles and lines on his face, and his hands were rough and calloused. A strange sensation came over all three of them.

"You'd actually give us a lift somewhere?" Roy asked.

"Why, of course I would. Is that not the courteous thing to do?" the man asked.

"Well, yes, it is, and you must forgive me. I'm not exactly from around here," Roy replied as they all climbed on top of the cart.

"Not from around here, eh?" the man asked, now with a hint of confusion in his voice. "And where exactly are you from?"

"I'm from Vermont," Roy answered as they all took their seats behind him.

"Vermont? You must be an off-worlder."

"You mean you've actually heard of Vermont?" Alexander asked.

"Well, of course I've heard of it! Not much I'm afraid, but my father was raised there before he ended up here on accident," the man answered.

"Your father was . . ."

"His name was Robert Givilray. Before that, if my memory serves me correctly, there was a man named John Dubby who was also from your world. I inherited my mother's last name, Altranus, when I was born, but that's beside the point."

*Robert Givilray?* Roy asked himself. *I've heard that name somewhere before...where have I heard that name? Robert Givilray was the name of the guy who abandoned the cabin years ago!*

"I'm sorry if I appear rude, but who are you?" Abby asked; the man smiled.

"Forgive me. My name is Gideon Altranus, and your names are?"

"My name's Roy Van Doren and these are the people who put me up, Abby and Alexander Reno."

"It's a pleasure to meet you all," Gideon said. "Now I suppose you'll need to be headed to Sayatta if you are new around these parts, eh?"

"Yeah, we do, but how did you know that?" Abby asked. "What's to say he's not already registered?"

"I just had a feeling," Gideon said, turning back to the strange creature in front and speaking another unrecognizable phrase. The creature started once again moving gently through the woods.

"Will you be joining the Hentar Academy then?" Gideon asked them. "You three look like you just got out of school for good."

"Yes, we did," Abby responded. "Our parents want us to join the academy this fall."

"But you don't want to, do you?" Gideon asked. They all exchanged glances, wondering how this man was able to know all this. What he had said was true, but they knew that if they revealed themselves and Gideon was with the Alliance, then it would all be over.

The answer was provided to Gideon by the uncomfortable silence that hung in the air. The three of them sat confused by the sudden feeling of trust that was coming over them. Why did they want to trust Gideon, who they had only met a few minutes ago?

"You don't want to go into the Hentar Academy, do you?" Gideon asked again. This time they didn't stay silent but nodded in agreement.

"No, we don't," Alexander spoke up. "And we're not exactly sure what's making us feel that way. I know by law we have to sign up, but we do not wish to do so."

"Feelings are a hard thing to understand sometimes," Gideon told them. "They are also a hard thing to change."

"What do you mean they're a hard thing to change?" Abby asked.

"If you truly believe in something, it is very unlikely that someone else is going to be able to change your view on it," Gideon explained. "And if they do, it is often over a long time period, is it not?"

"Good point," Roy commented.

"What are we supposed to do?" Abby asked. "If we don't go into the Hentar Academy, or at least register, we'll get in trouble, won't we?"

"Well, I can't tell you what you're supposed to do because it's not my decision," Gideon told them. "But if you honestly believe in your heart that there is another option besides swearing allegiance to the Alliance, then you'll just have to find another option. For by law, every person of age *has* to try out, even if they're not accepted."

"Are you saying that there is another option?" Alexander asked.

"What I'm saying is that if you look hard enough, you will find what you are looking for. Seek and you will find," Gideon told them. A silence came over them as they continued on. They all felt that there *was* something else out there – they just had to find it. It was then, in the silence, that they all knew for certain that there *was* another option. They lightly talked to themselves and to Gideon as they continued on their way until finally Gideon pulled the cart to a stop and turned around to face them.

"I'm afraid that this is where we part," Gideon told them. "I have business in a number of smaller communities just a few miles from here. If you head down the trail you will find Sayatta in twenty minutes."

"Thank you very much," Abby replied, climbing off as the others followed suit.

"Will we see you again?" Roy asked.

"Oh, I'm sure we will run into each other again. Good luck in your search; I hope that you find what you are looking for," Gideon said. They wished each other goodbye and then started off into the woods and disappeared from sight. Gideon meanwhile sat on the path and smiled.

"You will find what you are looking for," Gideon said aloud. He had found the truth years before with the same curiosity that these three had. Without speaking another word, the cart began moving and the man disappeared from sight.

Roy and Abby followed closely behind Alexander through the woods as they wound their way through the maze of trees and brush that covered the forest floor. They listened to the birds that chirped in the trees all around them, and could not remember a place more peaceful or beautiful.

Without warning they reached a tall line of shrubs and bushes that towered high above them, making it one of the more unusual sights Roy had seen since he had arrived.

"What is this?" Roy asked.

"City wall," Alexander answered. Roy shot him a look of disbelief. "When they built the city they wanted it to blend in with the surroundings, so they planted the vines and shrubs so that as they grew they would cover the walls of the city, camouflaging it."

"Interesting," Roy admitted. He had never before seen or heard of anything like this, but he was quickly learning to go with the flow.

They walked along the wall following the rows of trees and shrubs for what seemed like forever. Finally they came to a large steel gate. They stood outside for only a few seconds before the gates were opened by the guards and they were allowed to pass.

Roy followed Alexander and Abby timidly, surprised that they weren't asked any questions at the gate. Roy could do nothing but walk in silence and awe as he looked at everything around him. The buildings were unlike anything he had ever seen, towering hundreds of feet above him and built completely out of stone.

The streets were filled with people. They walked among the different shops and vendors along the way. Strange birds flew in the sky, almost appearing to have people on top of them.

The streets were empty of cars, instead filled with the noise of hundreds or even thousands of people who seemed to walk everywhere. Roy watched the city with confusion overcoming him.

"This is amazing," Roy exclaimed, getting a quick smile from Abby and Alexander."

"Haven't you see anything like this where you come from?" Abby asked. Roy shook his head.

"Nothing like this, we have cities sure. But they are made mostly of steel and concrete, and have cars and millions of people going everywhere. It's not exactly paradise."

"Sounds like a strange place," Abby agreed, "What do you think of this so far?"

"Different, but I think I could get used to it," Roy said, glancing around the city again. "So no one knows what a car is?"

"Never heard of one, off-worlder," Abby said with a slight smile.

"Sayatta is said to be one of the prettiest cities in the world," Alexander told him. "Not that we would know. We've only been to one city, and that's the one that we're in right now."

"Well, it sure beats the cities we have back home," Roy told them. They walked further and Roy slipped back into his thoughts. Back home a city like this was filled with crime, noise, and countless self-centered people. Here the people and atmosphere of the city seemed to be lighter and happier.

"Where are we headed?"

"We have to register at the senate building which is in the center of the city," Abby told him. "That's where we'll register you, since you're a new citizen, and where we'll sign up for the Hentar Academy."

"I thought we weren't signing up for the Academy," Roy said.

"True, but it is legally required for us to sign up. If we can find a way out of it in a couple of weeks then we'll do that. Otherwise, we might just skip out when it comes time to actually go to the Hentar Academy."

"I guess that makes sense," Roy agreed as they walked three abreast down the street. They wound through the numerous alleys and streets. Alexander claimed he knew a shortcut, but they seemed to get more lost by the second. Finally, they entered another street, and Alexander pointed to a building on the horizon.

"There it is," Alexander said. "That's the Senate building." Roy looked at it, almost confused, as it was much shorter than the buildings surrounding it. The building itself was only ten feet tall and didn't look very grand.

The guard held out a hand to stop them when they finally approached the set of wooden doors. The creatures stood only about four feet tall with strange, furry hands and a weird-shaped head with three eyes in the center of it. He spoke in a language that Roy was unable to understand; he just hoped that Alexander or Abby did.

"What is this creature?" Roy asked Abby in a whisper.

"How should I know?"

"Because you live here?" Roy returned.

"Well, *forgive* me but I'm not a expert on every creature that walks the earth," Abby said. "Good thing is Alexander knows their dialect. Fair warning, off-worlder, there's a good deal of what you will no doubt call *strange* stuff around here. I'm sure you'll get used to it eventually."

"I'm not so sure," Roy replied as Alexander started speaking to the creature. "What's he saying?"

"He's telling the guard that you'd like a big sucker and look like a giant mutant of a person," Abby answered. Alexander turned around.

"That's not what I said," Alexander said, turning his attention back to the guard.

"He doesn't know that," Abby said, getting a slight laugh our of Alexander. "Okay, what he actually was saying that you are new around here and need to register . . . what I said before wasn't true."

"Hadn't picked up on that," Roy said so sarcastically that even he couldn't keep from laughing. Alexander spoke for another minute to the strange creature before they were led down the hall.

"The ceremony and registration for the Hentar Academy finished nearly an hour ago. Thankfully because Roy's here, we're being given a special audience . . . though it will be given to us in the middle of the Senate session."

They turned to the left and walked down the corridor as it turned slightly. There were walls on either side of them with about twenty feet of open space in between to make up the hall. The floors were made out of a dull stone, which didn't reflect anything but made the building seem older than it might actually be. About eight feet above them there were small windows cut into the wall about two feet wide by two feet tall. They let in an enormous amount of light and created a slight breeze that cooled the building and its inhabitants.

They finally came to a stop outside a set of doors that looked more magnificent than the rest had. These doors were covered in gold with intricate carvings from top to bottom. The guards immediately opened both of the large doors, seeming to move them effortlessly, despite the weight.

The guards ushered them through and then closed the doors after they had passed. All three stood, not knowing what to think of what they were looking at.

The top of the building was open, letting in an uncontrollable amount of light and air. The entire complex wrapped around in a huge circle, including the hall they had been in. The walkway they were on was covered by a balcony that surrounded the entire structure, supported by wooden columns and a railing that went the entire length of the walkway.

Several staircases led from the balcony down to the main floor, which had been dug into a hole in the ground and slowly declined into a mass of chairs and desks to the middle. The seats and desks of people wrapped all the way around with one large desk sitting in the middle of the space.

They walked to the nearest stair and began walking down to the desk in the middle. Everyone stopped and looked at them as they approached, suddenly making them self-conscious. Roy looked at the people as they passed, never in his life having seen creatures like he was seeing now, with human as well as strange creatures sitting side by side.

Roy turned his attention from the hundreds of people in the desks to the five people in the middle of the room. They all wore robes. The person in the middle was a little shorter than six feet and had long, flowing brown hair and eyes that sparkled like diamonds, The entire assembly was completely silent.

They finally reached the five figures, stopping a few feet away as instructed by the guard. They stood waiting for something to be said as the silence stretched on, to the point where it began to get uncomfortable. Finally, the figure in the middle stood and walked around the desk.

“Leaders and members of the Senate,” the figure in the middle said, seeming to have a strong but soothing voice about him. “It appears that we have some visitors.” The Senate quietly murmured to themselves as the man approached them.

“It is such an honor to have you here with us. I'm aware there is a new arrival to our world here among us. Allow me to introduce myself; my name is Lucerine, and I am the leader of the Senate, as well as the Alliance, for the two are one entity.” Roy felt as though he shouldn't speak at all, not liking the feelings of insecurity and distrust that he was getting as he looked at Lucerine. Lucerine smiled warmly, further making Roy and the others want to leave. By the look of him, Roy thought that they could trust him, but his heart told him otherwise.

“Which one of you is new to these parts?”

“I'm Alexander, this is my sister, Abby, and this is Roy,” Alexander started, trying not to show how uncomfortable he actually was. “Roy's an off-worlder and needs to be registered under the jurisdiction of the Alliance, does he not?”

“Indeed he does,” Lucerine replied. The Senate became excited, trying to keep the noise down as they whispered and gossiped back and forth to each other. Roy's feelings of distrust and insecurity were growing stronger by the second. “You were wise to bring him here,” Lucerine told them. “For unless he is registered under the Alliance, he cannot do much of anything. Let's see what we can do for your friend here.”

Lucerine turned from them and began walking towards the desk where the other four cloaked figures sat silent. Lucerine stopped a few feet later and turned to look at them, motioning that they should come. They reluctantly began walking toward the desk, feeling uncomfortable as everyone in the building stopped talking at once.

"Well, Roy, I can't begin to tell you how excited I am to welcome you here to Sayatta," Lucerine started again. "We haven't had an off-worlder in many, many years. Now all you have to do is sign these papers, and you will be registered under the Alliance."

Lucerine handed Roy the papers and a pen unlike any that he had ever seen. Roy looked around, trying not to look too eager to sign the papers; something wasn't right. He signed the papers and handed them back to Lucerine, who smiled, not giving Roy any added comfort.

"Roy, on behalf of the Senate of the Alliance and all those in attendance I would like to officially welcome you to the Alliance!" All the people assembled applauded until Lucerine held up a hand to silence them. "Now that you are officially registered under the Alliance you will be graciously welcomed into the Hentar Academy, the finest school in all the world."

"Sounds good," Roy lied, trying to sound like was excited.

"Now Abby and Alexander, are you registered for the Hentar Academy? Because in just a few weeks the final selection will take place."

"Yes, we are," Alexander lied. They hadn't registered, and if they had anything to say about it they would never register. Something about the Alliance just didn't seem right. There had to be another option, and they were going to find it if it was the last thing they ever did.

# 4

**DESPITE ALL THE** odds stacked against them, they had managed to walk out without being registered for the Hentar Academy. They walked in silence for a few minutes, making their way through the people and strange creatures who went about their business.

Abby stole a glance at Roy when he wasn't looking and couldn't take her eyes off him. What was it about him that was getting her attention? He was just another average, everyday person, as far as she could tell.

He turned toward her, making her instantly look away, hoping that he hadn't noticed the way she was staring at him. Something about him was different and caught her attention; she wanted to know more about him. She shook her head, remembering the way they had met. He probably thought she was a strange, off-the-wall girl and wasn't interested at all.

Thinking back on how she had acted and treated him, she wouldn't blame him if he did feel that way. If she was in his shoes, she would be offended, too. Sorrow filled her as she hoped that somehow she would be able to make a better impression in the days to come.

She looked at the sun for another moment, watching it as it descended in the sky, wondering how they were going to make it home by the time the night was over. The sunlight was quickly vanishing, and the darkness was starting to cover everything in a blanket of shadow and mystery.

"What are we going to do?" Abby asked Alexander. "It's not likely that we'll get home before the sunlight disappears completely. And I don't know about you guys, but I really don't want to be wandering out here in the middle of the night.

"Why not, Abby? You afraid of the dark?" Roy asked, looking back at her with a slight smile and a sparkle in his eye.

"Yeah, that's right, smart guy," Abby replied, smacking him in the side. "No, I'm not afraid of the dark. It's not like I sleep with a candle lit or anything like that, but I've heard some strange stories of what happens out here after dark."

"What kind of stories?" Roy asked.

"There was one story where these people got lost in the woods, and then they just never came back, they were found a few years later completely-"

"Okay, Abby, we don't need to know the full details," Alexander told her.

"Roy was the one who asked!" Abby pointed out.

"Roy decided he doesn't want to know," Roy interjected. "But just out of curiosity, what's going to happen if by some strange chance we *do* get stuck out here after dark?"

"I'm guessing we'll find out soon enough," Abby told him with a chuckle.

"You're such a comfort," Roy replied. They walked until they reached the city gates and then entered into the forest which had fallen completely silent in the dusk. The trees were motionless and still, and the sound of the birds had vanished as they slept peacefully in the trees. The sky was dark and clear, making the temperature plummet.

They walked for hours, getting colder and colder as they went, wondering if they were going to make it through the night. They stopped in their tracks, too cold to go any farther.

"I've never been so cold in my life," Abby said as they all collapsed on the ground and shivered. "Alexander sat down across from Roy and Abby, shivering almost uncontrollably

"I think that's an understatement," Alexander replied, his breath visible in the cold night air. "Do you guys smell that?" Roy and Abby sniffed the air.

"Smoke?" Roy asked. Alexander nodded his head.

"From a campfire?"

"One can only hope," Abby replied, being the first to get up off the cold hard ground. They managed to stand, looking up the hill on their right. A small glow came to their sight identifying that a fire burned on the other side. The smoke could be seen rising up into the night.

"What if it's something we don't want to associate ourselves with, and we become a sacrifice or something?" Alexander asked, stopping Abby in her tracks.

"I'd rather take my chances than stay out here and freeze to death. And in the event that we do end up as sacrifices, I hope we taste good."

"You're so weird," Roy said as they followed Abby up the hill. They climbed to the top, slipping once or twice before they reached the crest of the hill. Abby stopped in her tracks as Roy and Alexander went to either side of her and looked down into the valley below.

Down in the valley was a small orange fire that glowed in the dark night, offering warmth and life to them. They searched the forest for signs that anyone else might be present.

They found no one in sight, and quickly began walking down the steep hill. Abby followed Roy with Alexander leading the way. The hill grew steeper still, as they tried to quietly make it to the bottom.

She slipped, lost control and slid down the hillside. She slid into Roy's legs, causing him to lose his balance and slide down the hill. Alexander jumped out of the way, nearly losing his own balance as Roy's leg brushed him. Abby and Roy grabbed each other as they tumbled down the hill, barely missing the trees that were in the way. They rolled onto the main ground and tumbled to a stop inches away from the fire that burned.

Abby looked at Roy and neither of them could help but break out in laughter as he rolled off her. Alexander smiled as he approached.

"The word *quiet* doesn't mean anything to you, does it?"

"We'll have to work on that," Abby replied.

"So I noticed. But seriously *quiet* might be a good thing. We still don't know whose fire this is. I mean we could end up chopped into a thousand pieces or cooked alive."

"This is a serious concern for you isn't it?" Abby asked. Alexander's mouth dropped open.

"How is it not a concern?"

"Rest assured, I'm not in the habit of eating people who look to get warm by my fire," a familiar voice said from the other side of the fire. "Though I may charge a small fee."

They looked to see the man they knew as Gideon coming out of the darkness, with some pieces of wood in his hand. He put the wood on the ground and sat down cross-legged as if he was ready to listen to a great story.

"What are you doing here?" Alexander asked.

"Sitting by my fire," Gideon replied with a smile. "Looks like we have a knack for running into each other."

"Indeed," Abby said. "Do you live around here?"

"No, I don't live around here. At least not during the summer months," Gideon told them.

"So you live around here only during the summer? Surely you must have some kind of a house, or a place to stay."

"Correction; this is what I do in my free time. I stay out here and rescue people from anyone who might have nefarious intentions. My wife often joins me, but she is away on other business at the moment. "

"What do you do when you're not on free time?" Abby asked.

"During the school year, I am a teacher at a school," Gideon answered.

"The Hentar Academy?" Alexander asked.

"No. The Alliance and I do not see eye to eye. In fact, I am glad to say that I do not stand for anything the Alliance stands for; in fact the school I belong to stands for everything that the Alliance works so hard to destroy," Gideon answered.

"If you don't mind me asking, what does the Alliance stand for?" Roy asked. "I know I'm new here, but even I can tell that something about the Alliance isn't right. What do they stand for?"

"A good question, and one I can answer. You see, the Alliance is not what it seems to be. They put on a good face and seem to be goodhearted, only concerned about the welfare of the land and it's people. However, I have discovered disturbing truths about them. They have a far different plan than anyone could even begin to guess. They seek death, destruction, evil. They put on a face of compassion, but they show no mercy to those that displease them."

"So if you don't stand for the Alliance, then who do you stand for?" Alexander asked. Gideon studied them all for a moment. "Is there another option out there?"

"There's always another option," Gideon told them. "It's just a matter of looking for it; seek and you will find. You have been looking for another option, now it is all paying off because you have found another option."

"We were right!" Alexander cried, trying to contain his excitement.

"Yes, you were right," Gideon replied. "You are wiser than you realize, for many people know the Alliance as I know them but don't bother to look for another option. They merely give in to what everyone else thinks they should do."

"What is this other option?" Abby asked.

"The other option I speak of is known to all, but in the grand scheme of things only a small number acknowledge him or accept him as the true king of everything," Gideon started. "You see, the Alliance is not at all happy or pleased with Chrystar and his teachings, nor the numerous followers all around the world, which is why, for now anyway, the school is a secret.

"Who's Chrystar?" Roy asked. An unexplained sense of peace and completion seemed to come over them with that name, even though they had never heard it before.

"Chrystar is the creator and ruler of everything and stands for everything that the Alliance is against; *he* is the other option."

"So does this guy really have a school, or are you pulling our leg?" Alexander asked; Gideon smiled.

"There is another school besides that of the Hentar Academy, and if you wish to go there you will begin your training to become a Chrystarian warrior. Are you interested in this school? There is always a risk of being found out by the Alliance."

"What do you mean?" Alexander asked. "If this is a secret school how would the Alliance even know about it?"

"Think of it this way. If you don't go to the Hentar Academy, it won't take the Alliance long to look up their list and notice that you haven't registered or even shown up. You must choose whether you wish to put yourself at risk, even if it is something that may be better than the Alliance."

"So if we don't stand for what the Alliance stands for, we become Chrystarian soldiers and then we can fight it?"

"More or less," Gideon replied.

"We're interested," Alexander told Gideon. "Now what do we have to do to be accepted into this school?"

"You've already been accepted," Gideon, answered; all three of them gave looks of confusion.

"How can we be accepted when we haven't even met anyone except you, from this school? How do they know we're even coming?"

"You've already been accepted because you honestly believe that there *is* another option," Gideon explained. "You *are* willing to put your life at risk in order to resist the Alliance. Your hearts are pure, and I can guarantee you that no one loyal to the Alliance would even consider doing something as bold as that."

"Where is this school, and how do we get in it?" Abby asked.

"You will be contacted a few days from now with all the details," Gideon told them. "But enough talk about this tonight, we'll get some sleep, and then I'll take you home in the morning."

Abby laid down on the ground. She could hardly contain her excitement as she lay there trying to get to sleep. The fire burned down until the logs were only a pile of coals before she finally drifted off to sleep.

# 5

**THREE WEEKS PASSED** without any further word from Gideon or anyone else from the school. Gideon had been gracious, and had given them a ride home, and explained to their parents why they were so late in returning. Their parents had looked the other way and had forgotten completely about that night, not knowing what had really happened.

Alexander and Roy had continued sharing a room, but had managed to find Roy a small sofa to sleep on to prevent any more accidental impaling when Alexander woke up.

Roy was still trying to adjust to the crazy lifestyle and people that he had met and was quickly realizing that even if it was strange, he wouldn't trade it for the world. Roy had managed to blend into the normal life so well that when people met him, some hardly noticed that he was an off-worlder as he worked and helped out around the house and with the harvest.

The time flew by like a strong wind, but it wasn't fast enough for the three of them. They patiently waited to hear back from Gideon or someone else from the school that they were planning on going to. The days passed, and yet another night came as the silence continued.

Now there were just three days until they would be leaving, making it one of the most anxious times of their lives as they wondered if they were actually going to make it to this other school or if they would have no choice but to go to the Hentar Academy.

They still hadn't told Cyrus about what they had found; he had already been attending the Hentar Academy for the past two years and wouldn't likely side with them. Cyrus helped them pack their things and tried to get the three of them excited about going to the Academy. The others played along and hoped that he didn't suspect anything.

“Maybe we'll hear back tonight,” Abby said, shutting Alexander's door as she sat down on the bed next to Roy. Roy nodded and stole a glance at Abby, whose long brown hair and personality was catching his attention more then he wanted to admit.

“I sure hope so; I really don't want to go to the Hentar Academy,” Alexander said from his spot on the floor. The others nodded in agreement.

“I think we'll be hearing back real soon,” Roy said. The others nodded and fell silent, listening to the cool, quiet night as a breeze came through the open window.

“What if we don't hear back?” Abby asked. “We can't exactly just skip out if Cyrus is with us; he'd rat us out in a second.”

“We'll cross that bridge if and when we get to it,” Roy assured. They fell silent, not speaking for a few minutes. Their thoughts were interrupted as their names were heard as clear as day.

“Who said that?” Alexander asked, looking around the room for anyone who might be playing a trick on them. Again, their names were heard, making them look around the room in confusion, almost wondering if Cyrus *was* playing a strange prank on them.

Roy stood up and made his way to the window. He looked out and spotted a lone shadow, standing and looking towards their window.

“Who is that down there?” Roy asked. The others crowded around.

“Looks like Gideon!” Alexander exclaimed. “Let's go meet him and see what he wants.”

"I'll second that," Abby replied with a smile. She jumped up from her spot on the bed, quickly reminded of just how low the ceiling was as she hit her head and came back down holding her head and laughing. "That hurt."

"At least we know there wasn't anything damaged because I don't think you had anything in there to begin with," Roy said, following Alexander to the door.

"I do too have something in my head!" Abby exclaimed, falling in behind Roy.

"I mean something besides open space," Roy said again, not noticing that Alexander had stopped. Roy ran into Alexander, pushing him into the wall.

"You're one to talk, Mr. Van Doren," Abby argued, also failing to notice that they stopped. She ran into Roy. "Why did you stop?"

"I stopped because Alexander stopped," Roy answered, turning to Alexander. "What did you stop for?"

"Everyone else is in bed; we might wake them and arouse suspicion if we are sneaking down the hall," Alexander pointed out. "We'll have to take an alternate route."

"What kind of an alternate route would that be?" Abby asked.

"Through the window," Alexander replied, pulling the sheets off his bed and tying them together into a rope. He handed it to Abby who tied the makeshift rope to the dresser and threw the rest of it out the window. "Who wants to go first?"

"You made the rope," Roy replied. Alexander gave him an *'Alright, I'll do it'* look and then climbed out the window, safely making it to the ground.

"You next, off-worlder," Abby said. Roy shook his head.

"Ladies first," Roy said. Abby half smiled.

"You act like you haven't done this before," Abby said. Her eyes lit up as the revelation hit her. "You haven't done this before!"

"Oh, would you be quiet and get down the rope!" Roy said, half amused at her expressions.

"Have you really never done anything like this before?"

"Sneak out a second story window with a rope made from bed-sheets? Doesn't ring a bell."

"I would say your childhood was missing some fun."

"Perhaps. But I'm still alive."

Abby climbed out the window and slowly let herself down the rope. Roy hesitantly started out the window, not waiting for Abby to be down the rope before starting his descent. Roy froze in place, his hands starting to slip.

He lost his grip and fell down onto Abby, grabbing her and pulling her off the rope. They tried not to scream as they both fell into the bushes that were directly below. They sat up, their heads spinning.

"Sorry," Roy said as she smacked him in the shoulder. "Nevertheless, I've proved my claim . . . never been down a blanket rope before."

"No worries. I just *love* behind yanked off a rope by an idiot off-worlder who can't keep his grip."

They turned to look at the shadow in the distance that had caught their eye. The shadow came closer. Gideon smiled at them as the shadow disappeared from his face.

"Good evening, my friends!" Gideon greeted in a whisper. They all moved further away from the house, until they were nearly in the forest.

"It's about time you showed up," Alexander said. "We were wondering where you've been."

"I apologize about the lateness of my visit. I've been incredibly busy with other students and last-minute preparations. I almost forgot to visit all the students who wanted to come. But, hey, I made it. Better late than never?"

“True. But could you try coming a little earlier in the day next time?” Roy asked. They all chuckled.

“I find that night works the best for this because usually the parents and other family members are set on the Hentar Academy. So if I come late at night, usually the only ones awake are the students themselves,” Gideon explained.

“What do you have for us?” Abby asked.

“I have your instructions on how to get to the school and what to do,” Gideon said, handing a piece of paper to Alexander.

“Platform three, take a step of faith,” Alexander read aloud. Abby and Roy gave Gideon a look of confusion. “What does this mean?”

“Well, you go to the same place everyone else goes, just as if you were heading to the Hentar Academy, except you find platform three. Once you find it only a step of faith will get you to the Chrystarian Academy.

“Tell me if I'm wrong, Gideon,” Abby started, “but there is no platform three. I've been to the station before, and for whatever reason there's no platform three.”

“Seek and you will find,” Gideon told them. They stood in silence, each waiting for the other to speak. “Sorry to just drop this off and run, but I've got many more late night visits to make in the next two days. “May the power of Chrystar watch over you.”

They briefly said goodbye before Gideon turned and climbed onto his little cart with the strange creature and started off into the night.

They all turned and headed back to the house without saying a word. They were lost in their thoughts, wondering about what the future might hold. They reached the rope and silently climbed up. Roy started up before Abby, hoping this time he wouldn't lose his grip and fall again.

They climbed back through the window without incident and sat down on the bed, each waiting for the other person to say something and break the uneasy silence.

"What do you think?" Abby asked. "Should we go, or should we change our minds now? The instructions don't seem to invoke much interest on my part."

A knock came on the door. The door opened, and Cyrus poked his head through the opening. He came in silently and closed the door behind him.

"You three are up late," Cyrus said, sitting on the trunk at the end of the bed. "Excited about joining the Hentar Academy?"

"Not really," Roy replied.

"Why not?" Cyrus asked. "I was excited my first day." They all remained silent. "I saw you talking to someone. Who came to see you? Who was he?"

"We'll tell you, but you have to promise not to tell anyone," Abby bargained. Cyrus nodded, and Abby continued. "He was a representative from a different school, a school other than the Hentar Academy."

"But there is no other school," Cyrus replied. The others hesitated and looked at each other; they knew differently. "At least not one worth going to. And even if there was, why would you be interested in it?"

"We don't like the idea of going to the Hentar Academy, and this new school we've found seems to be a better way. You're welcome to come with us if you want."

"Yeah, right," Cyrus retorted. "I'm not going to risk getting myself killed by going to a different school; the Alliance will come after anyone who doesn't join one of their schools. Besides, this year, I finally get the chance to become a real Hentarian Knight. I'm not going to give that up."

"Why not?" Roy asked.

"Because it's what I've always dreamed of. Everyone dreams about becoming a Hentarian Knight. At any rate you're safer with the crowd, the wide path. You shouldn't defy the Alliance. They're in charge, and you'll be criminals."

"Well, we are," Alexander responded. "If you want to come with us, then you can. At the very least, think about it."

"Fine, I'll think about it." Cyrus agreed reluctantly. "But I'm not making any promises." He got up and left the room, slamming the door.

"Maybe he'll come around in a day or two," Alexander suggested, doubtful that it would happen. Abby left soon after, and they all went to their beds, staring at the ceiling.

* * * *

The three days came and went slower than the three of them would've liked. They had tried on several occasions to get Cyrus to come with them, but instead Cyrus had barely spoken to them in the past three days, seeming to have more anger than any of them had ever seen in him before. He shut himself up in his room and refused to talk to them except at meals or if it was unavoidable when working.

Roy, on the other hand, was actually excited for the new adventure. He found it a little strange that he felt more excited for what lay ahead then when he had pulled out of his driveway for the last time. Only time would tell if his feelings of excitement and anxiousness would actually lead up to something, or if all his hopes and dreams in this new world would crash as they had back home.

Life went on as normal for the most part, even though they were packing to leave. Norah and Victor seemed to be handling the fact that they were all going to be gone better than Roy had imagined. He had been told several times that letting go was the hardest thing you had to do as a parent, but they appeared not to be having any problems.

The night before they were to leave, they had received yet another late night visit from Gideon. They spoke at great length and informed him of everything that had happened with Cyrus. Gideon asked if Cyrus would be coming. They shook their heads sadly and informed Gideon that it wouldn't be happening that way. Gideon nodded saying that it had to be his choice, and no one could make it for him.

Roy felt peace run through him like a river when he had heard those words. That, too, was unlike anything he had ever witnessed back in the real world. He knew some people who hadn't made a decision in their life because their parents had made them all—the college they were going to, or what they were going to major in.

Finally, Roy put the last shirt in his small carrying bag when Alexander came walking through the door, closing it behind him.

"Today's the day. You excited?" Alexander asked.

"You bet I am," Roy replied. "I'm just glad I don't have to go to the Hentar Academy. Something doesn't feel right."

"Agreed. What do you suppose that is? In your opinion?" Alexander asked.

"For me? I have a feeling that the Alliance is hiding something. I'm not sure what it is that's warning my heart, though."

"Same feeling here. Maybe someday we'll be able to figure it out."

"I hope so," Roy said, zipping up his small pack and getting a strange look from Alexander. "What?"

"We're going to this school for an entire year, and all you're going to bring is that small bag of clothes?"

# ALLIANCE

"This is all the clothes I have," Roy pointed out.

"True enough," Alexander replied, doing up the zipper on his bag. "I was just thinking you'd have bags like Abby does. You know, the bags that weight sixty pounds each."

"Sorry to disappoint," Roy replied. He grabbed his bag and headed out into the hallway. Cyrus came down the hall and brushed past them without saying a word.

They shrugged it off and made their way outside. The morning sun was just starting to peek over the tall trees to the left, filling the sky with beautiful red streaks. They threw their stuff onto the cart that had been provided for them and climbed up onto the back of it.

Cyrus came out and didn't speak to them as he threw the rest of his things on the back of the cart and hopped up onto the driver's seat, grabbing the reigns from Victor.

"We're proud of all of you," Norah said, with an uncontrollable smile across her face. "You have no idea how much we've looked forward to this day, when all of our kids would be accepted into the Hentar Academy." They tried to hide their real feelings and not how much they were bothered by the mention of the Hentar Academy. They hugged and said good-bye before starting on their way.

The house and their parents disappeared from their view, leaving them alone. For the first time it sunk in that it would be nearly a year until they saw them again.

"How is this cart going to get back home?" Roy asked curiously.

"The animal knows the way, *off-worlder*," Cyrus said. Roy grew uncomfortable. He had gotten somewhat accustomed to the term coming from Abby, but the way she said it was much different and more enjoyable.

"Have you thought about what you want to do, Cyrus?" Abby asked. "Coming with us, I mean?"

"Yeah, I've thought about it," Cyrus snapped. "I think you're a bunch of idiots. If you want to put your life at risk and defy the Alliance, then go ahead. I won't be making the same stupid choices you are." They fell silent as a wave of disappointment and sorrow came over them.

Alexander looked at Abby and knew she was feeling the same pain that he was. Cyrus was their brother and had been their best friend for years; now it was as if they had never met him. He was different from the brother they had known; he was angry and short tempered, and they weren't sure why.

They rode for an hour until finally they made the right hand turn into Sayatta. The city streets were filled beyond capacity as thousands more people than usual made their way to the station. Kids were being dropped off everywhere, and parents said their goodbyes. They wound their way through the crowded city streets until they reached the station.

The station was a building that stood about twenty feet tall with two more stories. The first floor was more of a long hall that spanned hundreds of feet in the distance, running right past each of the platforms. Every twenty feet there was a numbered sign, telling them what platform was on the second floor, along with a corresponding staircase that led to the second floor.

They got off, grabbed their bags from the back, and quickly realized just how many people *were* enrolled in the Hentar Academy, or one of the other schools that the Alliance approved of.

Cyrus was quickly lost in the crowd, leaving them alone in their new surroundings. They walked past platform one and two and then stopped in their tracks when they saw the number four instead of three. They put down their bags as they looked around in confusion.

"Alexander, do you have that piece of paper that Gideon gave us?" Roy asked. Alexander pulled it out of his pocket and opened it.

"It says platform three," Alexander told them, pointing to the words on the note.

"Where is it?" Abby asked. "Gideon wouldn't send us to a dead end."

"She's right," Roy concluded. Platform three has to be around here somewhere." They studied the surroundings, hoping that they might get lucky. Roy looked to the right, noticing a platform without a staircase.

Without speaking to the others, he picked up his bag, walked over to the platform, and studied it. He smiled when he saw the number three was engraved in the middle of the platform.

"Found it!" Roy exclaimed. They immediately came over to him, bringing along their bags.

"Good work, Roy!" Alexander exclaimed as they stood on the platform. "Now what do we do?" As if a magic word had been spoken, the world spun around them and then vanished. When finally the spinning stopped they fell to the ground.

They tried to get their bearings as they stood and looked around. They were in a well lit cavern, spanning thousands of feet across in every direction, forming a perfect circle. They were suddenly overcome with fear as they realized they were standing on a circular pad that was only twenty feet wide.

Roy looked over the edge of the pad and then quickly looked back to the others. They were suspended in the air with a drop to every side of them. The ground couldn't be seen. The pit of darkness spanned the distance between them and the wall on the other side.

"Anyone have any ideas?" Alexander asked, using his foot to push a small pebble off the side of the platform and waiting to hear it hit the bottom of the pit. No sound ever came.

"The instructions Gideon gave us said to take a step of faith, right?" Abby asked.

"Yeah, but this is insane," Roy said. Alexander nodded. He looked over the pit to the wall on the other side, seeing an opening with two lights on either side. Above the opening, one word was carved into the rock.

"What's it say?" Alexander asked.

"It says, 'believe'," Roy answered. "We have to take a step of faith, toward the opening."

"I'm not sure about that," Abby replied. "There has to be another way to get across the gap."

"If there's any you think of in the next thirty seconds let me know," Roy replied. "Who's going to try it first?"

"I vote Abby," Alexander said.

"I say we do it together," Abby said, taking Alexander's hand and then grabbing Roy's. They stood and closed their eyes for a moment.

"We'll count to three and then go, alright?" Roy asked; the others nodded. "One . . . two . . . three!"

They all took a step off the platform; their feet came down and stopped a second later. He looked in amazement as all of their feet stood suspended above the huge pit below them. They took another step and remained suspended. They walked out in confusion and wonder as they looked at the pit. They were walking on air.

"The whole thing is a glass floor?" Alexander asked, as they each walked farther and in different directions. "This is impossible."

"This is amazing," Abby replied wandering off to the left and smiling. "You can't even tell that the floor's here."

"I think that's the idea," Roy replied.

"How do you suppose that pebble fell through?" Alexander asked.

"Somethings don't need to be answered," Roy answered. They all went back to the platform and grabbed their bags. They turned toward the opening on the other side and stepped out onto the floor again.

# ALLIANCE

They reached the opening and stepped onto a small ledge just inside the exit of the cavern. Was this really happening? Or was all a dream? They walked through the opening and were suddenly on the side of a remote cliff somewhere.

They looked to their left and saw the forest and then saw thousands of people causally walking in a clearing which was surrounded by trees, giving them cover.

Without speaking, they joined the crowd, soon blending in with the thousands of people who milled about in the clearing. They were met by two men who kindly asked their names and then took their bags when they checked their names on a list.

"We're glad to have you here," the taller of the two men told them. They didn't say anything, still trying to process everything that was happening. "We will escort you to the Griffin you have been assigned too, and then we'll get on our way."

The man led them through the masses to a strange animal on the other side of the clearing. The Griffin stood on four legs and was about four feet tall. It had the head and body of an eagle and a long neck, all of which were covered with feathers. The tail was long and fanned with feathers at the end.

"Never seen one of these before," Roy said.

"Me, neither," Abby said. "The Alliance uses different animals." They were motioned to get on board. Seventeen other people climbed on the Griffin and took a seat. They held their breath as all the great beasts began flapping their wings and took off into the sky. The Griffins gradually raised up into the sky, keeping extremely level as they did so. They looked behind them, thinking for a moment that they could see Sayatta fading in the distance.

# 6

**ALEXANDER HAD NEVER** felt so good. He looked down over the side of the Griffin at the land below, which had now been reduced to almost a memory. The people appeared to be nothing more than specks. The fact that he was riding on a Griffin, an animal that had only been legend as far as he had been told, was amazing enough. He felt as if he had been born again.

Roy and Abby were sitting a little ways from him, talking, unaware that he was even watching them. They talked and laughed and had a good time, showing on the outside what he was feeling on the inside.

He couldn't hide a smile as it began to sink in for the first time that they were on their way to a place that wasn't the Hentar Academy. Ever since he had been a kid, he had hoped and prayed that there was another option. Now that he had found one, he felt the most joy he had ever felt in his life.

Yet despite his joy, disappointment and sorrow were slowly creeping into his thoughts as Alexander's mind turned to Cyrus. They had been best friends all their lives and now in an instant his brother had turned against him and had left in a storm of anger and fury. He wasn't sure what to think of Cyrus's sudden feelings of anger and hatred, but Alexander was sure that the change could only be attributed to the teachings of the Alliance and the Hentar Academy.

# ALLIANCE

"Are you as excited about this as I am?" a voice asked. Alexander was snapped out of his thoughts, his attention turned towards a mid-height person with curly brown hair.

"You bet I'm excited," Alexander told the stranger. "This is incredible."

"I know what you mean," the man replied. "My parents always spoke of this, but until I decided to not go to the Hentar Academy, I never felt this happy."

"Your parents came to this school, too?" Alexander asked.

"Oh, yeah. My family has been Chrystarian Warriors for at least three generations now. I guess it's a lucky thing the Alliance hasn't found out, otherwise, I'm sure we would've all been killed."

"My name's Alexander Reno." Alexander held out a hand.

"Jonathan Analai," he replied, shaking Alexander's hand. "It's a pleasure to meet you, Alexander."

"Likewise. So you heard about this school from your parents?"

"That's right. I knew about it all along, but they still couldn't choose for me whether I was going to go here or the Hentar Academy. How did you hear about the school? Did your parents know about it?"

"No, not that I know of," Alexander started. "I'm here with my sister and one other friend of ours. We kind of found this place by accident, but I'm sure glad we did. I had made up my mind to skip out and be on my own if it came down to it."

"That's good to hear," Jonathan replied. "I know some people that wanted there to be another option, but then didn't want to risk being caught by the Alliance and killed, so they didn't come."

"I know some people like that too. My brother, among them."

"I'm sorry to hear that. I wouldn't worry too much; maybe in the end he'll come join us and become a Chrystarian Knight."

"Maybe, but I doubt it," Alexander said as they climbed higher into the sky. They looked behind, noticing for the first time that there were probably a hundred Griffins in the sky. Despite how high they were, they all seemed to be warm and felt only a slight breeze as they flew.

"Jonathan, do you mind if I ask what a Chrystarian Knight is?"

"You don't know?" Jonathan asked. "A Chrystarian Knight, or Warrior—either term is acceptable—is the front line of defense against the Alliance. They're the good guys, so to speak. I'm not too sure on the fact of it just yet, but I know that one day the Chrystarian people will rule over everything and defeat the Alliance."

"How can you be sure?"

"Like I said, I'm not sure on the fact of it, but my heart tells me there's truth in it."

"I hope that's true, and I hope to see that day," Alexander told him. Unfortunately, if the Alliance would have to be defeated, then so would Cyrus, unless Cyrus reconsidered and decided to come with them.

They soared higher and higher, eventually climbing through the clouds. After a while a cloud came into view that was different from all the others. The cloud was as white as it could be, and the biggest of any cloud they had ever seen in their life. The cloud appeared peaceful, like a cotton ball causally floating through the air. They looked to the pilots and talked among themselves as they headed straight toward the cloud, but this time they began to think they could faintly see something in the cloud.

The image was hazy at first, only appearing to be a shadow, but the nearer they got to the cloud the more excited they became. They entered the cloud, running into a gentle shower of mist and water droplets that refreshed them. They clung to the Griffins, speechless, as the cloud seemed to disappear before their very eyes.

In front and slightly below them was a structure of immense size. The cloud they had just come through now seemed to surround the entire complex. Buildings floated in the air on a suspended platform. In every direction of the buildings were other suspended platforms with other buildings on them, with bridges connecting each one to another. The sprawling city reached far above them, spreading nearly as far as the eye could see.

"How is this possible?" Alexander asked, staring on in amazement.

"I have no idea," Jonathan said. "How they made the entire thing look like a cloud on the outside is beyond me, but it's a work of pure genius. They've made an entire city invisible."

Hundreds, if not thousands of Griffins flew in every direction, between other buildings and from platform to platform. They looked down below at the people who walked on the bridges and waved back as the people cheered and waved at them from the ground. Alexander's eyes were drawn to the bottom of the sprawling city, where under each platform he noticed a bright florescent light glowing. They continued to look on in amazement and wonder.

*How could something like this really exist without the Alliance knowing about it?*

Though Alexander's mind was sufficiently boggled, a sense of welcome and kindness came over them as they listened to the sounds of the new city. Griffins sailed through the air as they neared the biggest complex in the middle of the entire city.

"Welcome to Granyon, home of the Chrystarian Academy," the pilot told them, unable to stop a smile and a slight chuckle as all the newcomers looked at the city in awe. They slowly started to descend towards large platforms where the Griffins gracefully and gently landed.

Everyone got off the Griffins, and a moment later all the Griffins took flight and vanished into the sky. They stood on a large rock street of sorts that was met by a lush green lawn. Shrubbery was dotted here and there, along with several walkways laid out across it leading up to the large doors of the building.

The doors were at least ten feet tall with just one word carved into them: *Believe.* The building itself was five stories high with windows lining the entire bottom story. Rock columns ran up the side of the building and past some of the windows, covered with some sort of fancy carving work.

A man cleared his voice, and their eyes were all directed toward a man who had walked up to them without being noticed. The person was dressed quite nicely in a white suit; although his face was anything but human.

"Welcome to the Chrystarian Academy," the creature said. "Your bags have already arrived. Now if you will follow me, we will make our way to the main hall where many people are awaiting your arrival."

* * * *

Roy and Abby joined Alexander as they began following the guide. The walkways were all made of a dark marble with fancy designs winding through it. He stole a quick glance to the distance, staring at the bright lights that hung beneath each platform, noticing walkways winding beneath them, connecting them all underneath.

They entered the main building in complete silence. The floors inside were made of a white marble that had been polished to the point where everything was reflected back at them. A large staircase stood in front of them with fancy woodwork carved into the railing that appeared to be covered in gold. The staircase was wider than he had ever seen, easily being able to hold a thousand people at once.

Up above, more halls and corridors ran along with a railing and rock columns that went up from the floor every so often. The corridors were empty as a tomb as they turned to the right. They followed the guide farther and farther down hall, which was well lit by the windows.

Several doors were to either side of them – some leading back outside, and others leading into rooms that they didn't know. Strange lights were mounted every ten feet, glowing a florescent white and giving a new light to everything. The lights on the wall, even if they were a different color, appeared to be the same kind as the ones they had seen below the city.

They walked for a while until they reached another set of doors. The doors parted silently, giving them a view of what lay ahead of them. Before they could comprehend what they were seeing, they were walking into a massive dining hall.

Thousands of people sat at long tables and turned to look at them as they walked in. They tried to hide their smiles as the people started clapping and cheering for them as they entered the long rows of tables. The tables were made of solid wood, and finished beautifully with a long royal purple cloth that ran the length of them. They were led to the front, where they were stopped before a platform which was about a foot higher than the main floor. A large chair was the only thing that sat on the platform.

Behind the chair, another set of doors waited. These doors appeared to be made out of polished stone, which reflected every light that hit it. They waited anxiously as the guides motioned that they should stay, and then left them.

Roy glanced behind him at the sea of people, relieved to find that they weren't starting at him. Instead, they looked past him and the others to the set of doors, as if waiting for something spectacular to happen. Roy looked at Abby and wondered what was running through her head.

Not a noise was heard anywhere through the hall as the clapping stopped, and every person fell down to one knee where they were. Roy and Abby looked around, and eventually fell down to one knee to avoid standing out so much. Not a person moved in the silent hall, as they remained down on one knee.

"Do you have any idea what this is for?" Abby asked Roy. Roy shook his head.

"It's for him," Jonathan answered, pointing to the set of doors behind the chair. They slowly parted, making a noise sounding more like a gentle *whoosh* than a stone door opening. Their attention was captivated immediately as a middle height man entered the room. His hair was brown and neatly combed. His beard was nicely groomed. He walked tall and proud, and with certainty and conviction. Something about him struck Roy as different from anyone he had ever met.

Without a word being spoken, every person in the room stood to their feet and sat down at their tables. The people who stood at the front remained standing, not yet having been given a place to sit. The man moved around to the front of the platform.

"On behalf of everyone present and those who are not, welcome to the Chrystarian Academy," the man said. The entire assembly erupted into applause for a moment or two and then quieted down once again. "You are probably wondering who I am. I can answer that question. My name is Chrystar, leader of the Chrystarian Academy. I understand that some of you have gone to great lengths in order to get here, and I also understand that some of you are here without your parents consent, or knowledge. Although I would normally speak against disobeying your parents wishes, I applaud you for this. Standing up for what you believe and choosing your own path is not easy.

"By coming here, you have chosen to defy the Alliance, which I can assure you in the days to come the Alliance will not stand for. As of yet the Alliance appears to be harmless and innocent, but in the near future everything will change. Thank you all for coming. Your courage and your bravery will be rewarded. You will become the finest Chrystarian Warriors in all the earth!

"Your journey towards becoming a Chrystarian Knight, however, will not be as easy as you may have thought it will be. You will face pain and suffering and persecution, along with many other trials. In time, you will understand what I am talking about," Chrystar told them. "But for now, let us talk and get to know each other better. Once again, welcome to the Chrystarian Academy. All classes will begin tomorrow. Until then, fellowship and get to know each other as you settle in for a new life. Are there any questions?"

All the students looked at each other and wondered who was going to be the first; finally, one hand went up. Every eye moved to the person who spoke. "What about our parents? The creature asked. "They will write to us and send their letters and mail to the Hentar Academy, and then the Alliance will know that we didn't show up.

"The Hentar Academy is likely already aware that you haven't shown up, but as for your parents, this problem has been taken care of. Your mail will arrive here from our people down below and then be given to you. Your parents as well as the Alliance will be unaware of your whereabouts." Chrystar surveyed the group again for another who might have questions. Seeing no more hands, he turned and moved to the side of the platform and came down the stairs.

"Now talk and fellowship," Chrystar said. "For good it is for one to have friends." Chrystar made his way through the tables, talking to each of the students and groups as they ate. When Chrystar finally came to their table, it was all Roy could do to keep from telling Chrystar everything he knew or asking every question that went through his mind.

As they ate and took in everything around them their hearts swelled with joy. They knew that what would happen here would change their lives forever. This was the start of a great adventure.

# 7

**CYRUS PUSHED THROUGH** the crowd of people, trying his best to forget the situation that had unfolded in the past few days. He had dreamed of becoming a Hentarian Knight all of his life, and if he was lucky, that day would soon be coming. Yet as much as he wanted it, he couldn't make Abby or Alexander want it. He had pondered the situation night and day, not able to fully understand what it was that they didn't like about it.

The Alliance was the commanding force in the land. They were respected, powerful, and anyone who wanted to be anybody worked for them. The world had been at peace for as long as he could remember, which is why Cyrus couldn't understand their line of thought. Even if they didn't like the Hentar Academy, they could have still chosen to go to another school that the Alliance approved of. Instead, they were heading nowhere.

Cyrus mostly blamed Roy for this sudden change of heart. Alexander and Abby had never voiced any kind of discontent before he had arrived. Whether it had been there or not, Cyrus couldn't guess.

Regardless of what he thought, they had chosen their own path and would have to live with the consequences of their choices. Their choices would lead to death and exile, while his would lead to life, success, and riches; everything that everyone dreamed of when they were kids. He pushed all the thoughts from his mind, trying to forget the three of them.

He reached his platform and quickly scaled the large flight of stairs and came to the second floor, where everyone else was slowly making their way to the flying creatures that the Alliance used for transportation. Cyrus looked at the creature, having always been taken by the great beasts. The creature was that of a Dreygar. Someday, he wanted to have one of his own.

The Dreygar was large, but low to the ground, with four legs, a long gangling neck, and a long tail with six or seven large spikes on the end that you certainly never wanted to get impaled by. The head looked as though it should belong to a Dragon, with three rows of razor sharp teeth.

Cyrus walked up to the guard who looked at the ticket that Cyrus gave to him. A moment later, he motioned Cyrus on without saying a word. Cyrus climbed onto the creature's back, feeling the soft fuzzy hair that covered a Dreygar.

He sat, waiting for the rest of the people to climb aboard so that they could get going and he would be able to more easily forget Abby, Alexander, and Roy. As much as he hated to admit it, he was worried about them. To truly defy the Alliance was to become nobody. Would they become exiles? Would they be living on the run for the rest of their lives?

Whatever the answer was, Cyrus still felt as though they had made the most foolish decision they could have ever made. Still they had chosen, and if in the end Cyrus would have to fight them, then he would. The Alliance was in control, and they were doing a fine job with the power that they had been given. Trying to overthrow them would be useless.

Finally, the last person climbed up the stairs and onto the Dreygars, and they took off into the sky heading south, leaving the city behind them. Cyrus watched it vanish from his view, a smile coming across his face. He was on his way toward glory. If he was going to be chosen to become a Hentarian Knight, then it was going to happen this year.

He only hoped that he had what it would take to become a Hentarian Knight. He wondered and dreamed about what the future might hold, anxious to get to Bruden and continue his training. The city of Bruden was the Hentar Academy. The entire city had been built for the school specifically, and it was an amazing city at that.

He had never heard much about what it was the Hentar Knights did, but it was well known across the land that they were the highest form of official that you could become, unless you were Lucerine himself. If there was any one person Cyrus longed to be like, it was Lucerine. His fearless attitude and confidence in any situation made him the ideal leader. Cyrus longed to be like him, as did everyone who went to the Hentar Academy.

They flew for hours as the sun slowly dipped down in the sky and nighttime started to come over the land. Splashes of red danced over everything on the horizon, and darkness started to creep in. Cyrus could hardly contain himself, knowing that any minute now Bruden would be appearing on the horizon and he would feel as though he was returning home.

The city appeared on the horizon, still a long ways off, but he knew what we was looking for. Light smoke drifted into the sky, coming from the huge pillars that lit up the entire city whether it was day or night. Within a few minutes, they reached the city and began flying over it. It was an incredible feeling, flying hundreds of feet over the tallest city that he had ever been in. The buildings were beautiful and and flawless.

The people were far below them and paid them no attention as all the Dreygars weaved their way in and around the buildings, making their way toward the one in the center. They approached a large tower, and flew into a gaping chasm in the side of it.

Once inside, they found themselves in a large tunnel with statues of the greatest Hentar Knights carved out of stone. As they were flying he looked at the one he admired more than any other: Tarjinn.

Tarjinn was a legend among the Hentar Knights, having completed training in under a year. Tarjinn was also the youngest Hentar Knight and already had an impressive list of accomplishments and accolades.

They exited the tunnel immediately casting their eyes on an enormous golden statue, nearly sixty feet tall. The statue was of Lucerine himself, the person they all looked up to and wanted to be like. Cyrus looked around at the amazing city, noticing that the pillars had been lit for their nighttime arrival.

He welcomed the feelings of serenity that flowed through him. This was his home. He loved this city and he loved the Alliance. He wanted to become a Hentarian Knight. The Dreygars split up according to how long they had been coming to the Academy. The newest students went to the first floor, and the second years to the second floor and so on. His group headed toward the third floor, where platforms were waiting for them.

The Dreygars landed on the platforms as the pilots motioned that they should all get off. They did this, and then the pilots took to the sky again, vanishing from sight. They all waited for someone to say something, but instead they remained silent.

A set of doors parted and a single man walked out. He wore a black cloak and his hair was nicely combed, offsetting a few scars that were on his face.

"Come this way, students. Lucerine has decided to speak to you first. Follow me." Cyrus couldn't help but feel excited at what might lie ahead of him. Lucerine always spoke to the first-time students first. Why the sudden change?

Cyrus pondered the question that bounced around in his head and followed the guard until they came to a dozen sets of doors. The doors were opened, and they were allowed to enter, bringing them into a huge theater sort of setting. It was circular in shape and a hundred feet tall, with enough seats to easily hold everyone who stayed on this floor. Cyrus took a seat near the stage.

When the entire room was filled, trumpets sounded and two doors were opened to Cyrus' left. The corridor beyond was black with only a few orange torches coming from the inside. Everyone watched in anticipation as first one shadow became visible and then another, until five shadows in all came out into the light.

Everyone broke into applause and cheering as their leader came forward followed by his four assistants. There was a certain mystery about Lucerine's assistants. They always wore their dark cloaks and had their hoods up, and in all the years Cyrus had seen them he had never heard them speak before. It was a little strange, but even more intriguing.

Were they Hentarian Knights that were more powerful and famous than any others? If they were, Cyrus wanted to be one of them. The four cloaked figures took their spots in the large comfy chairs that were waiting for them opposite the doors that they had come in. Lucerine moved to a podium that was in the center of the stage.

"On behalf of the Alliance and the leaders and people that *are* the Hentar Academy, I would like to welcome you here for your third year!" Lucerine started, his voice easily heard by everyone despite the fact that he wasn't yelling. "This is going to be an exciting year for all of you, and I can assure you that it will be one of the most satisfying that you've had up to this point. You all know what this year is. What it means. This is the year that the people who are to become the Hentar Knights are chosen. The rest of you can still get employment under the Alliance, in practically any other position you might want, which is still an admirable job and worthy or remembrance. Or you may choose to join our armed forces which grows in numbers daily.

"The path toward becoming a Hentar Knight will not be an easy one, but I assure you that whatever struggles or pain you might face are well worth it. Once your training is complete you will be the crown jewel of the Alliance and life will never be the same. You still have much to learn, but it is now time for you to move on to a different kind of learning. The days of textbooks and learning in a classroom are over. From this moment forward the people chosen to become Hentar Knights will take up their training underneath a Hentar Knight, for three years, or until your master declares that you are complete in your training.

"However, it is not my choice who will become a Hentar Knight, or who will not. It is not even my assistant's choice. Instead you are chosen by a Hentar Knight. They have been watching you since the first day you stepped foot in this fine city. You may not have known that they were watching, but they were. Some of them were pleased or impressed with your performance, while others did everything all wrong.

"The selection day has finally come, and I will now announce the names of those who are to be chosen as Hentar Knights. I will not say who it was that chose you, until that Hentar Knight is present. But before I do, I will remind all that just because you are chosen by a Hentar Knight, it does not mean you have to accept. You are free to decline and give someone else the chance at glory. Also more people may be contacted afterwards, having been selected. So never give up hope that you may be chosen. Becoming a Hentar Knight means swearing your heart and soul to the Alliance, believing with everything you have that the Alliance is looking out for the best interests of everyone in the world.

"Now I will announce the names of the people who have been chosen. The first person to be chosen by a Hentar Knight to be trained is . . . Varno Huggat." The section of the crowd that Varno was in cheered for a moment or two. Lucerine went on and named forty other people and Cyrus felt his hope start to fade. "Now the last person to be selected for training as a Hentar Knight is . . . Cyrus Reno."

Cyrus let out a sigh of relief, unable to keep from smiling as pure joy rippled through him. This was the day he had waited for. His mind wandered, wondering who it had been that had chosen him to be trained.

"Thank you all for coming, to those chosen I wish to say congratulations, and to those not chosen I extend the greatest sympathies to you! Remember it does not matter what job you hold within the Alliance, you will not be forgotten by us. I now dismiss you to your various duties and tasks. However, I would like Cyrus Reno to remain behind if he will."

Cyrus felt like slapping himself to make sure that he was awake. Lucerine wanted him to stay behind? To talk to him? The excitement gnawed at him as he impatiently waited for the last person to exit the room. When finally the last person had left, Lucerine strode toward him gracefully, his four assistants milling around the stage.

"It's a pleasure to meet you, Cyrus Reno," Lucerine greeted, extending a hand. Cyrus shook it. "I've heard so much about you that I feel as if I've known you forever. Tarjinn talks of you as if you were her own child."

"Tarjinn?" Cyrus asked. Lucerine smiled.

"I don't mind telling you, ahead of time, that you have been chosen by Tarjinn. Someone no doubt you've looked up to. Am I correct?"

"Who wouldn't. I can't believe I was picked by her. She's like a legend."

"She is a legend. She is certainly one of the greatest Hentar Knights I've ever seen, and at so young an age? She's not more than five years older than you are. She has a great and glorious road ahead of her, no doubt.

"It is rare that a Hentar Knight takes an apprentice at such a young age, but then again I suppose she's an exception to every rule. She has spoken with me at great length about choosing you, and after looking at your record I could not find a reason you shouldn't have been picked. You will be the first to ever train under the great Tarjinn and truly learn from a master. You should feel very honored."

"I do," Cyrus replied. "I have a hard time wrapping my head around all that is happening."

"I will put those fears aside. It is indeed happening. Walk with us," Lucerine told him. Cyrus felt as if though he was living in a fantasy as they walked out of the stadium and into the hall that Lucerine had first come through. Once inside there seemed to be more light there than he had initially thought. Cyrus could see just fine, and the floor was smooth, as were the walls and the high vaulted ceiling.

"If I may be so bold," Cyrus started, "why did she choose me?"

"I'm not at liberty to discuss that matter. It may have to do with the assignment that she has been given, and that matter is completely confidential until you officially pass the initiation ceremony tomorrow night. All that aside, I was curious as to where your brother and sister are, as well as the off-worlder Roy. I believe they were supposed to be coming here today were they not?"

"They were supposed to, but they said that they have found a different way."

"That is what troubles me the most. If they did not want to be in the Hentar Academy, they could have easily enrolled in one of the other schools, but they show no records of ever being registered."

"That doesn't surprise me. I think that off-worlder poisoned their minds. I never heard anything about them skipping out until he came around."

"Roy?"

"Right."

Lucerine thought for a moment.

"This troubles me as much as it does you. We do not need anyone, let alone an off-worlder, spreading rumors about us. They have no reason to fear us unless their head is playing tricks on them. We are good people who only want what's best for everyone."

"Unfortunately they didn't seem to agree."

"It seems there are more than just your brother and sister who don't agree. Over the years hundreds of thousands, maybe a million students have not shown up to any of the schools that the Alliance approves of. This has troubled me night and day."

"Where are they?" Cyrus asked. "They can't just disappear?"

"I'm not sure. But enough of this talk. Tomorrow is the initiation ceremony, and then we will talk business when Tarjinn arrives."

Cyrus bowed to Lucerine before he was shown the way out. Cyrus was led away and back out of the theater. He walked through the hall, taller and prouder than he had ever been. He had started the day with doubts, only to find out that he had been chosen by a Hentar Knight, Tarjinn.

Maybe someday his name would be on the pillar next to Tarjinn's. Cyrus's head filled with ideas and thoughts that he had never thought before, but he didn't mind. Each of them was filled with glory and splendor as everyone would look up to him and declare him the best Hentar Knight in the world.

He walked out to one of the landing platforms, taking a quick glance down to the people who were nothing more than dots. Cyrus climbed onto one of the Dreygars and told the pilot where to take him. The beast lifted off and then gently glided through the sky as Cyrus thought about the initiation ceremony.

His mind wandered briefly to Alexander, Abby and the off-worlder Roy. He couldn't begin to guess where they were, but right now he didn't care.

# 8

**ROY COULDN'T REMEMBER** having a day where he felt so much joy. It almost seemed surreal, like a dream and at any moment he was going to wake up.

The dinner that had been prepared for them had been better than anything he could have ever dreamed of. The meat had been juicy, perfectly cooked, and filled with a flavor that awakened nearly all his senses.

How long they had sat in the magnificent hall and talked Roy could only begin to guess, but at last Chrystar stood once again to address those gathered. He smiled warmly, instilling the same undivided attention that he had the first time.

“I hope your meal was to your satisfaction?” Some of the people cheered their approval. “I hoped it would be. There is always something about a well cooked meal that hits close to my soul. In all seriousness though, I would like to inform you of a few ins and outs and how things work here.

“Today was for feasting, and celebrating! Tomorrow shall be a return to normalcy. Classes will begin tomorrow, the world of academia in the morning, and the world of combat and warfare in the afternoon. It is with a slightly heavy heart that I must announce that you are the first class who will be trained in both simultaneously. But alas, the time is quickly approaching when we will do as we have been called to do and stand against the corrupt evil that will threaten to destroy us. It is my fear that you are stepping not into a battle, but a war. A war of the heart. Every person in this room, and in fact every person in the world will have to choose for themselves where they want to stand.

"The options are many, and they are few at the same time. For while many place their faith in the teachings of the world. The teachings I give you are different, as they should be. But what sorrow awaits those who trust in their own faith, for who can save them in the end?

"In short, there is one very big difference between the Chrystarian and those who follow the Hentar or other cults and belief systems around the world. While the Hentarian company focus only on your thinking, and using and twisting that to get you to feel certain things, the Chrystarian is concerned about the condition of their heart. For it is by the renewing of the heart that the mind is refreshed and better able to make good decisions.

"But how does one keep their heart pure? For it is no secret that the heart is wicked and deceitful. Let us remember one very important thing, it's what goes in that makes the biggest difference in who you are. If you put bad things into your mind, by your conversations, or your actions, particularly when no one is looking, then you can expect bad things to follow. It's who you are when no one is looking that is important, if greatness is to be accomplished on any level.

"Now, please remain seated until you are approached. You will be split and taken to your rooms. Your things have already been delivered and will be waiting for you. You are all being assigned to a house, the leader of that house is to be your mentor as you are trained in the coming weeks. You may ask them anything you wish and confide in them whatever you wish. I wish you all a very good night's rest and goodnight!" Chrystar finished, walking off the stage and heading through the door behind.

The hall became a congested mess for some time as people were tapped and told to follow. Roy and the others waited patiently until it seemed they were the only ones sitting at their table.

Nearly twenty minutes passed until the entire hall cleared out, leaving only twenty students by themselves. Two people came forward and Roy let out a sigh of relief.

Gideon walked forward with a woman next to him. She appeared to be about his age with blond, graying hair. Her eyes were inviting and her demeanor calm.

"Don't worry, I didn't forget about you guys. I simply wished to avoid the massive crowds. This is my wife, Evelyn, and we are honored to host you in our house. Please follow us."

The remaining students stood and followed them out of the great hall and to the right. Eventually they entered onto a small platform where a Griffin was waiting for them. They all climbed aboard and the Griffin took to the sky.

"I can't get over how peaceful I feel being here," Abby said.

"I understand. I realize the prospect of war should have me freaked out, but after being here for only an afternoon my thoughts are at peace," Roy replied.

"Can I ask you something?" Abby asked. Roy looked at her and nodded. "I'm embarrassed to say it, but I feel like I need to ask your forgiveness."

"For what?"

"I've treated your rather horribly, and I haven't been fair to you. I guess I just ask that you forgive my rashness. It gets me in trouble far too much, and it's something I need to get better at."

"Of course I can forgive you," Roy replied. "But I think I, too, need to ask forgiveness. You may have been harsh on me, but I had written you off and tried to avoid you for a while. When we were flying here I realized that you are not quite as rough as you appeared and I hope we can know each other as friends."

"I can forgive you," Abby said, looking away, a smile tugging at her lips. "You can call me Abigail if you want."

"Really?"

"Yes," Abby answered hesitantly. "It's an exclusive deal though. If anyone else calls me that I might have to get in touch with my rash side." He laughed.

"I feel honored, Abigail," Roy said, she smiled shyly and looked away. "However, I think most of the time I'll call you Abby anyway. Unless it's just the two of us." She smiled at that.

Eventually they descended to another large platform and they swiftly got off the Griffin and followed Gideon and Evelyn through the bustling town square. If they didn't know any better they would've said this was the same town they lived in back home. The buildings were built out of the same material and the atmosphere was the same.

They entered into a large building that was more basic than the previous one they had been in, but was still cozy and inviting. They turned to their left and climbed a small stair up to a second story. Here the floor turned to carpet and the strange phosphorescent lights that had shone all through the previous building also shone in this one. Although, here they looked more like lamps would in the real world.

Finally they turned down yet another hall, where a set of doors was opened for them. They walked into a large living space with plenty of couches and chairs for all of them. A shelf of books, old and worn, lined one wall and in the wall directly in front of them was a roaring fireplace.

"Welcome to your home away from home," Gideon started. "This is obviously our living room, there's a small kitchen over to the right. The halls to either side of the fireplace will lead to your sleeping quarters while you're training. Girls on the right, boys on the left. Your things are already waiting for you, go ahead and get comfortable. Evelyn and I are here for anything you need, and we're always glad to lend an ear or have a good stimulating conversation."

*　　　*　　　*　　　*

The night grew late and though Roy felt as though he should go to sleep he was unable to do so. For lack of anything better to do he went out to the roaring fireplace and grabbed a book off the shelf. He opened it up and read before he was aware of someone watching him.

He looked up to see Gideon walking towards him. Without speaking he sat down in a chair adjacent him with a cup of tea which he neatly put on the table next to him.

"Late night reading?"

"Couldn't fall asleep."

"Anything on your mind? I'm always here to talk."

"I have a lot on my mind. As you know I'm a newcomer to these parts and overall, I feel a little conflicted or confused."

"What are you conflicted about?"

"Is the Alliance really bad?" Roy asked. "I chose to look for another option because I *felt* they were bad. Let's face it, I certainly haven't had near enough time to do the research. Right off hand I'd say the Alliance is not bad . . . at least they don't appear bad."

"The Alliance, at it's core, is very deceptive," Gideon said. "They say one thing and put on a good face; meanwhile, behind the scenes they are doing some rather horrible things. I for one should know better than anyone, for I was a Hentarian Knight for nearly ten years."

"You were?"

"Yes, in fact it was Evelyn who helped me see the light of day. At that time Chrystarians were broken into twenty factions. Minor disagreements on a lot of things. They were divided. My job was to find where these factions were and destroy them. Everyone. Not one was to be left alive. All of this was done in secret, the public did not know.

"But when I came to Evelyn's faction and specifically when I looked in her eyes a terrible flash of light filled my vision, and I became blind. For three days I was blind, but I did not wander in darkness. Evelyn and her family took me in, cared for me even though I was sent to kill them. When finally my sight returned I threw away my sword and vowed myself to the Chrystarian way."

"What is the Chrystarian way?"

"Others first. Self last. Love your neighbor more than yourself. There is no greater purpose than this. It is what the Alliance lacks, and in time I'm sure you will come to see that."

"So what does the Alliance have against a teaching like that?" Roy asked. "It sounds honorable and good."

"Oh it is, and it is in the light of such a teaching that the flaws of the Alliance are exposed. They play favorites. In the Alliance, you're either a success or you're nobody. In their eyes there are some who will never be *equal*. The Kingdom doesn't believe in a philosophy like that. Each person has their flaws, but with the help of Chrystar, they can each overcome those flaws.

"So the Alliance puts on a good public face, that I'll admit," Gideon said.

"The Hentar Knights though . . . watch out for them. They are the black sheep of the Alliance." They both fell silent for several minutes as Roy mulled everything over.

"You said in the past there was twenty factions. Did the factions get reunited?"

"Don't quote me on that number, but yes, there were many. The factions were reunited by Chrystar about ten years ago. More so, he helped us see our similarities, rather than our differences. We have been building up our numbers and peacefully sharing our hope with people. Now, it appears war may happen and though I hate it, it may be the only way to fix the world."

"I've never been in a war," Roy admitted.

"War is ugly. No other way to put it," Gideon replied. "But no matter what happens in the the war, we must never loose our hearts for what is right and what is just."

* * * *

Morning came and so did the smell of fresh eggs and bacon. Roy woke faster than usual and stumbled out into the main living area seeing a table and chairs set in the middle of the room. Evelyn and Gideon were fast at work in the kitchen, cooking up a storm.

"Good morning Roy, have a seat, breakfast will be in a few minutes!" Gideon called out. Roy took a seat, soon joined by Abby who came and sat next to him.

"Good morning Roy," she greeted in her normal cheery self.

"Morning Abigail," Roy said quietly. She smiled shyly at use of her full name. "Sleep well?"

"Almost didn't want to get out of bed," Abby replied. "I've never had a bed that comfortable, as you can attest to."

"Your parents could definitely stand to upgrade a few things in their house," Roy agreed. "Comparably, I don't think my bed back home feels half that good."

"Back home in Vermont?"

"Yeah. Small cabin in the mountains."

"Sounds like a nice place."

"It is. If I ever figure out how to get back there I'll have to take you along. Show you the sights my world has to offer."

"Would you want to go back?" Abby asked, taking sip of coffee.

"Right now, no. I'm having far too much fun trying to keep up with this new world. Besides I'd miss you – I mean, all my friends, if I was to go back." They didn't say anything else, instead getting lost in their own thoughts.

"I'd go with you," Abby said in a whisper.

"I—"

"Hey, Stranger!" Alexander exclaimed, coming down the hall. "Long time no see."

"Oh yeah, really long time," Abby remarked. "It's been what eight hours?"

"And it was a long time," Alexander replied. "Besides that, any day that starts off this way is just strange."

"Explain that?"

"First off sis, you didn't make fun of Roy – you know, call him any weird names or something like that . . . and secondly, I didn't get to yell at you and use your full name. Call it strange, but those have become very important rituals in our family."

"Very well," Abby said, getting up and walking away. "I'll solve both problems." She disappeared from sight and then came walking back into view, sitting down again and glaring at Roy.

"Hello?" Roy asked.

"Hey, dork brain," Abby started.

"Abigail!" Alexander scolded. The three of them chuckled as Alexander sat down. "Thank you, my morning is now complete."

"Is dork brain really the best you could come up with?" Roy asked.

"I was working on short notice, Roy. It was either that or scuz bucket."

"I'll take dork brain," Roy replied. Just then Jonathan came walking down the hall.

"Listening to you three, I really wish my parents had more kids," Jonathan said as he sat down.

"Do you have any siblings?" Roy asked.

"No, I'm an only child," Jonathan answered. "At least now though I feel like I belong to a family."

"As you should," Gideon said, coming over with the first plates of food. "It's by design that the twenty-one of you who are in our dwelling should become like family. You'll do everything with these people. Live, eat, work, relax. All your training will be in this group."

"Like a family," Jonathan said.

"Exactly. A single strand of rope is easily broken, but a cord of three strands will not easily break," Evelyn said.

"Also, we will select three of you to become pilots and eventually one of you will be chosen to be a Captain. You'll report to me directly as I will be your commanding officer."

"Are we to assume war is imminent then?" Jonathan asked.

"It would be safe to assume that, yes. The Alliance won't stop until they've eliminated all threats, but there will be more about the war in the second part of your day."

They said nothing further on the subject. They enjoyed the meal that had been prepared for them and enjoyed talking with everyone else as they came out of their sleeping quarters.

The meal finished up and many people were clearing their plates when the last person came out of the hall, having nearly missed breakfast. She was a short girl with straight long red hair.

Although nobody else saw it right away Alexander's eyes were fixed on the attractive woman, nearly with his mouth hanging open. Roy took notice and nudged him, though it didn't get any rise out of him.

"Earth to Alexander," Roy said, quietly. Abby perked up, noticing Alexander's dumb expression. "Are you in there?" Roy knocked on his head lightly.

"I'm here!" Alexander quietly exclaimed. He leaned in Abby's direction. "Who is she?"

"You like her?" Abby asked.

"Obviously, I haven't talked to her yet, but do you believe in *love at first sight?*"

"No, I don't."

"Well, knock me over. I thought of all people that you would believe in love at first sight."

"Why would you think that?" Roy asked.

Alexander leaned over to Abby. "What's her name?"

"Savannah," Abby answered.

"I need to talk to this woman," Alexander quietly exclaimed.

"Savannah!" Abby cried. The woman came and sat down across from them, her food brought to her a moment later. "Come sit with us."

They talked for nearly a half hour as Savannah helped herself to the delicious meal that had been prepared. As much as they talked however Alexander seemed to be perfectly tongue tied, and hardly could get a word in without stuttering or fumbling over his words like a nervous school boy. When Savannah was done with her food she got up and disappeared down the girls hallway to prepare for the day.

“Cat got your tongue?” Roy asked.

“Yes, it seems so,” Alexander said. “Made an utter fool out of myself.”

“That you did,” Abby agreed.

“You're such an encouragement, sis.”

“I wouldn't worry too much. First conversation is the hardest. Right, Roy?” Abby asked a sparkle in her eye.

“Right,” Roy said nervously.

“I'm sure the next one will go better.”

“I guess we're bound to have a better conversation in the future, seeing as we're living in the same group.”

“Exactly. Way to think positive!” Jonathan said.

“Just remember, Alexander, things could always go worse,” Roy said. “This reminds me of a saying that my dad had. He didn't have many good ones, but this one has always amused me. Can I share it with you?”

“Certainly. Any advice is welcome.”

“Always remember . . . '*if the cat's got your tongue, it's your own fault! You were the one making out with the cat!*'” They all laughed, while Alexander turned red.

“Roy, that is possibly the worst advice or saying that I've ever heard in my life.”

“Made you laugh though, didn't it?”

“You guys think you're so clever,” Alexander teased. “With friends like you, who needs enemies?”

"Exactly. You have two for the price of one!" Abby said.

"I'm glad to be a part of this group," Jonathan said with a chuckle. Roy smiled, having been thinking the same thing for some time.

# 9

**THE MORNING PASSED** swiftly and soon they were back in their rooms, eating the lunch that had been prepared. Gideon sat at the head of the table, while his wife Evelyn sat at the other end. They talked and laughed jovially, only slightly nervous about the next part of their training.

Roy had always been good at book studies, and had found the classes, which were mostly on history and logic, quite fascinating. But now he found himself anxious, as he knew nothing about combat.

He had a couple of cousins that had joined the military and had heard horror stories from boot camp, but would this be similar in any way? Roy had his doubts, but for now his mind was still getting the better of him.

When their half hour for lunch was up, Gideon led them through the city to an assembling area, where large numbers of students stood in their groups. Griffins streamed through the sky, swooping down, each picking up another group of people, before taking to the sky again.

Gideon and Evelyn stayed with them until their Griffin landed and they all climbed up on its back. They waved goodbye, and the Griffin took to the air, heading east over the city towards the cloud wall.

To their surprise, they didn't fly through the cloud wall as they had expected. Instead the cloud seemed to part and separate creating a large tunnel that could easily take any number of Griffins at once. The tunnel twisted and turned in ways that didn't really make sense to them at all. Were they going anywhere?

Finally they reached the end of the tunnel, exiting into a brilliant sunrise. The sky was lit up with the colors of dawn, confusing all of them greatly. But when they looked down, their confusion and amazement became even greater.

A massive cliff rose up beneath them and then reached far above them, creating an arch or an entryway of sorts. They passed through the arch, their breath taken away by the sights.

In front of them, as far as they could see, was an enormous canyon. Massive rock columns jutted up into the sky and cliffs, crags, and rocky plains made up the floor of the canyon far below. Roy looked over the edge of the Griffin, barely able to see the bottom. A few sparse canyon trees and shrubs dotted the grey and red rocks. In the distance, forests and even mountains were seen. Griffins flew everywhere.

“How is this possible?” Abby asked. “It feels like we've stepped into another world.”

“Maybe we have,” Alexander replied. “The air smells different here, and unless I'm mistaken, we just flew into a sunrise, which is impossible seeing we've just had lunch.”

“Maybe we were traveling longer than we thought and we're in a different time zone?” Roy asked. The others looked at him strangely. “What?”

“What's a time zone?” Jonathan asked. Roy stumbled over his words for a moment.

“I'm not sure quite how to explain it,” Roy finally answered, starting to become amused that they had no idea what he was talking about.

“I can see that,” Alexander said. “Though it does sound intriguing.”

“Tell me more,” Abby said.

"I don't know too much about them, except that they were started in the eighteen hundreds."

"Eighteen hundred what?" Alexander asked, now completely perplexed.

"The year eighteen hundred."

"But in the *'year'* there's eighteen hundred....what?"

"No, it's eighteen hundred like you're counting."

"Well, of course you're counting!" Alexander exclaimed, Roy smiled to himself. "What are we counting?"

"Years. Here try it this way...how old are you?"

"Eighteen."

"Right, now just add seventeen hundred, eighty-two and then you have it."

"So someone in your world is eighteen hundred years old?" Alexander asked.

"Back up everyone," Jonathan cut in. "What world are we talking about?"

"Roy's an off-worlder," Alexander said.

The rest of the conversation was one of the most amusing ones Roy had ever taken part in, particularly so because he was trying to confuse them, and it was working. Abby eventually caught on to what he was doing and just watched the three of them go back and forth for the next ten minutes.

They finally began descending into the canyon and landed in a large flat area with nothing else special about it except one rock pillar in front of them. Griffin after Griffin landed and dropped people off until as best as Roy could guess, there was probably close to a thousand of them on the floor of the canyon.

A few moments passed before horns echoed through the canyon and seven people on large white horses came riding up from behind. The mass of people parted to make way for them. The seven people quickly shouted out orders, instructing everyone to line up in formation, in their respective groups that they came with. They did as they were told, standing tall as a large Griffin approached from the east.

The great shadow passed over them all until a Griffin with a single rider landed at the head of the great company. He effortlessly slid off the Griffin's back and stood before them. He wore a uniform, which Roy thought looked like a flight suit. It was dark blue with red on the fringes and around the collar.

In an instant, the color changed and he was standing before them in a light brown flight suit, which was decorated with many medals and ribbons on the right breast pocket.

"I am Uri," the man started. His voice was deep, commanding, and intimidating at the same time. "As Commander of the Eritis Canyon, I welcome you. I am in charge of all operations in this canyon, and I am steward over the three hundred thousand people who call Eritis Canyon their home. I will be overseeing your training as we prepare you for the war which is likely to come.

"Unlike the Alliance, we believe we should teach *all* our people to fight, in all forms of combat. A one-stranded rope is easily broken, but a triple-strand cord is not easily broken. Training is for everyone, even if you don't think you'll ever have to use it.

"The groups you came in are now regiments. From among your group three people have been selected to become pilots. One of the pilots will become a Marshal, and be responsible for the other two pilots in the regiment. Still another person will become a Captain. The Captain shall watch over the entire group and report directly to their Regiment Officers, whose house you belong to."

"Does that mean Gideon and Evelyn are our Regiment Officers?" Abby whispered to Roy.

"I believe so."

"You should know that the three people from your group who are to become the pilots have already been chosen. Later in the day you will be presented with a card. Some will be blank and others will be green. If it is green you have been selected as a pilot and will receive an additional two hours of training everyday.

"You will be met by a Sergeant shortly, who will start you on your training journey." Everyone saluted as instructed and when the Commander had left they relaxed and talked anxiously to each other.

"I'm not sure if I should be excited or scared," Jonathan said.

"I'm leaning towards the scared side of things," Alexander said.

"I'm sure it'll be okay," Roy reassured.

"How can you be so sure?"

"I'm not. But when in doubt, bluff." Their conversation was brought to a halt as a man in a dark green uniform came up to them. His uniform was more simple than the Commander's, but he walked with just as much purpose as the Commander had. They fell back into their formation and saluted him. Once they had, he began speaking.

"I am Sergeant Parks. Your training begins now. Please follow me." He turned at once and began walking across the canyon floor. The others followed him two abreast as they had been instructed to do. After a few minutes, hundreds of different buildings waited for them. The buildings were large and there appeared to be one for each regiment.

They entered one of the buildings and let the door close behind them. The building opened up to a long hall and then quickly descended down into the ground. They scaled the flight of stairs, coming into a large open area that appeared to connect all the buildings. The other regiments could be seen from where they were.

They walked forward, entering into a still large, but more private room.

The room was wide enough for all of them to line the back wall. Sergeant Parks stood in front of them with a long table covered with different cloths in between. Behind him the space was open and stretched on for quite a distance.

"You will have ten weeks of vigorous training. In which time you will be trained in both armed and unarmed combat. We hope that all-out war can be avoided, but we must take every precaution necessary just in case.

"As a group you will be graded throughout your training. Should war break out, the highest ranking regiments will be selected for special operations. Understood?"

"Yes, sir," they said in unison, though clearly not loud enough for Sergeant Parks.

"I said, am I understood?"

"Yes, sir!" they boomed.

"Step forward." They did as he said, coming to the long table. "Now I will show you the weapons that you will be trained in." He pulled the first long cloth from the table. Directly in front of them was a three inch wide sphere. It was shinny and dark blue.

"What are these?" one person asked.

"These are called sactalines. They are a rare phosphorescent rock that is mined from the ocean city of Merodia. They come in an endless array of colors. Within the last couple of years we have discovered that each color has it's own unique set of attributes. The lights you may have noticed on your initial approach to Granyon were sactalines.

"The most important sactaline for you will be the one in front of you." He motioned and they picked them up, surprised to find that they felt nearly weightless. "Dark blue have attributes that help with concealment. Give the sactaline a tap and sees what happens." They all tapped on the sphere they were now holding, amazed, astonished with what happened next.

In the blink of an eye their clothes were transformed to a material that was bright orange. It was lightweight, flexible, but a few taps of the finger revealed that it was tough as steel. The Sergeant let them experiment for a minute as they tapped the sactalines repeatedly. If Roy watched closely enough he almost thought he could see the uniform coming through the air.

"For safety reasons. Your uniforms will be bright orange until you complete training. As you are only training right now, you will leave these uniforms here and pick them up every day. Next weapon." The Sergeant pulled back the next cloth. Everyone except Roy gasped.

"Crossbows. Nice." Roy commented, having never used one before but having seen them many times. The Sergeant looked at him warily.

"How is that you know of these weapons when this is the very first time they have been shown publicly?" The Sergeant asked. Roy considered his reply.

"I'm an off-worlder," Roy said. "I've seen crossbows before in the other world."

"Have you ever used one?"

"No, sir."

"With the exception of the off-worlder, has any one else seen this weapons before this moment?" Their silence and looks of awe on their face gave him the answer he had been hoping for. "Yes, this is called a crossbow and will be the main weapon you resort to when you are not using your sword. Then there's these." He pulled another cloth off the table, revealing arrows no more than twelve inches long. He picked one up and motioned that they could look at it.

"This is a small arrow," Alexander noted. "Why does it sparkle on the side?"

"Though they were banned by the Alliance some fifteen years ago, some of you may be familiar with Tantine arrows?" A few snickers went up from the team, primarily from Alexander and Abby. "These are something similar, but safer. They are coated in Tanterite, which is an explosive mineral. When they are shot from the crossbow they give off light as they fly. These are safer because unlike Tantine arrows these have to use the energy quickly in order to explode. Softer targets will get an arrow stuck in them, while harder targets will cause an explosion. Demonstration."

They looked to see three targets at the end of the room, one was an animal skin of some kind, the other was a piece of wood, and finally the last was stone. He grabbed a crossbow and quickly loaded and fired three shots. Two small explosions ensued, but the animal skin did not.

"Next." The Sergeant pulled a cloth off a large box sitting on a separate table three feet to his left. It held more black shiny sactalines, like the ones they had used for their uniforms. The only difference was that these ones were dark green. "In battle you will have to use many arrows, and won't necessarily have time to stop and gather them. Now, that will not be a problem . . . *BOLT*." In an instant one of the sactalines flew towards him, and seemed to strike him in the chest. In an instant a belt full of arrows appeared around his waist. "Any questions so far?"

"Is there any defense against Tantine arrows?" a person further down the line asked.

"Your armor will repel over thirty continuous strikes, but there is one other way to defend against the arrow." He pulled back the last cloth, revealing swords which they all carefully picked up.

"Our swords can stop arrows?" Abby asked, skeptically.

"Yes, they can. They have many attributes you may not guess just by looking at them. What is your name cadet?"

"Abby."

"Come help me demonstrate." Abby walked around to the front where the Sergeant was standing. "Draw your sword." Roy watched as she nervously drew it out of its sheath. "Strike my blade as hard as you can." Abby hesitated for a moment before raising her sword high and bringing it down on the Sergeant's sword. A small flash of light came from the impact point. The Sergeant held up a hand for her to stop. "Study the blades intently and tell me if you see any flaw, chip, gouge, or any damage at all." Abby inspected it carefully.

"I don't see any damage," Abby said.

"Thank you, fall back in line. The sword, for lack of a better term, is called a Super Sword. Once again there is a small sactaline of varying color in the cross guard of your sword. The color of flash you see depends on what color stone your sword has."

"So does each sword have a specific ability then?" Jonathan asked.

"No. As far as I can tell the designers threw that tidbit in just for the fun of it. This sword will block against the Tantine Arrows, without detonating them." They all strapped them to their waists as the Sergeant pulled out three cards. "Now. One last piece of business before we get started. Three people have been chosen by your Regiment Officers, Gideon and Evelyn, to be trained as pilots. When I say your name please step forward, take this card and go down to your left towards orientation. The rest of you will be dismissed for the day and taken back to the city until tomorrow when we will fully start your training." Roy held his breath as the Sergeant pulled three green cards out of his pocket.

"Jonathan Analai," Jonathan stepped forward, waiting as instructed. "Roy Van Doren." Roy's mind spun and nervousness immediately coursed through him as he stepped forward and took his green card. "Savannah Clives." She came and took the card. "You should feel very honored to be chosen to become pilots and you can start your journey down there. You may go." They started walking. "To the rest of you. Tap your sactalines, and you are dismissed."

Roy looked behind as Abby caught his eye for a moment. Everyone put their uniforms back and then were escorted out of the room.

"Anybody else nervous?" Jonathan asked. They all chuckled.

"What's the worst that could happen?"

"Fall off?" Savannah asked.

"There's nothing wrong with falling in my book," Roy said.

"What do you mean?

"It's not the fall that kills you, it's the sudden decrease in speed." They chuckled

"As factual as that is," Jonathan started. "It hasn't made me feel any better."

"Made you laugh, though."

# 10

**DARKNESS SETTLED OVER** the city of Bruden. The city that never slept was still bustling, despite the late hour. Dreygars were flying people here and there, and some of them flying just for the sheer joy of it. Cyrus stood dressed in his best cloak, waiting for one of the many Dreygars to come pick him up.

Nervousness mixed with anticipation raged inside of him. He had hoped beyond hope that he would be chosen to become a Hentar Knight and tonight if everything went well, he would join in a ceremony to welcome him to his new life.

He had heard that the life of Hentar Knight was hard, but he wouldn't have it any other way. To be a Hentar Knight would be the greatest honor. They were unlike any other people who lived and breathed in the world. They were known through the world for getting the job done when no one else could.

His mind had drifted often to the short conversation he and Lucerine had had the day before. Where were all the people that hadn't registered for the Alliance schools? What had happened to all of them?

Over the years there had been a few uprisings against the Alliance, but they had always been small and short lived. Cyrus had no doubt in his mind that any enemies of peace and of the Alliance would be crushed beneath the iron grip of Hentar Knights. The Hentar Knights were supreme and so was the Alliance. They were indestructible.

No one could destroy the Alliance. The Alliance was both strong and swift and had influence on every level of government in the world. Everyone was ruled under the Alliance and the thought of anyone else being in charge concerned him. Why would they be against peace?

A powerful screech was heard in the sky, sounding like music to his ears as the huge majestic beast descended out of the sky and came to the landing platform.

Cyrus climbed aboard without speaking. In an instant the pilot told the Dreygar to take off with a single one word command, and said nothing else. The air blew through Cyrus's hair as he admired the creature that fascinated him so much.

The Dreygar flew through the city, the bottom of which was only a blur, but still the tallest buildings were far above them. They passed through the city until they finally were within sight of the main central building that he had been in the day before.

As beautiful as it looked during the day, Cyrus had always thought it looked more mysterious and intriguing during the night. Lights came from every window, and the beams and other supports appeared to have red or blue lights behind them.

To Cyrus's surprise this time they climbed further into the sky, reaching the very summit of the building. Six pillars of rock rose into the sky, each of them with a blazing torch atop it. In the center of the landing the symbol of the Hentar Knights and the Alliance were engraved, glowing a vibrant orange.

The Dreygar passed overhead and then landed twenty feet lower on a landing platform. Cyrus thanked the pilot and got off, quickly getting out of the way before the Dreygar took off.

"I know it's likely a sign of respect, but you need not thank the pilots," Lucerine said approaching from the building.

"Sorry, just the way I was raised," Cyrus said.

"I know, and it's an admirable thing, but what can I say? The lower class is here to serve the higher class, and tonight you will get to join the higher class," Lucerine said. Cyrus tried to hold back a smile and shook Lucerine's hand.

"So, how does it feel to be here? To have nearly made it? You're only an hour or two from becoming part of the most elite group of people in the world."

"Surreal," Cyrus answered. "I'm having a hard time keeping up with all of it."

"Trust me, Cyrus, you have nothing to worry about. A simple matter of ceremony and you will become a part of greatness. And when your master declares your training complete, you will get your own Dreygar and pilot, who will serve you in whatever way you wish."

"I'm honored, sir," Cyrus said.

"Come. Let's get started." Cyrus tried to keep himself calm as he followed Lucerine inside the building. The building was well lit, but otherwise completely empty. Every noise echoed through the silent chamber. At length they came to a large door. They entered through it and Lucerine motioned for him to take his place along the wall. The other recruits were already here, standing, evenly spaced along the wall of the room.

The room was dimly lit, but for dramatic effect the floor glowed orange, while around other beams had different colored light behind them. The floor was black and shiny, reflecting the unique lighting back on itself. Lucerine quietly strode to the middle where a podium was waiting for him. He looked about the room as he began speaking.

# ALLIANCE

"Welcome, chosen ones. Today is the greatest day of your life. Today you will become a Hentar Knight. A Hentar Knight has chosen you for a specific reason, and only your new master knows what that reason is. If there is any reason that anyone wishes to give up their spot, this is your time to choose. Once you become a Hentar Knight, you cannot escape the wondrous life you will be introduced to. To break your oath is punishable by death.

"First, I feel as if I should dispel a few popular myths among commoners. Hentar Knights are not invincible, but they are very close to it. In a way of speaking, a Hentar Knight is just as much someone else as he is his own person. Serving others and looking out for their well-being is our utmost privilege and obligation.

"Part of what makes a Hentar Knight so great is their ability to see things before they happen, and act accordingly. With this *one* special ability the world is at our fingertips.

"The ceremony will begin shortly. What you are about to see is something that few people are ever able to behold. You will be seeing raw power in action. It is looking for a soul, a good strong soul to fill up so it can be used. Please look directly at me and do not look at anything else until I say to."

They did as he said and silence fell over the room for an interval of time, which Cyrus could not measure. It felt as though it was an hour, but it was likely only a few minutes. The silence was shattered by a new sound. Whispering.

Whispering filled the air, gently growing louder as something neared them. Cyrus tried to listen to what the whispering was saying, but it was unintelligible.

He flinched for a moment as something lightly touched his cheek. He stared straight ahead, able to see out the corner of his eye a mist or cloud of red slowly moving past him. It wrapped around in front of him, and the whole time the whispering was heard. Cyrus refrained from smiling.

The cloud of red had come from every direction, wrapping itself around each of the recruits. Finally the whispering ceased and Lucerine held his hand out. The cloud made its way towards his hand. The cloud condensed, appearing to be no larger than a ball. The cloud of red shifted and moved in the spherical shape that it had formed, now starting to slowly change colors, though still dominated by red.

"What I hold in my hand is nothing more than raw power. As much as it is a Hentar's choice to select you, this power I hold must also select.

"You are about to be tested beyond anything you could imagine. This will examine your mind, your memories, and your motives. For this power in my hands contains the purpose and passion, reason and understanding that you have been selected for by your master. It will hurt as they look at everything, things you don't want them to see. It won't last long, and if you pass this test then you will join your Hentar Knight as an apprentice. I ask that no one speaks until this test is done."

Lucerine looked at each of them for a moment before he finally released the power from his hand. It slowly drifted out of his hand and fell to the ground, creating a fog that quickly spread over the floor and drifted to each persons feet. For some people it was red, while others was a dark purple. Cyrus noticed his was a bright green.

It stopped and then took form, making a person of a sort in front of them. The person was unrecognizable and when you thought you knew what it looked like it would shift features. The eyes pierced into his soul, slowly eating away at whatever confidence he had.

Cyrus closed his eyes unable to look into the green form any longer. A searing pain filled his mind as his memories were opened and examined, making him look at things that he hadn't seen in years.

Alexander was before him, smiling and laughing, having a good time. A moment later, he was looking at himself walking through the halls alone. He saw himself from a new point of view, as if he was watching himself from someone else's point of view. He almost felt as if *he* was the green cloud that was examining him.

He looked over everything that had ever happened in his life in a matter of seconds. Looking at all his memories, Cyrus wished he knew what the green cloud was looking for specifically. Finally the pain ceased and he was able to open his eyes. The green form nodded and then flew up to the top of the room, waiting.

Cyrus watched in silence as all but one of the people finished their examination. The fog had all joined back together at the top of the roof and in an instant vanished. Around them they could see the person who hadn't finished the examination being led away in chains.

"You have all passed the test!" Lucerine declared. They all smiled and celebrated, while not making too much noise. "You are now officially a part of an elite group that is the crown jewel, and in many ways the very essence of the Alliance. Now comes the time for celebrating, and one more thing. A special gift from your masters to you."

He motioned for them to follow and they were led out of the room into a much more lavishly decorated room. Long narrows boxes were arranged on the wall, each one with a name over it.

"Please enjoy your new swords!" Lucerine said. Cyrus moved to the one with his name on it, undoing the latches. He opened the lid as it revealed a hand and a half sword. A red stone was set into the cross-guard which was lavishly covered in emerald and sapphire stones. He and the others experimented a little with them, watching the brilliant flashes of light as they struck each other.

Lucerine looked at them, pride beaming from all of their faces. Finally they put away their swords and strapped them on their waists.

“You have all done well and should be very proud. Now, you will be given very extravagant accommodations for the night as you celebrate. Whatever you ask for you shall be given. Your masters may arrive as soon as tomorrow, but it could take a week for them to get here. The world is a big place after all.” They chuckled.

“I look forward to working with all of you in the days to come.” They followed him to a set of large doors where they entered into a great hall filled with thousands of people. They erupted into cheers and praises as they stood on a large balcony. Cyrus and the others couldn't help but smile. They had done it.

They were Hentar Knights.

# 11

**"LOOK WHO SURVIVED** orientation!" Alexander exclaimed as Roy entered the room. Jonathan and Savannah came in behind and closed the door. They were greeted by smiling faces.

"How did it go?" Abby asked.

"We didn't die," Savannah replied.

"We also didn't fly anything," Roy interjected. "Today's instruction was mostly informational, procedures in the canyon, rules, regulations, things of that sort. Boring stuff, really."

"I expect a full report tomorrow!" Alexander exclaimed. "No excuses. You might think it's boring, off-worlder, but I've always thought flying sounded amazing."

"Jealous?" Jonathan asked.

"Hardly," Alexander said. "I might have said I think flying sounded amazing . . . But I did not say that I wanted to do the flying. If I fall off and die, I want it to be someone else's fault."

"I see how it is," Roy teased. "Always got to throw somebody under the bus."

"What's a bus?" Alexander asked.

"Never mind."

"I must say your world has very strange words that I don't think I'll ever understand."

"That's not exactly surprising," Roy retorted. Alexander started to talk but stopped as he clued into what Roy had said.

"You know, I think I'm done talking to you," Alexander stated. Heading down the hall. Jonathan and Savannah also dispersed.

"I'll talk to you," Abby said. Roy smiled.

"I don't know if that's safe. After all, apparently you and your brother manage to get contraband arrows for amusement's sake."

"That's not fair!"

"It is too, you little swindler. Time to fess up, where did you get them? If they've been *illegal* for so long."

"We know a guy, who knows a guy, who knows a guy."

"I figured that much. Name, I need a name."

"Not telling you," Abby declared.

"Why not?"

"I can't tell you all of our family secrets just yet."

"Okay," Roy said. Looking down the hall. "Alexander!!" A moment later Alexander came back into the room. "Where do you get the Tantine arrows from? Back home?"

"We know a guy, who knows a guy."

"Oh, come on!" Roy exclaimed. Those who were listening chuckled and snickered. "You're not going to tell me?"

"Nope," Alexander asked.

"Why not?"

"I don't know his name."

"What do you mean you don't know his name?" Roy asked. "How does that even begin to make sense?"

"Roy. I literally have no idea what the guy's name is. Abby met him on the road peddling arrows and other such things. We traded him with some apples, but Abby is the only person who's ever talked to him before."

"Which leads me back to square one . . . Abby." She smiled.

"You want to know his name?"

"Yes, I want to know his name."

"How much is it worth to you?"

"You're going to charge a poor off-worlder who doesn't have any money?"

"You bet," Abby replied. "And . . . You just played the *'poor little old me'* card, which means I'm going to charge you double."

"Is there any part of this scenario where I don't pay you money?" Roy asked. Abby gave him a sinister smile.

"It's not looking promising."

*   *   *   *

The remaining daylight faded and gave way to night, and soon everyone drifted off to their beds. Roy lay awake looking at the ceiling, still surprised and taken with everything this world had to offer him. He had never imagined himself in a position like he was now.

He got up and walked down the hall where the fireplace burned brightly, but no one else was up. He stepped through a door to the left and entered out onto a wide open porch, overlooking the city that was, for the moment, his home. The red sactalines glowed beneath each platform of the city, which despite the late hour, was still lit up with lights.

"Not the whole city is a school," a voice said. He turned to see Abby stirring in one of the chairs. She slowly sat up and looked out at the city. "I think only this platform is a school. The rest of it is normal life."

"What are you doing out here?" Roy asked. She looked away.

"I have trouble sleeping sometimes. I came out here to look at the stars, but the cloud we're in blocks most of them."

"It's a shame really. I love looking at the stars."

"Looks like we're in the wrong place."

"Perhaps," Roy said. "Then again, I would've never dreamed anything like this could exist before a month ago."

"Does your world have cities like this?"

"I suppose, but they don't fly. And they are much noisier. I prefer the countryside to a city any day."

"Tell me about your world," Abby said.

"What would you like to know, Abigail?" She smiled.

"What's it like? You've mentioned a lot of things from your world that have thoroughly perplexed my brother and intrigued me. You even knew what a crossbow was."

"It's true," Roy said. "Really there's not much to tell. Parts of my world are wonderful, and others have been destroyed by war and corruption. In reality, this is a more peaceful place than my world back home." Silence fell between them as they looked out on the city.

"Do you have a family? Back home, I mean," Abby said.

"My father recently passed away," Roy said, emotion coming to the forefront of his mind for the first time. "I have one brother who's still alive, though we're not really on the same page, if you know what I mean."

"I understand. Look at us and Cyrus." Roy nodded his agreement and a moment of silence followed.

"Are you scared, Roy?"

"Scared of what?"

"War? Flying? Anything."

"Afraid of flying, yes. As far as war, I can't say I've given it too much thought as of yet." Silence fell between them. "What do you think of everything we've been told so far? The classes this morning cleared things up a little bit, but I haven't lived here long. What do you think of the situation?"

"I think there's a lot the Alliance hasn't told us," Abby said. "If the Alliance really is hiding an army with intentions of taking down everyone who opposes them . . . I have a hard time supporting that, because what happens to freedom?"

"I agree. It could quickly become very much like a dictatorship. Do you think your parents know what the Alliance is up to? What they stand for?"

"No," Abby answered. "If they knew half of what we found out today, they'd have left the Sayatta region long ago. As I sat there listening in class today . . . I could see the pieces were moved into place. Nothing struck me as surprising. It made sense. Now I guess we know who's moving the pieces."

"Everyone seems to be fully expecting the Alliance to strike the Chrystarians. Why do you think that is?"

"I'm not sure," Abby admitted. "I have never even heard the name Chrystar before we met Gideon. My gut says, the fact that Alliance thinks that we're such a threat . . . means there must be something real about all of this. Something that goes beyond the implications of everyday life."

"Something bigger." She nodded. Roy pondered it for a moment. "I take it as a good omen that we are joining the Chrystarians, and the leader bears the same name."

"Indeed." A moment of silence passed. "Be careful, okay? As far as flying is concerned. I don't want them to have to peel your body off a bunch of rocks at the bottom of the canyon." Roy chuckled.

"That makes two of us. I'm a little freaked out by the notion of flying," Roy admitted. "I'm not afraid of heights, by any means. I just don't know what to expect."

"I understand," Abby replied. "I don't know what you should expect either."

"Can I ask you something, Abigail?"

"Anything."

"What do you think qualified me to be a pilot? Gideon doesn't strike me as one to just randomly pick someone for a job like that . . . but he's only known me a few days, really. What does he see in me?"

"I don't know," Abby said.

"Let's change the question, what qualities do you think would qualify me for the job?"

"I haven't even known you that long."

"After knowing me for a month what would you say?" Roy asked. Abigail fell silent and bit her bottom lip.

"You're stable. You're not rash or stupid like I can be. You seem to think things through well. You're confident. The whole time you helped us with harvesting the Gonshoesas, you never complained, even though I personally hate harvesting those pesky things.

"I would also say that you are gifted with foresight. Whether it's because you've seen similar things in your world, or whether it's simply that you're not as attached to this world. If my home was under attack, I would want to drop everything and run to save it. But if you, an off-worlder, saw my house under attack, you might run to save it, but then again you might be better suited to see a bigger picture that I would miss. Does that make sense?"

Roy nodded.

"I may not have known you long . . . but I'm glad to know you Roy Van Doren."

"I'm glad to know you too, Abigail."

"I don't know what time it is. Do you think we'll be able to stay awake in class tomorrow?"

"I'll know you've fallen asleep if you don't show up to the canyon tomorrow."

"You're not going to class?" Abby asked. Roy shook his head.

"First time pilots have their first session during the first half of the day. Then I'll join the others for regular training. The day after, I'll have a normal schedule and two hours of flight training at the end of the day."

"Good luck staying awake."

"Lot's of coffee," Roy commented. They both smiled. "If I fall asleep during flight class I think I've got issues."

"Who says you don't?"

"Hey, now."

"Just stating facts. After all you have me as a friend. That's dangerous stuff right there."

"To that, I have no argument."

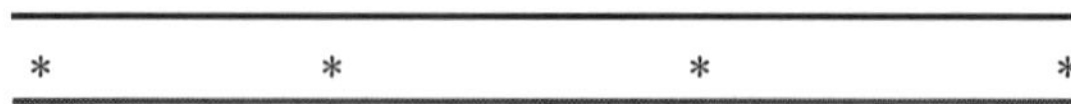

Despite the morning being full of sunshine and warm temperatures, when Roy and the others arrived at the Canyon, they found it to be near freezing and completely dark. The buildings illuminated the darkness, and in areas they could see light from other buildings scattered along the canyon floor.

Roy shook his head, trying to convince himself that he wasn't tired even though he knew he had been up way too late talking to Abigail. Something had changed in her recently, and he wasn't entirely sure what to do with it just yet.

They descended to the canyon floor, where all the other cadets were being dropped off and left to mingle in the large lighted section. Jonathan and Savannah were the first to slide off the the Griffin and join into one of the five lines that had formed only moments earlier.

"Here we go," Roy said, half to himself and half to the others. They nodded silently and stepped forward as they were directed to. When they reached the front of the line they were handed a small sactaline similar to the ones they had been given the day before.

The three of them tapped the sactalines, finding that they were instantly dressed in a flight suit. This one was heavy and thick, and covered all along the backside with small flat pieces of a dark purple material that Roy thought might be metal. All the pieces were uniform in color, shape and size. They slipped the sactaline into their pockets and stepped into formation.

"Good evening, cadets." Commander Uri said, quickly coming into view ahead of them. They saluted him. "Welcome to the first day of flight training for the Griffin Flight Corps. This will be the most important day for you as a pilot. If you fail to complete today's assignment, you will fall desperately behind as this course will not stop for anyone. If you repeatedly fail this assignment you will be dismissed from the G.F.C. immediately. Am I understood?"

"Sir! Yes, sir!"

"G.F.C. was created with the foresight that if war became inevitable, the Griffins would become an essential part of it. Our intelligence units have spotted an increased number of Dreygars flying in the airspace near the city and this canyon. It is because of this that we believe the Alliance is now actively seeking us out. That is why we will train you harder than you've ever been trained, and for that matter harder then we've trained any other group of cadets!

"The most important characteristic of a pilot is integrity. The G.F.C. cannot exist without this quality. In the G.F.C. you will be exposed to some of our greatest secrets and knowledge. We humbly ask that you do not speak of it to anyone. If the information that you learn in this course were to fall into the wrong hands, then it may be the end of the Chrystarian existence.

"I must also inform you that this canyon is the only place in the world where Griffins naturally live and breed. This canyon is their space, as much as it ours. Respect them, and they will respect you.

"Your assignment is simple in instructions, but not easy to complete. Currently you are in the region of the canyon knows as the Concord. It is the largest nesting place of the Griffins. You now must go and find your Griffin!"

"How are we supposed to do that?" Roy quietly asked. Jonathan shrugged.

"Did you have a question, cadet?" Uri asked. Roy stood tall.

"Just wondering how we go about doing that, sir!"

"Walk and explore anything you wish on the canyon floor. As much as it is a pilot's job to choose a Griffin, the Griffin must also choose you. You will know they have chosen you if they approach you. Once the bond is made the Griffin will remain loyal to you for your entire life, or until you retire from the corps.

"Before you leave, you will be given one of these," Uri pulled a thin metal plate out of his pocket. "Place it on the Griffins back and then let the Griffin go. Return to this point and check in. Then you will be able to join everyone else in their normal training routine. Cadets, you are dismissed!"

The Cadets murmured to themselves as they were once again assembled into lines, which slowly snaked their way through a narrow archway to a dark forest and valley beyond.

"Okay, so let's all walk into the forest in the middle of the night," Jonathan said.

"With no weapons or protections of any kind," Savannah added.

"I think we'll be okay," Roy said, sounding more confident than he felt. "If it was truly dangerous, they would give us weapons. If I understand everything clearly though, I don't think the Griffins are afraid of us. In fact I think they're here for us."

"What are you talking about?" Jonathan asked.

"This is the only place in the world they live and breed. As if they were designed for it. As if they have a purpose . . . whoever tamed the first one . . . it was no accident." Roy was lost to his thoughts, not noticing any questions that Savannah or Jonathan might be asking him.

Roy was overcome with a sense of familiarity. He had never been here before in his life, but something was tugging at the strings of his heart. Silence came to him and blocked out all other sounds. Strange as it was, Roy welcomed the silence.

In the silence he began to understand two things: the Griffins had been created for this moment, and he was meant to be here.

Chills swept up and down his spine as he remembered some of the conversation with Abigail about feeling as though they were in the very midst of something bigger, even though it seemed like this was just the beginning.

# ALLIANCE

He was overcome with a sense of conviction and purpose, coming to realize what might be expected of him in the future. He still was unsure why Gideon had chosen him to be a pilot, but in the dark corners of his mind, understanding was beginning to grow.

Perhaps he hadn't discovered the cabin and this world by accident after all; perhaps he was meant to be here for this very moment. The implications of the thought struck him, and for a moment he wished he hadn't thought of it.

What would happen if he was meant to leave this world? What if he wasn't meant to live here forever. What if it was like the world of Narnia, whose books he had read as a kid? He would be here for a while and then leave?

He hoped not. He didn't want to leave. The people, the places—somehow it wouldn't seem right without them. Strange world or not, it had captured a piece of his heart, and he felt like it was becoming a part of who he was.

He was pulled out of his thoughts as the three of them reached a small archway with metal gates. Guards stood at the post and handed them a metal plate, and then ushered them through.

Their breath was taken away as the valley was lit up with hundreds of thousands of lights. Each slowly moving in one direction or another. Some were blue, some were green, others still were florescent orange. They walked down into the valley, following a well worn path.

Deep growls and rumblings were heard from different places in the forest and despite the late hour, small birds chirped strange but comforting songs in the trees. Flashes of yellow would flutter through the sky and when they looked closer they could see that they were birds, whose wings lit up when they flew.

"This is something else," Savannah said. "What do you think the lights are?"

"Griffins," Jonathan suggested. "I read in a forbidden book that ancient Griffins would light up in the night. I thought it was just a myth though."

"Apparently not," Roy said.

"Do you think we're supposed to do this together or separate?" Jonathan asked.

"I think separate," Roy answered. They didn't speak any longer as each one of them slowly drifted off on their own path. Once they were into the valley a bit, there were no paths and each of them had to find their own way. Roy walked up a steep hill and looked down on all the different lights and oddities in the valley.

*I guess I just start walking towards one of them and see what happens*, Roy thought. He spotted a set of three green lights a little ways off and headed in that direction. He held his sactaline in front of him, illuminating his path. He entered into a steep ravine. The ground was rough and uneven, the traveling made difficult by trees and other debris that was knocked down.

An hour later he reached the bottom. As if the bottom of the ravine had sensed his presence, lights appeared everywhere. Some were birds like before, others were fireflies, but fireflies that glowed purples and vibrant reds.

A small stream to his left started to flow, the water changed colors and seemed to sparkle in the moonlight. He followed the bottom of the ravine, walking along with the stream until it went into a large cave.

He entered into the cave, his boots splashing in the colored water. He walked for several minutes, until finally he came out on the other side. A large lake was before him, The entire thing was surrounded by trees that were far larger than Roy could have imagined. Their trunks were more than ten times as wide as he was.

# ALLIANCE

In the distance he thought he could see a great number of trees, lined in rows, but he couldn't be sure. Down by the lakes edge there were a dozen Griffins drinking from the lake. He walked down to them but they all moved away from him.

Another hour passed as Roy continued to search the area and look around the lakeside for a Griffin that would like him. Time after time, they walked or flew away without making a sound.

*This is great,* Roy thought, sitting down on a large rock overlooking the water. He pulled the metal plate out of his pocket and stared at it, wondering what it would do.

A stick fell next to him. He scrambled to his feet and whirled around, looking into the face of a Griffin. The Griffin sat on the rocks like a dog. Its glowing green eyes staring at him.

"Hello," Roy managed. The Griffin seemed to nod. "I'm not sure what I'm supposed to do. Does this mean you've chosen me?" The Griffin put his head down and nudged the stick towards Roy. "You want me to throw it?"

The Griffin didn't move but stared intently as Roy picked up the stick and held it in the air. Roy chucked it over the lake. The Griffin bolted past him and dove into the water. No more than a second later the Griffin returned to the shore with the stick in his mouth. The Griffin put it at Roy's feet again.

The game continued for ten minutes until finally the Griffin took the whole stick in his mouth and chewed it vigorously and swallowed it. Roy reached out and touched the feathers of the Griffin.

"Don't suppose I can put this on you?" Roy asked, holding the metal plate for the Griffin to see. The Griffin dropped down onto his stomach, allowing Roy to reach up and set it on it's back. As soon as it touched the Griffins skin, the entire plate was pulled onto it. Roy quickly yanked his hand away as the gap between the Griffin and the plate ceased to exist.

Four circles, placed in the middle of each edge of the plate appeared.

*I wonder what that's for?* Roy asked himself. The Griffin stayed with him for some time before finally taking flight and vanishing to somewhere else in the canyon. Roy turned around and headed back the way he had come, exiting to the same place he had started the night. Roy looked around in confusion as only the Commander and a few other officials were present. Commander Uri straightened, his face showing surprise.

"Welcome, cadet!" Uri greeted. Roy saluted as he felt he should. "Have you found a Griffin?"

"Yes, sir," Roy replied.

"Very impressive!" Uri complimented, holding his hand out to Roy. "Never before has a cadet completed the task in so little time. Most people spend the entire day inside. Since you are so early, please come join us as we sit and talk."

Roy accepted the invitation, joining the others at the table. Food and drink were offered and he gladly accepted, strangely hungry.

"Gideon speaks very highly of you and now it is obvious why," Uri said.

"I'm glad he speaks well of me."

"He says you are from an off-worlder territory. Is that right?"

"Yes, sir."

"We've never had an off-worlder join the G.F.C. before. We are honored to have your participation."

"I'm honored to have been nominated. It's taking me a bit to get used to everything here."

"Where are you from?" Uri questioned.

"Vermont. Small cabin in the mountains."

"It must be hard being so far away from your home."

"It's been rather easy actually. I had just moved there. My family and I weren't on the best of terms."

"A family dispute is never an easy thing. I know I've had my fair share of them over the years. But with time, patience, and growth of character, they can improve."

"I suppose, though I'm in no real hurry to go back. I've been thoroughly enjoying life here."

"You're an unusual case," Uri stated. "Gideon's father almost went insane trying to get back to your cabin before he finally settled down and married."

"Interesting," Roy commented. "How many cabins are there?"

"Come again?" the Commander said.

"You said Gideon's father was trying to get back to *my* cabin. Is there more than one gateway between the worlds?"

"According to all records, there are three of them. People who come through them are few and far between, and it's been many centuries since anyone came through one of the other gateways."

"I'm glad I'm here," Roy said, unsure of where to direct the conversation. "I hope I can do the G.F.C. proud."

A while later another person came stumbling out of the valley. Within an hour everyone else returned from the assignment. They ate and talked, waiting for everyone from Granyon to join them as the sun started to rise in the canyon.

# 12

**“GLAD TO SEE** you're alive!” Alexander exclaimed as he slid off the Griffin. Abby followed close behind. Jonathan and Savannah greeted them cautiously.

“Where's Roy?” Abby asked.

“Things didn't exactly go as smooth as we would have liked,” Savannah said.

“Oh my goodness, is he alright?” Abby asked.

“See for yourself!” Roy declared walking up. The end of his sleeve was covered in red and his left hand was missing. Abby rushed to him.

“How did this happen?”

“It didn't,” Roy said, popping his hand out the end of his sleeve. They all started laughing at Alexander and Abby, who looked amused and embarrassed at the same time.

“And the red is?” Alexander asked.

“Grape juice that was served at lunch,” Jonathan answered. “He spilled the entire thing on himself.”

“You know how I said that I was happy to know you, Roy Van Doren?” Abby asked. “I think I might have to take that back.” Roy laughed as she smacked him lightly and moved past him. Savannah moved up and walked with Abby, while Alexander and Jonathan remained with Roy.

"Good one!" Jonathan exclaimed, giving Roy a high five.

"Whose evil idea was this?" Alexander asked.

"He's the brains," Roy said. Jonathan took a bow.

"Well played, very well played. What was Abby talking about, though? I can't recall any conversation where she said she was happy to know you."

"Have you been living under a rock?" Jonathan said. "They've been talking all the time. They were up most of last night talking."

"They were?" Alexander asked. He looked at Roy. "You were?"

"We're going to be late for training," Roy said turning on his heel.

"You think training will get you out of this?"

"No, of course not, but I could go over and tell Savannah some interesting things about you if I wanted to."

"Oh, please don't!"

"I'm glad you see it my way."

"I just don't see how I can argue with blackmail!"

"That's the beauty of it. You can't."

"Roy Van Doren, at least answer me one question?"

"One question," Roy agreed.

"Are you two in love or something gross like that?"

"The best way to put it is right now we don't hate each other anymore, but that's all there is at the moment. Satisfied?"

"I think so," Alexander said. They tapped their sactalines and were adorned in their training uniforms. "Just a word of warning though." He picked up a crossbow. "If anything does happen, you'd better watch yourself. I have one of these." He waved the crossbow.

"Do you even know how to use that thing?" Jonathan asked. Alexander scoffed.

"Of course I do." He set it down on the table accidentally hitting the trigger. An arrow released flying ahead of them and the girls before striking a rock column to the side of a door. They flinched and everyone ducked for cover as a ball of flame ensued and rock splinters were sent flying through the air. When the smoke cleared, they saw that half of the column was missing at the place of impact.

“Your threat, Alexander, has lost some weight, seeing as you seem perfectly capable of taking out your sister and therefore, alleviating all potential for romance.” The three of them were surrounded by a number of Canyon officials and soon were joined by Sergeant Parks.

“Who fired the shot?” the Sergeant asked.

“Him,” Roy said. Alexander smiled sheepishly.

“Hope you're satisfied, recruit!” Parks boomed. “If that column had been completely broken that whole building could have fallen down. I'm sure, now, you won't mind running thirty laps around it before you join us for today's training!”

“It's right at the top of my list,” Alexander said. Parks glared at him. “Sorry, I meant to *say,* Right away, sir!”

“That's better.” The Sergeant looked around. “Cammer!” Another man came running. “Make sure this recruit does thirty laps around compound A.”

“Yes, sir.” Cammer led Alexander off to the side.

“Gentlemen,” Parks said moving past them.

“Sergeant,” Roy said. Parks stopped and looked back at him. “I'm not t0o knowledgeable about engineering, but would that building really have collapsed if one column was gone?”

Parks smirked. “Of course not.”

"We will begin today's training with sword fighting," Parks bellowed. "Sword fighting is far more simple than you might think. In fact fighting in general is not hard. However it takes a lot of work and practice to become good, but fighting of any kind is about muscle memory. The more you do, it the less you have to think *as* you do it.

"Fighting is not a sprint, it is a marathon. You may get lucky and defeat your opponent quickly, but this is not likely and does not happen as often as you might think. People like to embellish their stories."

They chuckled.

"Endurance will be your friend. So we will train you as hard as and vigorously as we are able."

The next two hours were devoted solely to sword fighting and all the moves that they needed to memorize. They practiced them over and over again until finally Roy felt like his arms were going to fall off. Parks ordered them to rest for several minutes.

Roy rested against the wall and Abby joined him, both of them feeling more tired then they had ever been. They didn't speak, but both let a smile come to their lips as Alexander finally staggered into the training. He was drenched in sweat from head to toe.

"Look who survived consequences," Roy mocked.

"I would threaten you, but I've run far to long for that," Alexander managed.

"How big is this place?" Jonathan asked.

"The *entire* compound is very large. What have I missed?"

"Endless hours of sword fighting practice," Abby replied. The Sergeant walked up to them at that moment.

"Back to work everyone. Alexander, you'll train with me for the rest of the day so I can catch you up on everything you missed while you were running."

* * * *

The day passed and evening came until they once again found themselves gathered around a crackling fire. Savannah was asleep on the couch next to Alexander, who sat there half comatose. Each pondered their own questions which had started to grow within them.

Gideon came and took his customary seat in a large arm chair and had a cup of tea in hand.

"I'm surprised you are all still awake. I know what the first day of any training is like."

"We're surprised, too," Roy said, holding up his mug. "Coffee helps, though perhaps you might say it's helping too much." Gideon chuckled.

"Hard to resist a good cup of coffee."

"Never really drank coffee before I came here, but I've learned to like it pretty well."

"It's better than other stuff one could drink," Gideon said. Evelyn came and sank into an adjacent arm chair. "What's on your minds tonight?"

"Pain," Alexander said. "Lot's of pain. I will be much more careful with *crowbows* tomorrow."

"I think they're called crossbows," Roy corrected.

"Whatever. You know what I *bent*."

"What?" Roy asked.

Alexander waved his hand at Roy. "I'm done talking for the day!"

"Don't worry, the first day's always the hardest. From here on out it will only get easier," Evelyn told them.

"I have a question for you, Gideon," Jonathan said. Gideon looked up from the book he had brought and placed it on the table next to him. "What is the end game of the Alliance? I know they're hiding something. I know they're not what they claim to be . . . but what are they trying to accomplish?"

"The Alliance has ultimately a very simple goal. It's to stay in power at all costs. Therefore they attempt to target anyone who threatens that power. There is a backstory between Chrystar and Lucerine, the leader of the Alliance, but I don't bother you with it right now."

"If we win the war that everyone says is coming, what will victory look like?" Abby asked. "How will we know we've won? What is the plan for life after that?"

"You seem to ask good questions," Evelyn complimented. "The very basis of the Chrystarian beliefs is that everyone deserves to be free. At the very least to have the *choice* to be free. Chrystar has already saved us from ourselves by uniting the factions and resolving the hurt and conflict that had plagued us for centuries. Nonetheless, even though Chrystar brought us together it was still our choice to join. I know many people who refused to join together . . . my own sister among them. But now, we seek for the Kingdom to come and for the choice of freedom to be available to all, if only they choose it."

"What's the Kingdom?" Abby asked.

"The Kingdom is the reign that Chrystar will set up after the defeat of

Lucerine. Just as Lucerine has created the Alliance to his own designs, Chrystar seeks to set up the Kingdom. But unlike the Alliance, it will not be a kingdom ruled by him and him alone. We were made in Chrystar's image so that we could rule with him. We are not slaves to him, but out of the conviction of our hearts we want to serve him."

"I'm not quite sure what you mean," Jonathan said.

"Nowhere is it written that I have to help train you. To teach you anything," Gideon started. "It is not demanded that I answer any of your questions. But I do. Why?"

"Because you are loyal to Chrystar?" Abby asked.

"Partially, but not completely. I believe in Chrystar and everything he stands for, so much that I cannot sit back and idly do nothing while the world falls to waste. I am convicted in my heart about the truth of Chrystar and everything he stands for, to the point that I'm willing to risk my life to help others in need."

"It's not a safe job, doing what we do," Evelyn said. "Teaching and reaching out to those who have never heard of Chrystar. If the Alliance found out who we are or what we are doing, no doubt Lucerine would order us tortured and even killed if we would not be moved.

"The point is that Chrystar is risking his neck to help us. To lead us. To make a better world for others. So why wouldn't we do the same? We fight these battles not for ourselves, but for other people. So that they have the chance to learn what we have learned."

"So this 'Kingdom' that Chrystar wants to set up," Abby asked, "is meant to serve other people and help them, not serve him?"

"They are one and the same," Evelyn replied. "With his values at the heart of the Kingdom, we can serve both him and the Kingdom at the same time. We are the Kingdom. At the core, we are changed, and then we can go out into the world."

"Whereas the Alliance seeks change from a governmental to a dictatorship reign, the Kingdom is a personal choice?" Abby asked. Gideon nodded.

"Now you've got it!" Evelyn exclaimed. "There is a place for everyone. If only they choose it." They all were silent for several minutes pondering.

"So in this case, one would even say that there is room for mercy for our brother?" Alexander asked. "He has attended the Hentar Academy for three years and refused to come with us when we left."

"Yes, he still has the chance and still has the choice. But where some people get it wrong is the mercy and grace cannot last forever. Eventually war and dark days, both in reality and in thought, will come, and it is in those moments that a person must choose what it is they want to believe. The decision is theirs and theirs alone. No one can make it for them."

# 13

**THE SETTING SUN** shone down on the city of Bruden. When Cyrus had first come to Bruden three years ago, it had been overwhelming. But now it was a place he cherished and was glad to call his home.

Especially now that he was a Hentar Knight.

The thought and memory of the past few days still sent chills through him when he thought about it. His dreams had become a reality. The next chapter of his life was starting. Where it would take him, he didn't have a clue, but he secretly hoped it was to all the glory and prestige that was said to come with being a Hentar Knight.

A Dreygar landed on the platform in front of him and Cyrus climbed on. The platform soon disappeared from view as they began descending into the lower levels of the city. Cyrus was captivated as he watched everything with keen interest.

They continued their descent, putting Cyrus on edge. He had never seen this part of the city before, and even by a few of the things that were happening even on the streets, it made him uncomfortable.

They leveled off, flying just above the crowded streets, so close that Cyrus felt like he could reach down and touch their heads. He refrained from doing so as the Dreygar and pilot continued their course through the streets, turning several corners that wrapped around countless buildings, all of which stood tall and proud, despite the part of the city that they were in.

"Where are we headed?" Cyrus asked, wondering if something had gone wrong and his new master Tarjinn, was somehow displeased with him. Cyrus couldn't block out the thoughts, knowing that according to the code of the Hentar, a master who was displeased with an apprentice could at any time have them publicly executed in any number of ways.

"Don't worry. Nothing's wrong," the pilot said, but Cyrus still didn't believe it. "We're headed towards that two story building about a half mile off." Cyrus looked and saw the building, only feeling a little bit of comfort in his gut as the building at least seemed to look respectable, even if it was small and in a bad area.

The pilot landed the Dreygar on top of the building and took off moments later. Cyrus was left alone, listening to sights and sounds he had never heard in this city before. He walked to the edge of the building watching everything below him.

This wasn't the Bruden he knew, or was it? Cyrus turned back, trying to wrap his mind around everything. Peace, and serenity had been all that the Alliance had ever provided and everything Cyrus hoped to provide with his service. But what he was seeing in this part of the city was anything but.

Cyrus went back and looked over the edge again, as if expecting to see something different the second time. Instead, he saw only detestable practices, mixed with every crime you might imagine. In all his life he had never seen anything like this. A door opened on the far side and Cyrus turned to see Lucerine striding through, a large smile on his face.

"Good to see you again, Cyrus. I hope your trip was well. I'm sorry for being late. I was not informed when you were arriving or that you had been dropped off, but have no doubt, it was I that sent for you. Have you enjoyed yourself the past few days?"

"Yes, it was a good time."

"No doubt enjoying the spoils of victory and celebration?" Lucerine asked.

Cyrus smiled. "Yes sir."

"Everything to your satisfaction?"

"Quite so. The Alliance was very generous," Cyrus replied, beginning to regret the things he had done the past few days.

"Good. Only the best for the best, that's what I always say." Lucerine motioned for Cyrus to follow him.

"Where are we exactly?" Cyrus asked. "I'm not familiar with this part of the city."

"It's not something most people are familiar with, but Hentar Knights know it only too well." They entered inside to a long, slowly descending staircase. "There is a price to pay in order to have peace and serenity in all the cities of the world, and that price is that a portion of this city must be used to house those deplorable people who do not conform to the ideas taught by the Alliance. The area is completely secured, no one has ever gotten out and should they manage to they would be killed immediately."

"So what do these people do?"

"When they're not killing or destroying each other, they are put to work in our factories and laboratories. They help with many things. Truthfully, most of them are quite well behaved and good. To those who are good, we reward with better jobs and living conditions and to the bad ones . . . well, they can reap what they sow, can they not?"

"Seems fair," Cyrus said, his insides beginning to churn.

"Naturally we try to give our prized citizens the greatest care and privileges. Admittedly, we do sometimes struggle to reach the rural areas, but we are making great progress in that regard."

They reached the end of the stairs and turned a sharp corner where a door was opened for them. They walked into a vast open room and a large walkway with a railing that went across the entire area. They walked out to the bridge. Cyrus looked down, his mind reeling. Hundreds of thousands of people of every race, marched in formation. Crates and boxes in places were stacked nearly to the bottom of the walkway they were on. From the far end of the room they could see piles of sactalines, letting off their brilliant light.

"What is this?" Cyrus asked.

"Preparations, my boy," Lucerine said. "This is called the Costnas. It's an old term for storehouse. We have been training an army to squelch any opposition that we fear may spring up in the future."

"Does anyone outside of the Hentar know this?"

"No, and it needs to stay that way," Lucerine said. "We could tell the commoners and we will, but it'll be best to not tell them too soon. This is a matter of security and safety."

"Safety and security from who?" Cyrus asked.

"Those who seek to overthrow us! I once mentioned to you that there were a large number of people over the years who had not shown up at any of the Alliance affiliated schools?"

Cyrus nodded.

"That number is well over a million souls, and that was as of two years ago! Intelligence reports hint that the problematic groups, which were once separate, are now joined together as one. Such a fighting force would be devastating to the world. Being in a leadership position, it is my duty to protect those I hold dear."

"Do you know where these people are hiding? It seems impossible to hide that many people anywhere."

"You are quite right. We don't know where they are hiding, but we are desperately trying to figure it out. In a way we hope they will attack us first."

"Why?"

"Because then *they* are the bad guys, and we get to come to the rescue."

"But won't there be loss of life on part of the Alliance?"

"It is likely, but I'm not too concerned. They'll be acceptable losses as it were." They walked in silence across the expansive room. Cyrus felt more and more uncomfortable as a voice in his head told him this wasn't right. Did this happen to all the Hentar or was it something only he was feeling?

"So what will people—"

"Enough talk about that subject Cyrus, you can take it up more with your master shortly."

"Tarjinn's here?" Cyrus asked.

"Yes. She likes to hide in the library, when she's on her break, which she is now. I have new orders for both of you to get to work on immediately." Cyrus wished he could feel better about that but inside his heart was in turmoil.

They finally exited the great room and entered into another room just as big, but very different. Below were dozens of desks and chairs, all neatly arranged through hundreds of bookshelves.

"Welcome to the library of the Hentar!" Lucerine announced. Cyrus took it all in, not minding this part so much. They walked for some time through the rows and rows of desks and shelves. Although it appeared to be a very random path they were taking, Lucerine seemed confident in where he was headed.

"Every Hentar Knight is given their own special room, where they can fill the shelves with whatever books they want or need. We are headed for Tarjinn's library."

They came to a door on the far side and they quickly went through it, coming into a smaller room maybe two hundred feet wide, by two hundred feet long. Shelves of books filled the space and on the back wall a fireplace and two deep armchairs could be seen. A person in a dark black cloak, with the hood up sat reading next to the fire.

"Greetings, Tarjinn!" Lucerine exclaimed. Tarjinn stood and bowed to him as he approached. Cyrus didn't speak, growing more nervous with each second that passed. "Cyrus Reno, I would like you to meet Tarjinn. Tarjinn, Cyrus. I hope you will benefit from this arrangement and here are your orders once you get everything settled and get to know each other a bit. No immediate rush on these as they will take some time." He handed Tarjinn a small rolled up piece of parchment. "I'll leave you to it."

Lucerine quickly left and Tarjinn stood and strode to a window where she could look over the library beyond. She stood there silent for some time, and then turned suddenly.

"Come," Tarjinn told him. Her tone was harsh and cruel. Cyrus reluctantly followed her. They swiftly exited the library and climbed aboard a Dreygar and took to the sky. They headed towards the west, flying an unknown amount of time. All the while Tarjinn's heavy cloak didn't budge and her hood didn't come down, despite all the wind.

An hour later, they descended and put down on the slopes of a mountain. To Cyrus's surprise, a modest, but tasteful house sat in the shadows of the mountain. A lake lay to their right. Without speaking, she motioned for him to follow and stormed inside.

She unrolled the parchment and crumpled it in her hands a moment later, throwing it on the floor. In an instant she pulled off her cloak and hood and threw them to the ground. She sank into a deep arm chair next to a fireplace. The fireplace started itself immediately after. Cyrus stood in the doorway confused. He hadn't known what to expect, but so far he hadn't expected this.

"Sit!" Tarjinn yelled. Cyrus hastily closed the door and hurried to a chair across from her. He looked away for several moments, unsure if he should look at her. When finally he did he was looking into vacant eyes that stared ahead, as though there were things going on in her mind that he would never know about. The silence became uneasy and uncomfortable the longer it persisted.

"Sorry I yelled at you," Tarjinn said. Cyrus remained speechless, trying to find words. "Not a very nice start to a relationship is it?"

"Ah . . . it's okay I wasn't sure what to expect," Cyrus said. A moment of silence passed by them.

"Being a Hentar Knight is not an easy road. It requires sacrifice and discipline and cannot be achieved by the common everyday yokel. I am glad to see that you passed my test."

"Your test?"

"Yes, the green mist, the raw power. I can program it to seek out any character traits that I want, no questions asked. I've been watching you come up through the ranks and had my eye on you for quite some time."

"Thank you," Cyrus said. "I'm glad it all worked out."

Tarjinn scoffed and looked away. "Now I have someone to share in my suffering."

"Pardon?"

"Truth hurts, but this truth will only hurt you a little bit. You would've never passed to be anyone's apprentice if it hadn't been me who sought you out."

Cyrus remained silent, unsure of how to respond. "I take offense to that."

"Of course you do, but I will make my case and prove my point," Tarjinn said, leaning forward till her elbows were resting on her knees. "What did you think of the Costnas?"

"I was glad to finally see them. I had heard about them. And I love books, so a library was neat to see."

"What did you think of the location of the library? The setting, the things you saw and took note of?"

"I can see how much the Alliance loves its people. The values of the Hentar are the only thing keeping the world from falling to pieces," Cyrus said, his heart pounding.

"Nice try," Tarjinn replied, sitting back into her chair. "You said that because you thought I wanted to hear that. Any other master that would work . . . not with me."

"What am I suppose to say?"

"Go get the orders that I crumpled up and threw on the floor; then read them aloud."

Cyrus did as she said. Picking up the piece of parchment and carefully unfolded the orders, he silently read them.

"Read them aloud."

*'By order of Lucerine, his supreme majesty of the Alliance, the orders to Tarjinn and her new apprentice, Cyrus, are as follows: Our enemies are growing stronger and more cunning, and it is believed that we cannot wait any longer, for fear that they will try to overthrow the Alliance by year's end. Use all resources necessary to find the rumored hidden cities of the Chrystarians. When found, send word with reports on the quickest way to dispatch of the city and all its inhabitants.'*

Cyrus folded up the paper and put it on the coffee table between them. Tarjinn looked at him knowingly.

"What did *you* think of the orders?" Tarjinn asked. "Honestly."

"Honestly?"

"Yes. I want to know."

"They seemed a little drastic to me," Cyrus said. "With what I was told today, I'm not sure what to think. I don't like the word *dispatch*."

"I agree," Tarjinn said. "They should just write the word *murder* in there. It would be more truthful."

"Why don't they?" Cyrus asked.

"Because they have to look good. If the note were to fall into someone else's hand it would be perceived differently. Now I ask you . . . how do *you* feel about that?"

"I would have a hard time believing I could kill everyone," Cyrus admitted. "I would try to at least leave moms and their kids—"

"That's not the orders!" Tarjinn said forcefully. "Now tell me honestly if you could do it."

"No, I couldn't," Cyrus admitted. Tarjinn smiled, and for the first time warmness and life began to show in her face, even if it was only for a second.

"I knew you were going to say that."

"How?"

"I've watched you, Cyrus. Even as you were on your summer vacations. The way you interact with your family would've come back to haunt you. Your mom and dad make good efforts to look supportive of the Alliance, but I doubt their loyalty. Also, you have a brother and a sister who were of age this year. They were supposed to be here at the Hentar Academy. They did not show up. Here or at any Alliance affiliated school for that matter."

"You know a lot," Cyrus said.

"That's why you're alive. Do you know where your siblings are?"

"No, I don't."

"They could be among the Chrystarians. Would you be able to kill them? Your own kin?"

"What's your point?" Cyrus asked.

"My point is, I have a plan, and I need to know that I can trust you. My plan is risky. If it fails, we'll be dead. If it goes wrong in other matters I will be forced to kill you as the code requires me to. However, *if* we succeed, we may come out of this with some part of our souls and dignity intact."

Cyrus pondered her every word, confused and intrigued by the woman who sat in front of him. His expectations had been shattered, and he honestly didn't have any idea what to think of anything that had been said.

"What's your plan?"

"As far as my plan is concerned we need to figure before we go any further, how far do we want to go? This is the point of no return. Once again I remind you that before this is all said and done, I may be forced to kill you."

# 14

**"TO FLY A GRIFFIN** is one of the greatest experiences in all the world," Commander Uri boomed. "It is also going to be one of the most dangerous." Roy, Jonathan, and Savannah stood tall in line with the others as the Commander paced in front of the large group. The sun shone brightly in the canyon, illuminating all their uniforms.

"I do not say this to scare you. I say this to prepare you. While you have no doubt ridden Griffins in comfort up until now, you will be expected to fly in any conditions, at any moment, in situations that will be less than ideal.

"If you are standing here, it means all of you successfully tamed a Griffin and put one of these on its backs two weeks ago." Uri held up a piece of metal like they had been given the other night. "Once it was taken into their back four circles, one centered on each side, appeared. This is one way that you will fly your Griffin."

*Buttons?* Roy thought to himself.

"There are two ways to command a Griffin. One is by voice commands, and the other is by using these circles. They highlight pressure points in the Griffin. When pressed, they will move in that direction. It takes about two weeks for the metal to be fully integrated into the Griffin, which is why as of yet, you have not been instructed in the art of flying.

"Each Griffin is different and as such, has a different personality; therefore, you will only train and fly the Griffin you tamed two weeks ago. If your Griffin dies in battle, you will have to tame another.

"The typical Griffin can carry roughly an entire regiment, or twenty people in addition to the pilot. However this will tire your Griffin out quickly if it is a long fight. That is why from each regiment, three pilots are selected. If one Griffin is taken out, the other two can continue, and if two Griffins are taken out then at least three people can carry on with the mission. A triple braided cord is not easily broken!

"You may notice that the flight uniform you were given today is different from the ones you've been wearing up till now. You'll notice three small holes on the front of your chest guard. I will tell you now what these are for." He motioned for people, who stood with nicely decorated boxes to come and present one to each pilot. As instructed, they opened it revealing three sactalines. One green, and the other two orange.

"The orange sactalines are armor for your Griffin. They are small and compact; designed to fit in the small holes on the front of your chest guard. Put the orange ones in!" They did as he said. "These work just like the other sactalines, tap them and your Griffin will be protected in armor. Like your own, the armor does wear out after so many direct hits. For this reason you've been given two of them

"Now for a new innovation," Uri said, pulling a green sactaline into view, they picked up their own and waited for instructions. "These green ones are still mysterious to many people, but it has been discovered that they will pass your voice to whoever you say."

*Radios? Nice!* Roy thought to himself.

"Put it into your chest guard." They did as he said, all three sactalines glowed brightly. "As pilots you will be required to be able to use these flawlessly. It will take some getting used to if you're familiar with the hand signals that have been customary up until now.

"Pilots will be able to speak directly to the Regiment Captain, and Regiment Leader who will also be adorned with such a sactaline! Questions?"

"What happens if we fall off?" Savannah asked.

"You die," another cadet said. Some snickers went off.

"It may be amusing here," the Commander scolded. "But it would not be funny if it were happening to you. For those who found that answer particularly amusing, I order you to stay after I release everyone else to their assignment. Understood?" The group who had laughed fell silent and were clearly nervous.

"To answer your question, your suit has many attributes, one of which is that it is magnetic. To be more specific the blood of a Griffin has an unusually high iron content and your suit is designed to be drawn to that only. Unless you are doing something highly stupid, falling off your Griffin should be impossible. Next question?"

"How many Griffins are there in the canyon?" another cadet asked.

"The main flock of Griffins number around three hundred thousand. There are other flocks both in this canyon and at other secured sights around the world, but they all number less than fifty-thousand each. Next?"

"Does the Alliance have anything that compares to a Griffin?" Roy asked.

"Yes, they have Dreygars, which have similar attributes, though they are not nearly as graceful or majestic as a Griffin. Wouldn't you agree?"

Roy nodded.

"Do they come bigger than the ones we saw yesterday?" another student asked. "I've seen some Dreygars and that are absolutely massive." Others voice their agreement.

"They come in many sizes and there are mutant classes of both creatures.

Currently, nearly five thousand Griffins of this size are known in the world today. They can carry nearly six hundred people. Our top breeders and researches are trying to increase their numbers as we speak. Any more questions?" Uri asked. No one answered. "Very good. Today's assignment is simple. Left face!" They all turned to their left.

"From this point, you can see the cliff known as the Cliff of Rekum." Climb to the top of it, find your Griffin and fly it back to this point. Take it easy when flying for the first time! Today's flight is not about speed, it is about determination. You'll be tested to see if you truly have what it takes to become a pilot." Uri looked over the group one last time, searching each of their faces carefully. "You have your assignment. I wish you luck, and I will see you soon!"

The group dispersed from the area, all of them heading towards the Cliff of Rekum, which was nearly a mile away. By the time they reached the cliff everyone had split into their regiments, and all were trying to find their own way up.

The cliff was made of a dark brown rock. Roy pondered how they were supposed to scale it at all, when there appeared to be no particular stairs or doorway for them to use.

"Looks like we're supposed to climb it?" Jonathan asked.

"How?" Savannah asked.

"One rock at a time," Roy said, extending as far as he could reach and grasping the rock. They climbed and struggled their way up the cliff, often having to help one another reach the next landing. In some places there seemed to be narrow ledges on the border that they could walk on, but still they didn't seem to lead in any specific direction. An hour later they reached the top, letting themselves collapse on the hard rocky topside of the cliff.

"For a while I thought we were all going to die, climbing up that cliff,"

Savannah said. Jonathan nodded his agreement.

"Triple braided cord—" Roy started.

"Not easily broken," the others finished. They stood to their feet looking around the barren and empty top of the cliff. They mindlessly wandered for a few minutes, taking in the beautiful view of the canyon below.

"Where are our Griffins?" Savannah asked.

"Maybe we have to call for them," Roy suggested.

Jonathan shrugged and faced the open canyon. "Hey Griffin! Come here!"

"I don't think that's going to work." Roy said.

"What else are we supposed to do?" Savannah asked. "It's not like they have names."

"Maybe we should give them names," Roy suggested.

"What do you name a Griffin?"

"Anything you want," Roy answered.

"In that case I'm calling mine Griff," Jonathan declared. "Griff, come here!" Jonathan laughed, thinking he had made a great joke until a griffin landed behind him on the cliff. Jonathan's look of amusement turned to awe as he gently stroked the powerful creature.

"Dawnchaser!" Savannah cried out. Immediately, her Griffin swooped down onto the cliff.

"What are you going to name yours Roy? Vermont?" Jonathan asked.

Roy shrugged. "I have no idea! Any suggestions would be welcome. I have to be careful not to name it anything that sounds like an off-worlder or I'll be the laughing stock of the cadets."

"So my suggestion of naming it Vermont?"

"Denied." Without warning the Griffin Roy had tamed two weeks ago landed next to them and sat down like it was a dog. "Did you like the name Vermont?" The Griffin seemed to shake it's head.

"Me, neither. Let's see, how about Skywalker?" Roy asked. The Griffins expression was unchanged. "Never mind, forget that one."

"Now that would've made you the laughing stock of the G.F.C." Savannah said. "I've never heard of walking on a sky before."

"We are flying through the sky," Jonathan pointed out.

"Yes, but that's not the same as walking."

"Good point," Jonathan agreed. "Would that be an off-worlder name, Roy?"

"Yeah, it would've been very popular back in my world," Roy answered, amused.

"Interesting." Roy turned his attention back to his Griffin.

"Well, I do like the idea of having sky in your name, because obviously we fly . . . that makes sense right?" The Griffin seemed to nod. "I could call you Skylark?" The Griffin coughed. "Skyquill?" The Griffin stood to his feet like the others were doing. "Nice to meet you, Skyquill."

"I think that Griffin must be an off-worlder too," Jonathan said, from atop his own. "I think he's a little off in the head."

"We'll see who's laughing when we beat you guys back to the Commander," Roy said, starting to climb up on the Griffin's back. "Alright, let's go!" Skyquill jumped into the air before Roy even got on his back, sending Roy tumbling backwards onto the top of the cliff once again. All three of them laughed.

"I don't think you'll be winning any races with him," Savannah said through her own laughter.

"Skyquill!" Roy yelled. In an instant the Griffin was back on the ground in front of him. "Maybe I said the wrong thing, but I need to actually be on your back before you take off."

"This is where I remind everyone to put their helmets on," Savannah said. They did so and then laid down on their stomachs, positioning themselves where it would be comfortable to use the pressure point pad to steer.

"On three we go, okay?" Roy asked.

"Dude, I can hear you amazingly well, even with the helmets on. You don't have to yell," Jonathan scolded.

Roy smiled. "Sorry I forgot we have radios now."

"What in the blazes is a radio?"

"Why don't you try to catch me, and I'll explain it to you Three . . . Two . . . One . . . go!" Their Griffins leapt into the sky, spreading their enormous wings. Within seconds they had accelerated at speeds which were far greater than anything they had experienced so far.

They all cried out and pushed the down pressure point. In an instant all three of their Griffins were in a nose-dive, the ground racing towards them. They clung to the Griffins desperately, forgetting that they couldn't fall. They tried their best to level out, now flying only fifty feet off the bottom of the canyon.

"This is way faster than I thought it would be!" Savannah said as she and Dawnchaser raced overhead Roy and Jonathan.

"This is awesome!" Roy said, hitting the button to the left. Skyquill leaned sharply, as if to miss oncoming arrows. Roy let go and he leveled out.

"I'm officially freaked out!" Jonathan exclaimed. The three of them raced over the canyon floor, some of it no more than a blur. They climbed into the sky a little and then each tried their hands at turning and swerving. After a while they all turned around and headed towards the Commander who they knew would be waiting.

"Looks like it's just ahead," Savannah announced, pointing it out to everyone else.

"How do we get them to land?" Jonathan asked.

"Land!" Roy said to Skyquill. In a moment, Skyquill descended sharply to the ground and abruptly landed on the canyon floor. Roy, who had not expected such a rough landing was thrown over the Griffins head and awkwardly tumbled. Roy groaned as he sat up and looked at Skyquill who looked rather proud of himself. For a moment Roy thought he would be the laughing stock of the G.F.C. But his fears were put to rest as both Savannah and Jonathan were thrown over their griffins

"That was a very rough landing," Roy announced.

"I perhaps should have informed you that a Griffin who has never been flown sometimes takes a while to break in, so to speak." They looked to see the commander standing over them.

"Does this happen to everyone?" Savannah asked, groaning as she stood to her feet. Uri smiled.

"Most people," came the reply. "That is all for your training today. Roy please stay behind. The rest of you are dismissed." Roy swallowed hard as he stood.

"Have I done something wrong, sir?" Roy asked.

"Wait here until I send the other cadets back for the night." Roy reluctantly took a seat next to Skyquill who seemed to be in no hurry to move anywhere.

The time passed slowly. Nearly an hour passed before the last cadets arrived and were sent home. Roy had been taken into one of the buildings and placed in a room with no tables or chairs. Just the plain brown walls and a few torches for light.

Roy tried his best to calm himself and keep his mind working as the time stretched on. Finally without warning Commander Uri came in by himself. Roy stood at attention as Commander Uri came closer.

"Cadet Roy Van Doren. This is your name, is it not?"

"It is," Roy answered.

"It is my duty as Commander of the G.F.C. to make hard decisions when they have to made. It's one of the unpleasant parts of my job, but nonetheless, it is. Therefore, I am required to inform you that effective immediately you are being dismissed from the G.F.C."

"What!" Roy exclaimed.

"I know this must be shocking," Uri said. "But according to rules and procedural protocols, I cannot reveal the reason behind this until they are fully investigated."

"Why can't I know? Why can't I defend myself?" Roy asked, indignant.

"The subject matter of the reasons for your excusal are such that it would give us a better picture of the truth of the matter if you do not know them."

"So what am I to do?" Roy asked. "Sit back and do nothing?"

"A review board will hear your case next week," Uri explained. "Until then you are to go about your normal business, but you are forbidden to step any foot into the G.F.C. buildings, or participate in training until then."

"I don't believe this!"

"A pilot and Griffin are being provided to give you a safe journey back. Cadet Roy, you are dismissed." Roy remained where he was, determined to stay and argue his case. Three guards entered the room, hands on their swords. Roy considered his options but then started his way out of the room. He climbed aboard the Griffin and was lost to his thoughts and hardly remembered anything about the flight until he landed outside his building.

He climbed the great steps and made his way back to his dwelling where everyone was huddled around the fireplace. They jumped to their feet and swarmed him immediately, peppering him with more questions than he could keep up with.

"Everyone! Everyone! Have a seat, let the poor man have a little breathing room, please!" Evelyn cried above the noise of the crowd. They mumbled to themselves, but took their seats and remained quiet. Gideon motioned Roy to a chair across from him.

"It's been well-reported to me that you had to stay afterwards. Why?"

"I'm not sure. But the fact of the matter is I've been dismissed from the G.F.C. effective immediately." Everyone started protesting, but Gideon held up a hand to silence them.

"Why?"

"No reason was given. The Commander said it was sensitive information and it would be better if I was not told."

"How does that even begin to make sense?" Alexander asked.

Gideon thought for a moment. "There are only one or two reasons action like that would and could be taken, but nothing that I can recall would spur either of those two reasons."

"Then why is this happening?" Roy asked.

"You didn't do anything wrong, did you?"

"No, sir."

"Didn't disrespect any rules?"

"I would never do that."

"I believe you. Now I just have to get Commander Uri to see it my way."

"Can you do that?" Roy asked.

"As your Regiment leader? I can request a meeting with Uri and see what I can dig up on the matter."

"He says the case will be heard by a review board next week."

"That's awfully sudden." The entire room was silent as Gideon appeared to be in great thought.

"What do we do?" Abby asked.

"I will do what I can to get to the bottom of this, but it may take a day or two to get everything arranged," Gideon explained. "I would advise that you enjoy your weekend, if that is possible. For now you must respect his actions and play by the rules. I've known Uri for quite some time and he can be an interesting person to deal with, but I know how. Don't you worry about that. You won't be suspended from the G.F.C. for long. Not if I have anything to say about it."

After that, everyone agreed that the matter was settled and there was nothing further to discuss. Roy slipped into his bed, playing through the events of the day over and over again. Finally after his mind was too tired to continue any longer, he fell asleep.

"Coffee?" Roy asked. He held a mug out to Abby who was once again sitting on the large balcony. She smiled and accepted it.

"You, Roy Van Doren, are getting to know me too well," Abby said.

"Not a bad thing if you ask me, Abigail."

"Me, neither." They fell into silence, watching the sun begin to peak over the tall buildings of the sleeping city. "It's amazing how they've managed to make this 'cloud' so the sun can still come through."

"It's a bit mind boggling," Roy admitted. "It's a nice place. But I think I'd take my cabin back home if I could."

"You want to go back?"

"No. If I could have a cabin here somewhere in the woods, away from the city . . . that would be nice."

"I miss the countryside," Abby said. "The smell of the dew in the morning. The light wind that rustles the leaves on the trees. It has a place in my heart. As nice as this city is, I hope I can return to the country someday."

"That makes two of us."

"I do have a bone to pick with you, Mr. Van Doren.

"Oh?"

"I told you not to die when you started the G.F.C."

"And I haven't," Roy defended. "To be fair you never said that I couldn't get kicked out of the G.F.C."

"I suppose you're right." Abby thought for a moment. "But that's not much better. What's next? You going to get kicked out of the Kingdom all together?"

"No, I think I'm content with getting kicked out of only the G.F.C."

Abby laughed. "Good to see you aim high."

"I try," Roy replied. "Besides if I were to get kicked all the way out I wouldn't get to spend as much time with you." Abby lightly scoffed and waved him away.

"Are you still clueless on why you got dismissed?"

"Pretty much. I can't think of a single thing."

"How'd you like to find out?" Abby asked.

Roy gave her a look. "How?"

"I overheard Evelyn and Gideon talking, last night after everyone was in bed. Gideon was irate about the whole situation and is meeting Uri in the city late tonight."

"How are we supposed to get there?" Roy asked. "New students aren't allowed to visit the city without special permission from their Regiment officers. And I'm not about to go forging any special permission either."

"I wouldn't do that," Abby said. "But I would consider making a little excursion away from everything tonight."

"Sounds like a reasonable plan. Do you know where this meeting is going to be?"

"No," Abby answered. "But I'm sure if I ask the right questions and listen to the right conversations, I can probably figure it out. Gideon will probably give some other excuse as to what he's doing, but he may not change the part about where he's going."

"You've thought this out, haven't you?" She smiled.

"We could casually take a stroll down in the park and then borrow a Griffin for a while."

"It's a date," Roy said.

"A date?" Abby asked.

"I-I-I meant it's a plan!" Roy exclaimed. "It's a good plan. We should do it. Never mind!"

Abby leaned closer to him. "I certainly wouldn't mind if it's a date," she whispered with a wink. "Albeit, an unofficial one."

"It's a date then. What are we going to do about your brother? Is he going to know?"

"Oh, good heavens, no!" Abby exclaimed. "I love my brother dearly, but when it comes to things like this he can't know anything. He horribly teased me about a crush I had a few years back and it ruined the whole thing. I will even go as far as admitting I became a bit obnoxious to new people (especially guys) just so he would never suspect anything; if ever I was interested again. So, no, Alexander is not finding out about anything, until there's something to find out."

"Agreed, but we're not going to be able to just slip away together or separate without him noticing."

"Leave it to me. I'll make sure he's properly distracted."

# 15

**AS ABBY HAD PREDICTED,** Gideon did announce plans to be gone for the evening, though he still had yet to announce where. Roy and Abby waited, looking for the right opportunity to ask where Gideon was going to be later that night, but do so without raising any suspicion.

In addition to everything else, Abby was also plotting how to distract Alexander long enough that he wouldn't notice that she and Roy were going off together for a while, before they tried to listen in on whatever meeting Gideon was going to do.

"Where's Gideon going tonight?" Abby asked, flipping through a newspaper.

"He has a meeting with an old acquaintance, most likely they'll spend the time reminiscing about the good old days," Evelyn said. Roy stood around the corner and breathed a sigh of relief, from watching her reaction she didn't appear to suspect anything. Roy nodded in her direction, able to be seen by Abby, but not by Evelyn.

"Favorite hot spot or something of the sort?" Abby asked.

"I have no idea. It's on the other side of the city. Where is he anyway?" Evelyn looked around the common room. "I'd better go find him."

"Is something wrong?" Abby said.

"No, but he has another meeting with Chrystar prior to the hangout with his old friend," Evelyn said. "He can't be late for that."

"Does it start soon?"

"He's not meeting his friend until supper, but he's supposed to be meeting with Chrystar in twenty minutes," Evelyn stood and hastened down one of the other hallways looking for Gideon. Roy came out of hiding and quickly sat down next to Abby.

"What do we do now?" Abby asked frantically.

"He's not meeting his friend till supper," Roy reminded. "That means unless it's a really long meeting with Chrystar he'll be coming back here. If we can get away we can have the entire afternoon to ourselves." Abby smiled, and then frantically motioned Roy out of sight as Alexander and Jonathan came through the doors.

"Hello, sister!" Alexander cheerfully greeted walking by her. He paused and looked back at her, seeming to be studying her. "Abby?"

"Yes."

"You look different," Alexander said. Roy muffled a snicker as the look on Alexander's face was nothing short of hilarious.

"And you look uglier than yesterday, but I wasn't going to say anything," Abby replied.

Jonathan let out a laugh.

"I know what it is! You have your hair done up!" Alexander paused as if pleased with himself. "And you're wearing a dress?"

"We might be in training, but does that mean I can't look and act like a girl during the weekend?" Abby asked.

Alexander nodded, seeming confused. "It would be a first for you . . . then again, to each their own." He started walking away.

"Actually, Alexander, I was supposed to relay a message from Savannah." Alexander stopped and looked attentive.

Roy smiled as he watched.

"A message? Do tell."

"She wanted to have a late lunch with you down at the Falls." Alexander's eyebrows raised and a smile came to his face.

"Oh, did she?" An uncontrollable smile came across his face. "Well, Jonathan, I know I had said I would whoop you at a game of Trium, but I think I will be spending the afternoon elsewhere! Can we play later though?"

"Hey, I hear you. Don't keep a woman waiting, because that's usually what they do," Jonathan said. Alexander cheerfully exited out the main door and was lost from sight, though whatever ridiculous song he was singing to himself could still be heard for a few seconds. "I'm not sure if that's a good thing or a bad thing."

"You don't like Savannah?" Abby asked.

"It's not that—she's just way too smart for a guy like him," Jonathan said. Panic came over his face. "Not that your brother is dumb! I didn't mean it like that!"

"I know. It's okay; as his twin sister I could never disagree with that sentiment," Abby said.

Jonathan breathed a sigh of relief and smiled. "*This* is the education I missed out on by being an only child."

Roy stepped out from his spot around the corner and waved at Jonathan. A second later Savannah came out of the girls hall. Jonathan's face showed surprise, but also confusion and he wasn't able to speak.

"Just the person I wanted to see!" Roy said.

Savannah stopped, surprised. "Me?"

"Yeah. Actually, I have a message from Alexander. He was going out on the town for the afternoon and wondered if you might join him?"

"Sounds lovely," Savannah replied, shock seeming to taint her voice. "When?"

"He's hoping you'd join him now. He said he would be waiting by the Archway, or was it the Tri-Gur?" Roy asked Abby.

"It was neither of those. He said he'd be down at the Falls. Though he mentioned likely taking you to either one of those spots later," Abby said.

"Huh?" Savannah said.

"Not sound appealing?" Roy asked.

"Oh, no, it does! I just am a bit surprised. We've talked some, but not that much."

"He can be a little shy when it comes to women," Abby said.

"Aren't we all?" Roy asked. "Who can blame us really?"

"How long has it been since he left?"

"Ten minutes," Abby said. "He was heading towards the Falls."

"I guess I'll see you later," Savannah said. Abby smiled and waved as soon she was out of the door.

"Now that was a good plan!" Roy exclaimed, high-fiving Abby. They both smiled.

"And what are you two going to do?" Jonathan asked, knowingly.

"Nothing. Roy was just leaving, I thought I might as well try to set up Alexander and Savannah. We both know he's got a crush on her."

"Nice try," Jonathan replied. "I can see what's going on here. You two are going on a date, and you don't want your brother finding out."

"Yes and we'd prefer him to not know about it," Roy stated.

Jonathan chuckled. "Don't worry, your secrets safe with me."

Roy shot him a look.

"No, really, it is. I saw nothing! I heard nothing! I was not even here!" They laughed. "Go on you two, have fun."

"See you outside?" Roy asked. Abby shook her head.

"I'd better come with you. Women take forever to get ready for stuff like this," Jonathan teased.

"I'm not that bad," Abby defended. "I need maybe ten minutes."

"Women have a reputation."

"I'm not worried about it," Roy said. "The way I see it, it won't take her that long, because she doesn't have to work as hard everyone else to look good." Abby smiled, but hid her face behind the news paper. Jonathan smiled at the two of them.

"Have fun."

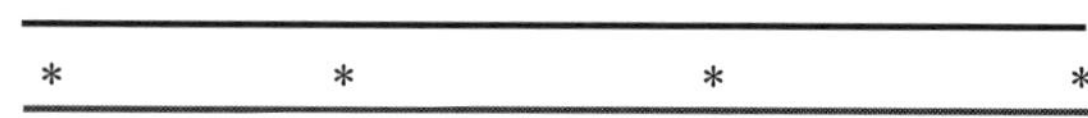

As Abby had said, it was only ten minutes until she came out the doors and found him at the spot they had agreed to meet at. She wore a nice, but still casual dress, and although they didn't do anything big or fancy. The afternoon had gone far quicker than either of them had wished it to.

For the most part they found themselves walking through one of the lush garden parks, or sitting at a table somewhere while enjoying drinks and each other's company.

The afternoon slipped on until evening, and they quietly sat outside their building, watching the doorway, waiting for Gideon to come out and head towards one of the Griffins. They hoped to follow him on a Griffin of their own, but were still contemplating how this was going to happen, seeing as new students weren't allowed into the city until their training was done.

"I had a good time today," Abby said.

"Me, too. I'll be curious to know if Alexander's been having a good time or not," Roy said.

Abby smiled. "I hope so, it'll make getting back tonight much easier."

They both straightened and fell silent as Gideon came out of the building and briskly walked towards one of the Griffins with a pilot. They spoke for only a minute before they both climbed on and took to the sky.

"So now for the part of this date that could kill us!" Roy exclaimed as they quickly darted towards one of the Griffins, whose rider was evidently at supper.

"I'm not too worried. You've flown before." Abby said, climbing up behind Roy.

"Yeah, but this isn't Skyquill. I've been told each Griffin is different and they will react to you differently. Do you still see Gideon?"

"Yeah he's over there." Abby pointed him out as Roy took one last deep breath.

"Let's do this!" Roy cried. He pushed the Griffin up into the sky, both of them clinging on for dear life as the Griffin climbed nearly straight up. After a moment Roy was able to balance the Griffin out as they both regained sight of Gideon.

"I know what we're doing is breaking a lot of rules, but this is fun!" Abby exclaimed. They followed Gideon, staying a comfortable distance behind him. As much as they could manage, they tried to enjoy the beautiful city that seemed like it towered over them no matter how high they were.

Without warning Gideon's Griffin dropped sharply, landing in a small alley between some rundown buildings. Roy circled around and started his descent, intending to land on the roof of the building.

"Brace yourself," Roy said. Before anything else could be said, they were thrown forward, getting a mouth full of feathers and fuzz. "That was better than I've done on Skyquill."

# ALLIANCE

"Well done, Mr. Van Doren," Abby said climbing down and heading towards the edge, where she could look into the alley. Roy dropped down and joined her, watching as Gideon knocked on the door of a darkened house. A few moments passed before the door was opened and Gideon was ushered inside.

They frantically searched for the stairs or a ladder to get down off the roof. They found a ladder to the left and they quickly descended, moving around to the front of the building. They kept to the shadows, surprised to find that the door of the building was wide open. Torch light flickered inside.

"This is a strange place," Abby said, looking at everything carefully. "What's Gideon doing in a place like this?" Roy held a finger to his lips as they crept forward to a small room with light coming from it. They quickly darted to the far side of the doorway, keeping in the shadows and listening to the conversation as it played out in the room.

"He's meeting with the Commander!" Roy quietly exclaimed. This time is was Abby's turn to hold a finger to her lips. Gideon and Uri both sat in deep arm chairs, which faced each other.

"So, do tell, Gideon. What is it that you want?"

"I'm sure you must know why I'm here?"

"Probably something to do with your pilot which was released from the G.F.C.?"

"That's right."

"First of all, let me just say that I can control a lot of things, but I cannot control if the council takes action without consulting me first."

"I got the papers this morning," Gideon replied. "They were signed by *you* and you alone, and unless regulations have changed, it is required for *all* members of the council to sign off in green ink."

"A new law goes into effect Monday, allowing me to dismiss anyone whom I wish for any reason."

"How could the council of the G.F.C. pass such a law?"

"It's a streamlining measure for war," Uri explained. "During war we cannot be bogged down with numerous petty and frivolous conversations about anything. We must be intentional and focused. I spend more time with the cadets than anyone else. Why shouldn't I be allowed to judge what I see?"

"Because that's not your role," Gideon retorted.

"Why shouldn't it be?"

"Because that's not how the Kingdom works, and you know that."

"The Kingdom can always be improved. This is just a security measure. The council can and will take it from me if I abuse it, or if they deem that it becomes unnecessary. This is well thought out. I don't see what the problem is." There was silence for a while.

*"Clearly Gideon's not going to win this on a matter of policy,"* Roy whispered.

"I plan to contest this to Chrystar!" Gideon announced.

"Go ahead. That's your right."

"I insist on knowing what is fueling his ejection."

"I can't disclose."

"Why?"

"Those reasons are confidential."

"Make them un-confidential."

"I can't do that—"

"The paper I got this morning said he's suspected of war crimes!" Gideon snapped.

"Yes!" Uri returned. "I'm bringing charges of treason against him."

"Treason?" Gideon boomed. "On what ground?"

"It's due to his abilities. Roy Van Doren has progressed unbelievably quick. Not only is he rising above the members of his own regiment, but he is on the verge of being the top cadet and recruit across the board. He is doing *too* well. He's breaking every record. No matter what I assign him, he and his companions always finish in a remarkable amount of time before everyone else."

"I would think that would be a good thing, seeing that a war is coming."

"He is too fast. I believe him to be a spy."

"A spy? It's a proven fact that for whatever reason off-worlder's catch onto things faster than most," Gideon said. "I don't see how your charges are going to stand up."

"As of Monday, it won't matter. The new law will take affect, and Roy Van Doren will become an ordinary soldier and you will be forced to comply and pick a new candidate as pilot."

Gideon sat back in his seat. "You actually think he's a spy?"

"Yes. He is training, as if he already knows much of it, but trying to be sneaky about it. I believe he is actually a Hentar, *coincidentally* placed into the care of you."

"Don't even try that one!"

"And why not? You were a Hentar once! You climbed their ranks and lived in much comfort. Who's to say you haven't kept in touch with some of the lowlifes you used to associate with?"

"I do keep in touch with them, because I care about them."

Uri scoffed.

"Isn't that what we're called to do?"

"That's not what I'm talking about—"

"Let's just cut straight to the chase shall we?" Gideon asked in a booming voice. "Your rejection of Roy has nothing to do with Roy. It has to do with me and my past, doesn't it?"

Uri was silent for a moment. "Off-worlders's are dangerous. Your own father searched endlessly for a way back to the other world and we both know he attracted certain attention that ultimately led to his demise. You were a Hentar—"

"Emphasis on the word *were*. Those days are behind me, and I have nothing in my past that I would hide from you now. Chrystar has taken care of everything and wiped my slate clean. He's given me a new start and a new life, and I've tried my best to make the most of it. Is that such a problem?"

"That is not the issue!"

"Apparently, it is," Gideon argued. "You forget, he did the same for you. You were no better than I."

"I had done nowhere near the evils you have," Uri spat.

"Evil is evil. The number of it doesn't matter. It's all the same. Yes, I was a Hentar Knight, but I had a change of heart, and Chrystar honored that." Silence fell over them for a moment. "All I ask you is this...if you are doing this because of a legitimate concern, than arrest him and try him right now. If you're doing this because you don't like that I've been able to start fresh, then leave him alone and take it out on me. Or, better yet, take the matter to Chrystar and see what he says. Your choice."

Roy and Abby listened for a while longer, the conversation drifting to things they didn't understand. Finally, Roy motioned that they should go and they climbed back to the rooftop, where their Griffin was waiting.

The sun had vanished from the sky and they began to realize just how long they had been following and listening to Gideon's conversation. They took to the sky and flew in silence, looking at the city lights which shone brightly.

"I'm glad to know that you're not being targeted for anything you've done specifically," Abby said, finally breaking their silence.

"I just hope I don't get kicked out for it," Roy replied.

“Gideon was quite firm that you weren't going to be,” Abby replied.

They flew for several minutes, winding their way through the city, but taking the slightly longer way, able to enjoy the sights of the city, as they weren't following anyone now.

“I had a good day with you, Abigail,” Roy said. They both smiled.

“Me too.”

“Not bad for a first date, I'd say.”

“It's hard for me to know one way or the other, as this *is* my first date.”

“Mine, too.”

A few minutes later they landed at the school platform, making sure to put the Griffin in the same spot they had taken it from. The rest of the platform was empty of people.

“We're later than we thought,” Abby said. “Looks like everyone is in their rooms.” They strode to the main door and tried to open it, but found it was locked.

“Oops.”

They searched for several minutes, walking around the entire platform as they looked for any door that might be open. Finding none, they stood pondering what their next move would be.

“Unless we sneak in with Gideon it looks like we're stuck out here for the night,” Roy concluded.

Abby shook her head. “Take off your shoes.”

“What?”

“Take your shoes off.” She slipped out of her own and he quickly did the same, following her around to the side of the building that Roy knew their rooms were on.

“What are we doing?” Roy asked.

“We're climbing to my window,” Abby answered.

“We're all on the second story.”

"So?"

"So that's like twenty feet up!" Roy exclaimed.

Abby smiled. "Afraid of a little adventure?" she taunted. "Don't worry, the side column there leads right to my window and has perfect design that we can put our fingers and toes into those cracks just like a ladder. My window is directly at the top of it. I keep it unlocked because sometimes I like to go for walks in the middle of the night. This will work."

"I'll try not to fall on you like I did the last time you took me out a window," Roy said.

"I'm going first, butterfingers." She put her shoes in the bushes and effortlessly began scaling the rock column.

"You could just use the door," a voice said behind them. They panicked as Gideon came walking up the sidewalk.

"What did you think of the conversation?"

Abby and Roy stammered.

"Come with me."

Abby dropped to the ground and Roy carried their shoes, as Gideon unlocked the door and they followed him up to their chamber.

"Would you guys like tea or coffee?" he offered.

Abby and Roy exchanged a glance, still stammering.

"Coffee, I guess?" Abby said.

"Sounds good, I'll get some started," Gideon said. He walked into the kitchen area, leaving the two of them by themselves.

"I'm confused. Are we in trouble?" Abby said. "Admittedly, everything that happened tonight was my idea." They cautiously walked over to the kitchen.

"Oh, you're definitely in trouble," Gideon said, their hearts sank. "In fact, I find you to be guilty of exactly what Commander Uri was concerned about. You're too smart for him." Gideon chuckled, and Roy and Abby's spirits started to rise. “Have a seat. I'll be right with you.” Abby and Roy took a seat on the couch as Gideon stepped into his bedroom for a few minutes.

“I'm not so sure we're actually in trouble,” Abby stated.

“It doesn't appear that way, but I don't want to jinx us. I'm still assuming we got busted and are going to get busted some more.”

Gideon came back out and soon brought a tray filled with three steaming mugs of hot coffee. He put a single lump of sugar in each and handed it to them, before settling in his chair.

“You two are really something you know that?” Gideon asked. Roy couldn't tell if he was happy or mad.

“Thanks?” Abby said.

Gideon laughed. “You two are certainly every bit as smart as Uri claims. I'm sure you heard the accusations against you?”

“Yes. Did you know we were there?”

“Let there be no mistake about it . . . I'm very proud of you both! I didn't know you were listening in on that meeting until you left and had to pass by the doorway. I'm assuming you took a Griffin and followed me?”

“Yes, sir,” Roy answered.

“My idea,” Abby admitted.

Gideon smiled all the more. “A brilliant one at that. As much action as I've seen in my life, I would've never thought I would be successfully followed and spied on by new recruits. A couple of 'youngsters' to a guy like me. I will have no disciplinary action against you two tonight, because you proved you are capable of great things.

“Roy, I plan on Monday to announce you as Captain of the Regiment. You are wise and smart, and are catching on to things amazingly fast, as Uri said.”

“I'm honored, sir, but am I still being expelled from the G.F.C.?”

"We'll have to wait and see on that, but when you go on Monday, I would completely expect for you to continue your training with the G.F.C." Gideon took a sip of his coffee.

"Thank you, sir," Roy said, relief flooding through him.

"Seeing that it appears Abby's brain was involved in the planning of your excursion tonight, I would appoint her Lieutenant Captain, should something happen to you." He turned to Abby. "That would mean you would be working directly with Roy. I'm pretty sure you wouldn't object to that?"

"No, sir. I'm very honored."

"As you should be. Now, I should mention, that although I am not taking disciplinary action against you tonight, if this happens again in the future, I will have to react."

"We understand," Abby said. "Sorry, Gideon."

"It's okay. I actually requested to have the meeting with Roy present, but Uri would not hear of it." Silence fell over them for a moment.

"Gideon, there were a few things discussed tonight I didn't completely understand. Why are off-worlders so dangerous?" Abby asked.

"They're not, but to people who like to control everything, off-worlders seem difficult to manage because some skills they have received from the other world translate to this one rather differently. I don't fully understand it myself. Once my father decided to live a good life here, he led a *very* good life. But unfortunately he had created some demons in his first years here. Eventually his bad choices, his demons, caught up with him and he was never the same."

"I'm sorry," Roy replied.

"It's okay. Now, I understand the bigger picture. People try to blame their problems on anything. It's always someone else's fault, when the truth is sometimes its us who create the problems with ill choices and don't realize we've done it." He took his last sip of coffee. "But now is the time for sleep. It's been a long night for all of us." All three of them stood to go their separate ways. Abby disappeared down the girls hall, while Gideon motioned for Roy to come back.

"Have a good time this afternoon?" Gideon asked. Roy couldn't hide a smile. Gideon smiled also. "I think you're good for each other and I'm assuming you want this kept under wraps for a while?"

"Yes," Roy answered.

"Your secret is safe with me."

* * * *

"Look what the cat dragged in!" Alexander said, standing next to Roy's bed. "What on earth were you up to yesterday? I didn't hardly see you at all."

"Correct me if I'm wrong, but you were with Savannah for a while right?" Roy asked groggily.

"Yes, this is true, but . . . I don't remember seeing you at supper last night."

"I was here. Jonathan can vouch for me, right, Jonathan?" They looked to Jonathan who was sound asleep.

"You're witness is not looking very reliable."

"One second." Roy picked up one of his shoes and threw it at Jonathan who jumped up and cried out before looking at Roy and Alexander with confusion in his face. “I was here at supper last night, right?” Jonathan glanced back and forth before a light came into Jonathan's eyes as he understood the situation.

“Yes, he was here,” he said to Alexander. “He was being all boring, reading books while you and I were busy playing Trium with Carl and David.”

“Ah, yes! Roy you would've been proud of us. We whooped their butts didn't we?”

“No doubt, probably the best game I've ever played,” Jonathan replied.

“What was the score?”

“Thirty-two to one!” Alexander exclaimed.

Roy raised an eyebrow. “Remind me to be on your team next time. Did things go well with Savannah?”

“Yes,” Alexander answered, all smiles. “However, it got off to a bit of an awkward start. Because Abby said she was waiting for me there, but when she showed up, which was after me, she said that I had told her to meet me there, which I don't recall ever saying. Anyways, long story short we made the most of it and had a lovely afternoon.”

“I'm glad to hear it,” Roy said.

“How did you like reading all your boring books yesterday?”

Roy smiled, remembering the day before. “It was a lovely afternoon for reading.”

“I suppose,” Alexander said. “You know me, I'm not quite the reading type.”

“I like reading.”

“What book were you reading?”

“Ah, some book about fishing in mountain streams.”

“That sounds really . . . boring.”

“I enjoyed it.”

"To each their own. See you at breakfast!" Alexander turned and left the room. Roy collapsed back on the bed.

"A book about fishing in mountain streams?" Jonathan laughed. "Pulled that one out of thin air?"

"Actually, Gideon does have a book on the subject sitting on his shelf. And I have read it."

Jonathan laughed. "Good cover."

# 16

**MONDAY CAME QUICKLY** and when all was said and done, Alexander remained none the wiser that Abby and Roy had spent any amount of time together the day before. Much to his and Jonathan's amusement, they found that Alexander had fallen asleep while attempting to read the book that Roy had mentioned.

They landed at the canyon for their training with Sergeant Parks. They walked in and tapped their sactalines, which were still orange. They also picked up all their weapons and strapped them on, waiting for Parks to arrive.

"How was your reading last night?" Roy asked.

"Any person who calls reading about fishing in mountain streams enjoyable is out of their minds," Alexander exclaimed. "How did you enjoy that book?"

"Like you said, '*to each their own*'."

"That's the last time I read a book that you recommend," Alexander said in a huff. Roy looked over to Abby and gave her a wink. She smiled and winked back, having been fully told about the book conversation.

"Good morning, recruits, stand at attention!" Parks said, striding in from behind them. They all saluted. "As you were." They relaxed into line. "You have been doing very well with basic training. Now it's time to take it to the next level. You will be randomly paired up with a person of my choosing for your dueling today. Then when you are practicing as you normally do, we will begin firing arrows at you."

Several of them exchanged glances.

"The battlefield will not be nearly as controlled of an environment as this is. We will start introducing other elements into your training. Today you will begin training by getting used to Tantine arrows being loosed at you."

They were immediately sorted into pairs with Alexander and Roy being paired together. They sparred fiercely, going back and forth across the large floor. An explosion shook the ground near them, and Roy stumbled on his feet and fell backwards. Alexander held the sword to Roy's neck, a childish grin on his face.

"Take that, Mr. Van Doren!"

"I tripped."

"Oh, right. Of course you did, twinkle-toes. Why can't you just admit that I am on fire!"

Roy smiled, seeing a slight flicker and a trail of smoke coming from Alexander's pant leg. "You are on fire."

"That's right," Alexander said.

"No, seriously, you are on fire." Roy now pointed out that his pant leg was starting to burn which prompted Alexander to scream and prance around as he frantically tried to smack out the flames. When finally they were out, he turned to face the Sergeant who had come over to them.

"Are you done screaming like a little girl, recruit?" Parks asked.

"I don't think I'm on fire anymore," Alexander said. An awkward silence settled over them. "I thought our armor would protect us from fire."

Parks looked at him funny. "These are just training suits. They're not as good as the uniforms you will be given at graduation. You can go get a different sactaline and uniform over there." The Sergeant pointed to the other side of the vast space.

"I'll be right back," Alexander said.

When it was clear Alexander was out of earshot, Parks turned to Roy. "He screams like a girl."

"Tell me about it."

They practiced for several more hours, with more and more arrows being shot near them. They still stumbled and faltered a little, but by the end of the session they were able to fight flawlessly no matter how many explosions were around them.

After that they moved outside, practicing with their crossbows, working on more focused and specific training now that they knew the basics. They looked for targets in trees as well as on the ground. As they had done everyday, Roy and his regiment finished the task far faster than the others.

At the end of the training for the day Sergeant Parks motioned for them to gather around. They quickly did so.

"I would like to congratulate all of you!" Parks said. "Your regiment has now been ranked number one out of every regiment in training." They all celebrated for a moment. "As a result, I am recommending that your regiment be put on the list for you to be assigned for regular security patrols and other small missions that may be completed within a day."

"So real jobs?" Carl asked.

Parks nodded. "Yes, real paying jobs. Now, a few housekeeping things before you go. Seeing as you've been selected to join the real workforce, you'll all need these." He motioned to a guard and the guard pushed forwards a small cart.

A large bowl was on the cart with a long grey cloth stretched over it. Parks removed the cloth, revealing new sactalines. These ones were still black, but they had a strange iridescent quality that made them appear neon green.

They tapped the sactalines and were instantly clothed in armor and their uniforms. Much to everyone's surprise and relief, these ones were not the same color of orange, but instead were a dark navy blue, and much like the ones Roy wore for the G.F.C. They had small indentations on the front to put extra smaller sactalines in.

“I much prefer this to the orange,” Roy said. The others all smiled and nodded in agreement. Parks smiled and pulled a small wooden box, out of his pocket and held it so they could all see.

“I have one more thing for all of you, before I dismiss you for the day. Gideon has selected Roy Van Doren to be your Captain. I now would like to present you with a special sactaline to commemorate the promotion. He opened the box and a single small blue sactaline glowed brightly. Roy knew what to do and immediately put it into his uniform. Instantly a dark green stripe became visible on each of his arms and the insignia of the Chrystarians became visible on the front. The others cheered and clapped when it was done.

“You're all doing very well. Congratulations, and I'll see you tomorrow. You are dismissed.” Parks smiled as they he turned to leave and they all migrated to the pickup area, where all the regiments were waiting for their Griffins to come pick them up.

“I do believe you are the only one I see wearing a Captain's uniform,” Abby said to him.

“I feel very honored,” Roy replied. “Now we'll see what happens when I show up at the G.F.C. today.”

“I'm sure it'll work out. Gideon seemed pretty confident that it would.”

“I know, but I'm still nervous.”

“Does this mean I have to call you Captain Roy?” Alexander asked.

“Probably, but only when we're working, and on every other Thursday.”

“Now that's ridiculous,” Alexander replied, laughing.

"You, my brother, are ridiculous," Abby said.

"Thank you. It is truly the best compliment one could hope to achieve in their lifetime." He turned and began talking to Jonathan.

Roy leaned close to Abby. "Sometimes, it is very obvious you two are related, and other times I think one of you was dropped off on the doorstep."

"Which one do you think was dropped on the doorstep?" Abby asked teasingly.

"Oh, look is that a Griffin coming? What good timing to keep me from answering that question." They both laughed.

"Good save Roy."

Soon the others were dismissed and Roy, Jonathan, and Savannah all stayed behind to join the other cadets in the G.F.C. Roy nervously stepped into formation, half expecting to be pulled aside and kicked out for good. Neither Gideon, nor anyone else had been able to fully confirm that he wasn't still expelled.

Nonetheless, Roy stood in line with everyone else waiting. The door opened to the right.

"Good afternoon!" To their surprise Chrystar stepped into view, while Commander Uri was nowhere to be found. "There are a few changes as of late that I am here to tell you about. First and foremost, Commander Uri has been removed from his position. I will not go into any further details on the matter, except to say that he is currently being investigated and it's being handled even as we speak.

"Next, our spies have spotted Dreygars within a reasonable distance of where you stand now. Right now they appear to be random coincidences and not premeditated attack plans. There will be a curfew for all citizens, young and old alike, of lights out by nine o'clock.

"As such, we will be accelerating your flight training and adding an extra hour to your flying schedule after today's class. You have achieved first flight, but how will you fare against the elements: Wind, Rain, Fire, Earth?

"You will be tested in all of these, starting now. Call your Griffin, but do so with a silent call. For in battle, thoughts will be better to call your Griffin, rather than words."

*Skyquill!*

A moment later the sky was filled with Griffins, all trying to get to the person who had called them. When they were all settled and everything had quieted down, a large white Griffin came and settled on the ground next to Chrystar.

"Today's lesson is about focus," Chrystar said, pacing in front of them. "You will each mount your Griffin and follow me on my flight. Anyone who passes me will automatically have to stay longer tonight." Everyone including Chyrstar chuckled. "I am not going to slow, or dawdle for you to keep up. Focus and keep your speed up, and we'll see what each of you has to offer."

In an instant, he leapt on the Griffin and took to the sky. The others quickly scrambled to get on. Jonathan and Savannah took off, and Roy just a moment later. Soon they were all immersed in a large cloud of Griffins as everyone jockeyed for position.

To the left. To the right. To the center. Roy followed Chystar's movements on his Griffin, trying his best to copy the movements as fluidly as Chrystar was doing them. They turned to the left, coming under a great cliff with a large opening in it. They entered single file, with Roy following right behind.

Sunshine shone through windows cut in the side of the rock and soon they were splashed in the face with ice cold water that fell through the rocks.

They eventually exited into the sunlight, welcoming the warmth, now that they were all freezing. Roy looked down, taking a moment to enjoy the view. They climbed high into the sky and then fell steeply down and pulled up at the canyon floor.

Soon Chrystar put down and landed, and everyone else did the same, fortunately much smoother than they had the first time. There were long tables and chairs set into the shape of a square. Chrystar waited for them in the center as they all took their seats.

"Roy?" Jonathan asked. Roy turned to him. "What do you think of Uri's dismissal the same time as the Dreygars appearing?"

"Not sure. It could just be a coincidence. Maybe Gideon will be more forthcoming with information tonight."

"The next part of your training is strategy and defense. This is best taught in a class room setting before we try it in the canyon," Chrystar said. "By the way, congratulations everyone on not falling off."

"Our suits are magnetic so we can't fall off right?" a cadet asked.

Chrystar smiled.

"Depends how reckless you're being." Everyone chuckled. "In coming days some of the training will be done over water because everyone falls off once." They chuckled again as Chrystar pulled out a large chalkboard with more figures, markings, and shapes on it than Roy had ever seen. In a matter of a couple seconds he could make out that it was a map of the canyon.

"First test of the day. Find the prisoner." Chrystar stepped back and let everyone have view of the board. Roy found it quickly, but a quick glance around the room told him no one else had. "Anyone find it yet?"

"I have," Roy said. The room fell silent. He could see Jonathan and Savannah staring at him with their mouths gaping wide open, but he ignored them for the moment.

"Come point out the prisoner." Roy did as he was told and pointed out the prisoner.

"How did you know that was a prisoner?" Chrystar asked.

"While there are hundreds of people on the board, this one stands out because of how he is standing-"

"How he's standing?!" Jonathan exclaimed.

"While everyone seems to be standing straight and appear to have something to do, the prisoner is standing alone and he's hunched over as if he's weighed down by a great burden. Also he's the only one that doesn't have shoes, implying that he isn't worthy of any, in the eyes of his master."

"Very impressive," Chrystar congratulated. "Now how would you rescue this prisoner?"

"Rescue in what way?" Roy asked.

"How would you set this prisoner free?"

"I could easily glide in on my Griffin and snatch him up."

"Do you think that would work?'

"No, sir."

"You don't?

"No."

"Explain."

"It would work for a while, but it wouldn't have been his choice to be free and it wouldn't make his master very happy. So although it might be the best first choice, it would have drawbacks."

"If snatch and grab is not a good tactic, what else would you suggest?"

Roy thought for a second. "I'd buy him from his master! If his master gets the money, then he will be happy and he won't hunt you, and if the slave knows that he has been set free by the person who paid his debt, then how could he ever doubt the person who set him free ever again?"

"Very good," Chrystar said, motioning that Roy could take his seat. "I tell you the truth. This is how we'll win the coming war."

"By buying slaves?" a cadet asked.

"In a sense. War is ugly and you are in the midst of one right now, even if you don't think you are. You're in a war for your mind, heart, and soul. In a war that *is* about the heart, you need to win the heart and that means serving the prisoner in love and showing them the way. Show them kindness, when the world shows them hate. Show them compassion when others dish them cruelty. You combat hatred with love, indifference with action, and loneliness with community. For a triple braided cord is not easily broken.

"Let it be known that the first war and greatest war is in you, for your souls. Being a Chrystarian Knight *does not* make you exempt from disaster, temptation, or trials. Rather, it gives you another way of dealing with something that would destroy most people."

* * * *

Roy let himself sink onto the sofa back in their room with Jonathan and Savannah still staring at him as though he was from another planet. Abby and Alexander came down the hall and stopped at the sight.

"Is something wrong?" Abby asked

"No." Roy replied.

"Are they *okay*?" Alexander asked, pointing to his own head. Roy looked at them for a moment.

"I think so." The silence grew both awkward and amusing as it got longer and longer, meanwhile Savannah and Jonathan stared at him.

"How was the canyon today?" Abby asked.

"How the heck did you know the answer to the questions!?" Savannah exclaimed, her voice almost to the point where it would wake someone if they were sleeping.

"Answers to what questions?" Alexander asked.

"They are upset that I answered all the questions at the G.F.C." Roy replied.

"Somehow in a matter of seconds he had figured everything out. Everything!" Jonathan said.

"I see," Alexander said humorously. "So you're all jealous of our Captain?"

"Oh, yeah that's right. You're our Captain now!" Savannah exclaimed.

"I guess he was picked for Captain because of his brains," Abby replied.

"You heard the woman. 'All hail your Captain!'" Roy cried. Savannah and Jonathan both walked off in a huff, and the three of them nearly died of laughter.

"So how did you know all the answers to the questions?" Alexander asked.

Roy shrugged. "To me it just seemed obvious. It made sense. I'm not sure how to explain it, but it felt like they were concepts that had come from my world."

"Do you think the two worlds are connected in some weird way?" Abby asked.

"I don't know," Roy answered. "But it's an interesting thing to ponder, isn't it?"

"You've been gone a long time," Alexander said. "I wonder if time in your world's been passing at the same rate it is here."

"To be honest, I've hardly thought about the other world recently." They fell silent and soon Gideon walked through the doors, his arms full of bags and boxes. They watched him as he struggled to close the door and walk in without tripping over anything. Finally he let them fall on the sofa.

"Don't anyone get up and help," Gideon said.

"Don't worry, we didn't," Alexander replied. Gideon flashed an amused and annoyed smile. "What are these boxes anyway?"

"Mail," Gideon replied. He rummaged through the pile and pulled three small boxes from it, and handed one to each of them. They quickly opened the boxes like it was Christmas time, each of them pulling out a bottle of liquid into the light. Abby and Alexander squealed in delight. Abby's was florescent Red, while Alexander's was Orange. Roy looked at his with curiosity as his seemed to change colors depending on how much light hit it.

"What is this?" Roy asked.

"Our favorite drinks. We usually get them only once a year, because they're so expensive. It's a real treat," Abby said, removing the cap from hers and taking a sip. "Mine is a strange mixture of tangy cherries, sweet huckleberries and perfectly balanced with a single drop of sourdum."

"What is sourdum?"

"I have no idea, but that's what it says on the bottle," Abby said, pointing to it. "It's good try it." Roy hesitantly took a sip and was surprised to find that it did taste good.

"Guess you can't judge a book by it's cover, can you?" Roy asked. "Alexander, what's yours taste like?"

"Bubbly bananas."

Roy burst out laughing. "Why on earth is a banana drink orange?"

"Hey, I don't make it, and I don't ask questions. I just drink it and enjoy."

"Anyone care to enlighten me about what this one is?" Roy asked holding up his own drink.

“I've actually never seen this one before,” Abby said inspecting the bottle.

“There's a note that goes with it.” Alexander said, pointing to the box.

Roy picked it up and read it.

*For the hot and spicy food lover. How about a spicy drink?*
*Love, Victor and Norah*

*PS: This is supposed to be hotter than that juice of the Cherinmu Flower.*

“So you've got yourself a spicy drink?” Alexander asked, grabbing the bottle only to have it grabbed away by Abby immediately.

“I have a hard time believing my parents claim that this is hotter than the Cherinmu Flowers,” Abby said, smelling it. “It doesn't even smell like anything.”

“I enjoyed the Cherinmu sauce your mom makes,” Roy admitted. “But I hardly thought it was spicy.”

“You're so weird,” Abby said. “That stuff burns my mouth off at the best of times.”

“Anyone game to try it with me?” Roy asked. Abby signaled no, while Alexander seemed to be considering the options.

“I'll try! Abby get us two glasses,” Alexander cried. She did and Roy split the bottle between them. “Rules?”

“First one to down the whole glass wins.”

“And the loser?”

“Has to show up to the canyon tomorrow with no shoes!” Abby exclaimed. Roy and Alexander looked at her in a funny way.

“No shoes?” Roy asked.

“Seems like a pathetic consequence,” Alexander said.

"Would you guys rather have to show up tomorrow with no pants?"

"No! The shoes seems perfect!" Alexander agreed. He picked up a glass. "My dear sister. Count us down."

"Three . . . two . . . one . . . go!" Roy and Alexander both put the glass to their lips and chugged the liquid down as fast as they could. Roy set his glass down, his face already red and his mouth on fire. Alexander screamed out in pain as the liquid burned, not even making it through half the glass.

"That stuff is horrible!" Alexander exclaimed. "I feel like a dragon!"

"I'm not feeling much better over here," Roy said, now sweating. "That stuff is HOT." Alexander and him both got up and walked around as though that would help the situation. "It doesn't even taste good! At least if it tasted like something I would feel like it was worthwhile."

"I know!" Alexander agreed. "Instead it's just a bottle of liquid fire."

"Just FYI," Abby said. "The bottle says effects may last up to twenty-three hours."

"Twenty-three hours? What kind of a number is that?"

"I'm just reading it." Abby defended.

"Well, my dragon friend there is one important thing we must remember from this contest," Roy said. "I won, you lost. No shoes at the canyon for you tomorrow."

"A deal is a deal. Besides anything's better than drinking that awful liquid." He left the room walking down the hall. A moment later they heard him cry out again. "Ah! SWEET HUCKLEBERRY TREES, that burns!"

"Good job keeping it clean, Alexander," Abby teased.

"THANKS. Oh, goodness, that's horrible."

# ALLIANCE

The next day proved to be one of the most amusing days that Roy could remember since arriving in this new world. They had gone about their business as usual for the morning, all the while still having to listen to Alexander complain about lingering affects from the drink. And even though Roy might have agreed with Alexander about all those lingering affects, Roy didn't complain, and instead chose to laugh about the hilarious scenario.

"Ready for the canyon today?" Roy asked. Alexander stood next to them, looking particularly pleased with himself for whatever reason.

"I was born ready."

"Not yet you aren't," Abby said, coming up behind them. "Shoes, now."

"I was kind of hoping you had forgotten about that," Alexander said, taking off his shoes and handing them to his sister, who proceeded to throw them in the bushes.

"I would not forget about something like that."

Nothing more was said on the subject until they reached the canyon and had landed. They walked into the building and tapped their sactalines, instantly dressed in their appropriate attire. They lined up in formation, waiting for Sergeant Parks.

"I can't believe you're actually doing this," Savannah said.

"Doing what?" Alexander replied.

"Showing up to training without shoes. You're going to get killed."

"I will not!"

"I'm going to be attending your funeral tonight. Mark my words!" Savannah warned.

"Two things, my dear Savannah—"

"Dear Savannah?" Abby interrupted. "Is there something you need to tell us about?"

Alexander turned to face Abby. "No." He turned back to Savannah. "As I was saying. First and foremost, I made a bet, and I lost. I must honor the bet. Secondly, prior to firstly, I'm not going to die, because it's highly unlikely that anyone, especially Sergeant Parks is going to notice that I don't have shoes on, because let's face it nobody ever looks at your feet!" They all chuckled, while Alexander tried to stand taller.

"Say what you want, but you'll have to eat your words. You watch and see!"

"Oh, we'll be watching!" Abby exclaimed. They fell silent as Sergeant Parks entered the room and strode across it like he always did. He walked down the line the regiment had created, greeting each of them with a nod as he looked them over. He nodded at Alexander and kept on going, Alexander gave Abby a thumbs up and an *'I told you so'* expression after they had been both passed. Sergeant Parks took his normal spot in front of them.

"Alexander, come forward!" Parks boomed. The others held their breath but had to admire Alexander's determination to not panic as he strode confidently forward until he was standing directly in front of the Sergeant.

"I'm going to ask you this only once, soldier." The Sergeant paused. Still, Alexander didn't waver in his serious expression. "Are you feeling prepared for the day?"

"Yes, sir!" Alexander said, saluting. The Sergeant nodded.

"Do you think I'm blind or I'm stupid?" Parks asked. Alexander's determined expression vanished in an instant. He fumbled over his words as Parks glared at him.

"I-I-I don't know, sir?"

"YOU MUST BE A SPECIAL KIND OF STUPID! Where are your shoes, soldier?!" Parks yelled. Alexander looked completely horrified as everyone else winced and tried not to chuckle at the same time.

"I lost them in a bet," Alexander said.

"You lost them in a bet?" Parks asked. He sounded mad and was still yelling at Alexander, but Roy thought secretly he was amused. "Your level of stupidity is one not achieved by many, soldier! What do you think this is, A DAYCARE! A playground for little babies? Because that's what your feet look like! Mathison!" He came at once and saluted Parks. "Mathison, take Mr. Sissy feet out and have him run thirty laps around the complex, making sure that he never sets foot on any grass, and steps on every rock and sharp pointy object in the path!"

"Yes, sir."

"And then, soldier," Parks said. "Have this man give us one hundred push ups on his knuckles and two hundred crunches. Then he must still perform all his required training for the day. Since he loves being without shoes, we're going to put his sissy feet to the test. Are you satisfied with your choices, soldier?"

"But, sir—"

"GET MOVING, BABY FEET, OR I'LL MAKE YOU RUN SIXTY LAPS AROUND THE COMPLEX!" Alexander took off running for the door with Mathison following directly behind him. Once the door was shut. Parks turned to face all of them.

"Whose idea was it?"

"Mine, sir," Abby admitted.

Parks laughed. "You're his sister, right?"

"Yes, sir."

"That was the best prank I've ever seen. I'll be laughing about that one for a long time. Come, let's begin." They fell in line behind him.

Roy leaned close to Abby. “I'm sure glad I won the contest.”

# 17

**BY THE TIME** Alexander returned, it was late evening. Everyone had already eaten supper and were talking or reading as the group always did. The door had been thrown open by Alexander who looked more dead than alive, yet he still had a stupid grin across his face. He let the door close behind him as he made his way to the fireplace where everyone was sitting.

"Hello, my dear sister!" Alexander exclaimed.

Abby looked up. "Hello, brother. You're late."

"If I didn't love you so much, I'd throw you right out that window! But," he paused as he lowered himself gently into a chair. "I'm enjoying more the fact that I did it! I beat everything that Sergeant Parks threw at me. So the joke is on you, dear sister."

"If it makes you feel any better, I am sorry for making a bet that caused you so much pain."

"Ah, whatever!" Alexander said. "I'm alive. That's the important thing, and it will make a great memory for years to come."

"You know me, always trying to make you good character building memories!" Abby exclaimed.

"Your kindness is overwhelming."

The door opened and Gideon came walking in.

"Hope you don't mind, but I need to borrow Roy for a couple of hours."

"A couple of hours?" Roy asked. "I can hardly stay awake as it is."

"I understand, but I need to give you a tour of the city you'll be patrolling in the coming weeks. And just so you all know, the days you're on patrol you will not have any other training. Or the next day, depending on what shift you're assigned to."

"I guess I'll see you later, if you're up," Roy said to Abby. Alexander still sat in the chair with his stupid grin on his face.

Roy grabbed his coat and slipped out of the door, following behind Gideon who walked briskly through the halls until they were outside.

"Is something wrong, Gideon?" Roy asked.

"Maybe. But I don't want to talk any specifics until we're truly alone."

"I understand." They stood in silence and walked outside, a griffin coming to them at once. They soon took to the sky, the city below them shining with all the lights and sactalines that were scattered throughout the city.

"I am still going to give you a walk through of the portion of the city you'll be patrolling. Mostly night shifts. They like to give those to the newcomers. But before I do that, I wanted to share some tidbits I've heard on Commander Uri."

"I was curious about what happened," Roy admitted. "It seemed like a sudden departure."

"It was. He's currently being investigated for corruption and espionage."

"Oh my," Roy said. "I can't say I expected that."

"Me, either. The fear is that he was connected with nefarious people back on the main land. As such, it is believed that he was the one responsible for the Dreygars being spotted so close, so suddenly."

"What does all of this mean?" Roy asked.

"It means I don't expect everyone will be able to finish their training before something big happens. I know you are about four weeks in, but I don't see ten weeks of training in your future."

"Why not?"

"If Uri truly is loyal to the Hentar in any way, than they may know of the location of the city. There is an announcement going out at the end of the week. I don't know the nature of it in full detail, but it may call us all to arms."

"You think it will come to war so soon?"

"In my experience we must assume that there will be an attack, and hopefully we're wrong." They flew in silence for another minute or two. "There is one more thing I'd like to tell you, but you must promise to tell no one, not even Abigail."

"Anything," Roy agreed.

Gideon smiled. "My father was not a Hentar Knight, but he was captured by them."

"What happened?"

"I've never known. But with all the mysteries, of his disappearance and life, I've been stuck on one question, and only recently do I believe I've figured *why* he was captured."

"So why did you became a Hentar Knight, then?"

"Looking for answers about my father. About what the Alliance was really up to behind the scenes. Long and short of it is I played with fire for too long. You pretend something long enough, even if you start out with good intentions and it can destroy you. In the beginning I did a lot of bad things for good reasons, tried to play the middle road, or the Robin Hood of the era."

"Robin Hood?"

"My father loved Robin Hood," Gideon said. "But all that aside. It corrupted my soul. But back to my point, I believe my father was taken by the Hentar Knights because he *was* an off-worlder."

"How can you be sure?"

"I've gone to the tedious research, looking through thousands of years of Hentarian control, even if they haven't claimed to be in control. All said and done, you are the thirty-third off-worlder to come to this world. Each one of them was eventually hunted down or mysteriously disappeared."

"So I have that to look forward to?" Roy asked. "You sure know how to cheer a person up."

"I say this to warn you. It's always been my belief that an off-worlder would be able to go between worlds. I have no proof of my claim, as my own father was never able to. But if it works, it might just be what keeps you alive."

"How could I leave everyone here?" Roy asked. "What about Abigail? And the others, too?"

"I didn't say it would be easy," Gideon admitted. "I also didn't say that you would have to stay there. Assuming you could come back, it would be a brilliant way to be unseen, while still living your life here."

"I suppose. Why would I want to do that, though?" Roy asked. "I love it here."

"Perhaps you were made for both worlds."

"I don't have many connections in the other world," Roy admitted.

"Any family?"

"One brother. It's been hard talking to him since my father's death."

"I'm sorry to hear that."

"Thanks."

"I do have one more thing to say on the matter and that is that Evelyn and I both have a very strong feeling that you're supposed to live in both worlds. Keep that in mind." Silence fell over them for several minutes.

"You really think I'm going to be hunted because I'm an off-worlder?"

"I do," Gideon said. "You are the best Captain I've ever had the privilege to watch over. You're outperforming everybody in training and the regiment itself is, in higher circles, considered one of the best, and you haven't even finished your fourth week of training. If there is a war, we all might be targeted. If that happens, consider it my official advice to hide out in the other world for a while."

"It'll take me some time to digest this," Roy admitted. Gideon nodded and they descended lower and lower in the city, until finally they landed in the middle of one of the large platforms.

The city bustled with life all around them as Gideon led Roy into the tallest building. Once they were through the door, they turned toward a small locked door on the left. Gideon produced a key and turned it in the lock.

The door swung inward to reveal a long spiraling staircase that went down. Sactalines were mounted on the walls, evenly spaced down the entire structure. They walked for what felt like forever until they at last came to a large landing. One door stood at the end of a small corridor and Gideon once again produced a key.

"You'll be required to check this area once per shift," Gideon said, unlocking the door. Only take those which you trust the most. Which, I certainly hope you trust everyone in the regiment." They both chucked as he opened the door and the area was flooded with light.

Roy shielded his eyes for a moment and then looked ahead. In the distance a large red sactaline glowed brightly. Gideon motioned for Roy to follow and they stepped out onto an expansive platform. Railings circled around the edge and a smaller barrier wrapped around the center two feet.

"This is the heart of the city," Gideon said. "The red sactaline if you remember, is what keeps this city in the air. Walkways connect all of the *stations,* as they're called, to each other. There are also three support braces overhead, connecting every platform together."

He pointed up to the support beams which were larger than Roy had imagined, being nearly two feet thick in most places.

"So if one of these sactalines goes missing, will the whole entire city fall?"

"Each platform is connected to a minimum of three others in order to ensure that if one of the sactalines fail, the other two would be able to support the structure. A triple braided cord—"

"Is not easily broken?" Roy asked. Gideon smiled.

"Are there regular patrols down here?" Roy asked. "It seems like a point of weakness, anyone could fly a Griffin or perhaps even a Dreygar and land right here."

"Trust me. You may not see it, but the security is there." Gideon handed him a pencil. "Throw it off the platform." Roy attempted to throw it over the railing but instead the pencil bounced back as though it had hit a wall.

"Didn't expect that," Roy admitted. Gideon chuckled.

"When you first arrived did you see walkways beneath the city, or just the red lights?" Roy thought for a minute.

"Just the red lights, but I wasn't really looking for walkways though."

"From the outside, you can't see the platform. Only the light and anything else that may pass in front of the light."

"Isn't that partially a security risk?" Roy asked. "Someone could be down here and not be seen."

"As Captain of the Regiment it would be your job to oversee the others. They will have regular routes and patrols. You will check down here at the start and end of your shift, and then stay in what's called the *'bridge'*, which I'll show you. You'll have clear sight of the base you're watching and be able to listen to everyone's chatter on the sactalines."

"We were told that the radio sactalines were still rare and so only pilots and captains would have them."

"That's true, but security has a number of them. You'll check them in and out like you do at training," Gideon told him. Gideon led him back the way they had come, except instead of climbing the stairs all the way to the top, they went through a door that Roy hadn't noticed the first time. The door opened up to a large room with chairs, a long desk along a window that ran the entire length of the room.

"This is the bridge," Gideon explained. Roy looked out and could easily see the sactaline underneath the platform.

They toured the rest of the 'normal' spots that they would all have to check and Gideon assured him that he would be with them for the first couple of nights. After the tour was done they went back home, where Roy found Abby having fallen asleep, reading a book on the couch.

He smiled as he looked at her and laid down on the couch across from her. Gideon's warning and advice went through his head. Roy tried to push it from his mind as he tried his hardest to find sleep. As he lay there thinking, Roy became certain of one thing...this was his home, these were his friends, and he wasn't going back to the real world.

# 18

**TO SAY THEIR TRAINING** picked up intensity would be an understatement. The next two weeks went faster than any of them would have thought, and altogether it hardly seemed like anything more could be squeezed into the day.

"Good work," Sergeant Parks told them. "I have to give a report to my commanding officer. Rest until I get back, then we'll get back to it."

"Great!" Alexander exclaimed once the Sergeant was out of ear shot. "More work."

"Can't take it?" Abby asked, elbowing him in the side.

Alexander smiled. "I can take it, but this is almost insane. I'm glad to be trained so thoroughly, but does it have to be this vigorous?"

"Everyone thinks there's a war coming," Roy said. "And I think they're right."

"Does Mr. Captain-Fly-Boy know something we don't?" Alexander asked.

"The Dreygars have been spotted consistently during the day, but just the day before yesterday one of them approached in the night."

"You never told us that," Jonathan said.

"I was asked not to," Roy replied.

"Seriously, you were told not to tell us?" Alexander asked.

"That's right. Now, I could always tell you, but I'd have to kill you afterwards, so I'm not sure I want to go there."

"How considerate of you. However, didn't you just tell us something that you weren't supposed to?" Alexander taunted.

"No."

"How's that?"

"You heard Sergeant Parks. We're on break. I'm no longer Captain Roy Van Doren, and I'm not flying, so I'm clearly not Fly-Boy. The one thing you could conclude from this line of thought is that you are the delusional one because the person you were talking to a while back doesn't exist." Abby laughed.

Alexander looked befuddled as he processed everything. "I would love to argue that, but I don't think I can."

"So, just to be clear?" Roy asked.

"We heard nothing. We saw nothing. In fact, we were never even here!" Jonathan exclaimed. Abby and Roy laughed while Alexander snickered and gave them a confused look.

"What?" Roy asked. "Not funny?"

"Not as funny as you think it is."

Abby and Roy both laughed again, this time Jonathan joined in.

"I'm missing something aren't I?" Alexander asked.

"Haven't you always been?" Abby asked.

"Look whose talking, sister!" Alexander fired back.

"Hey now, we don't need any wars among family members," Savannah teased.

"Why not?" a voice said. Startled they turned to see Chrystar coming up behind them. "That's what I've come to do."

"Turn family members on each other?" Savannah asked. "How does that make any sense?"

"It's the side-effect of war." Chrystar sat down with them. "Wars make people choose their side and fight to the end. Everyone is bound to have their own opinion, even if it's wrong."

"And the strongest army wins?" Carl asked.

"No."

They gave him confused looks.

"Though the stronger army may appear to win, if they have gained the whole world and yet still lost their soul, their heart, their conscience . . . what does it matter? I've said it many times this war which is coming is a war—"

"Of the heart," Jonathan interjected.

"Exactly! If you want to see what a person is truly like, look at their interactions, more than their actions. People can intend their actions, but to fake interactions is much harder to do."

They were interrupted by Parks, who came back from his errand. He bowed to Chrystar in the customary way. "I'm sorry for not knowing you were coming. If I had I would have made sure everything was fully in order."

"So many say." Chrystar sighed heavily and they wondered what he was thinking. "I leave you with this for today. Many wait for tomorrow to do what should be done today. There are some who always wish to be notified when a disaster is coming before they prepare and defend against it. People like that are like a castle in the sand. They are easily washed away with the tide. But a shack on a rock will never be moved. Which one do you want to be?"

"The shack on a rock," Parks replied. "Forgive me, my lord."

"It's not a problem, Parks. I know your heart and you have provided a most compelling illustration."

"Thank you, my lord," Parks said. "Announcement for all of you.

Starting tomorrow everyone is going to be attending G.F.C."

"Everyone?" Roy asked.

"Everyone is doing quite well with the flying lessons. Now it is time to add archers to your Griffin and see if you can hit anything from the air," Chrystar explained. "From here on out, your training will be together. It will combine everything you've learned both at G.F.C. and with Sergeant Parks. For the sake of this training. Sergeant Parks will be your Regiment Leader, calling the shots and relaying orders as if it was war. Two weeks from now we have the 'War Games'."

"War Games?" Jonathan asked.

"Every Regiment will be assigned and arranged as though it was actually war," Parks said. We'll have a mission to complete and real troops trying to stop us. First one completed wins the prize."

"Can we die during this game?" Alexander asked.

"No. Everyone will have special uniforms for the day. They will cause the arrows to bounce off with no affect. Though you might get a good bruise at the impact point." Parks dismissed them and Chrystar bid them farewell.

Roy walked with everyone as they went to the landing place of the Griffins.

"You have a plan to keep Alexander amused tonight?" Roy whispered to Abby.

"Jonathan will be starting a Trium contest right after supper. We'll have all the time we want."

"Looking forward to it."

The next morning, Roy was sitting on the balcony when Alexander found him. Roy sat with a cup of coffee in his hand and another cup of coffee sitting on the table next to him. Alexander collapsed into the chair, rubbing his eyes.

"You look like you're still asleep," Roy commented.

"I think I am asleep." Alexander grabbed the coffee mug and held it up. "I don't like coffee, but I need caffeine and I need it now!" He took a sip and then proceeded to screw up his face and gag. "How can you drink this stuff?"

"You'll get used to it," Roy replied.

"I'm not so sure," Alexander said, taking another drink, with equally humorous facial expressions. After a moment or two, confusion spread over his face. "Who's coffee is this?"

"I'm not sure."

Alexander looked at him skeptically.

"It's still warm. You're having coffee with someone?"

"No comment."

"You *are* having coffee with someone!" Alexander exclaimed.

Roy smiled. "Alright you caught me."

Alexander proceeded to take another drink of coffee into his mouth.

"I'm having coffee with my girlfriend."

Alexander choked on his coffee and ended up spitting it out in similar fashion that Abby had done the first day they had met.

"You Reno's. I'm not sure what I'm going to do with you. You keep spitting stuff in my face!"

“Girlfriend?” Alexander asked. “What girlfriend?”

“The only one I have.”

“Yes, I gathered that. But I am baffled at who this woman is. Though it might explain why you've missed most of the Trium tournaments.”

“Indeed it would!” Roy agreed.

“Who is she?”

“You know who she is.”

“No, I don't! If I knew, I wouldn't be asking.”

“What I meant was, you've met her before.”

“Met who before?”

“Yes.”

“What's her name?”

“Who?”

“Your girlfriend.”

“Who?”

“YOUR GIRLFRIEND!”

“My girlfriend?”

“Yes,” Alexander answered. “She has a name doesn't she?”

“Of course she has a name.”

“Well, what is it?”

“What is what?”

“What is her name?”

“Who's name?”

“Your girlfriend?”

“Oh, her. It's a nice name.”

“You're killing me, Roy! Just tell me her name,” Alexander started, he held up a hand to stop Roy from speaking. “I realize the error of my words. You are not *actually* killing me, but depending on how this conversation goes I might want to kill you.”

"You can't do that."

"Why not?"

"My girlfriend wouldn't like that."

"That's okay," Alexander said. "Because if she didn't like it then she would have to find me in order to get her revenge, which means I could learn her name. Now tell me her name!"

"Who's name?"

"Roy Van Doren—"

"Alright, alright. I'll tell you her name."

"Then tell me already!"

"Abigail."

"Abigail?"

"Yes."

"I wasn't aware of another Abigail."

"That's because he's talking about me," Abby said coming up from behind Alexander. Alexander looked completely dumbfounded. He remained completely speechless as Abby sat down in the chair on the other side of Roy, while grabbing her coffee from Alexander on the way.

"I'm not sure what to say," Alexander said, after a few strange moments of silence.

"So we noticed," Abby said with a smile.

"I didn't . . . I mean, I wouldn't have . . . uh . . . wow."

"I hope you're not upset about this?" Roy asked.

Alexander shook his head. "No, certainly not. Just surprised. I'm shocked, but happy for you guys."

"Good, because it wasn't going to change anything even if you didn't like it." Abby said. They all smiled.

# ALLIANCE

* * * *

Later in the day when they flew to the canyon they didn't stop at their normal spot. Instead they flew further across the vast expanse of land. Roy looked at Alexander, who looked surprisingly nervous.

"Something wrong, Alexander?" Roy asked.

"We're training with the G.F.C. which means we'll probably end up flying with you . . . I'm not sure what that's going to be like."

"Don't worry, we've all become pretty good pilots," Jonathan said. "That being said, this canyon is much larger than I thought, and I have no idea where we are going."

They flew for another half hour until they descended to just above the great shelf of rocks that made up the canyon. A dense forest of pine trees stretched out before them. Finally, a hint of blue could be seen up ahead.

Within minutes they found themselves on the shores of a rugged rocky coastline of a lake, which had a hundred islands of rock laying scattered throughout the massive lake. They landed in the main assembly area, where Sergeant Parks was waiting for them. A box of black sactalines was by his side.

"Good afternoon!" the Sergeant greeted. "Suit up and we'll get started." They all grabbed their sactalines and tapped them, soon adorned in their armor and weapons.

"Today we'll introduce you to air strikes. Jonathan, Savannah, and Roy have already become well-versed in tactics, and maneuvers, and let me tell you, you have some of the best pilots from this year's recruits. Split up into three groups. Each group will complete a three mile run to an area where you will call your Griffin. Once there, get into the sky and search the islands. You're looking for rocks that have been painted purple. There are thirty rocks in all. Once you've struck all of them with your arrows, return here. Understood?"

"What happens if we fall off?" Alexander asked.

"We're training you over water for a reason. Swim to an island and your pilot can land and pick you back up. You'll each be given a pack to strap on your Griffin, which will have more Bolt sactalines in it. If you run out of arrows without striking all your targets, return to the loading area. Understood?"

"Yes, sir!"

They completed their run at a comfortable pace and soon they were all waiting in the assembly area. They called their Griffins, who happily landed on the hard rocks. Roy, Savannah, and Jonathan took their places, laying down on their stomachs.

Alexander remained on the ground, even after everyone else was on board. "I'm not sure about this."

"It'll be fine. Your armor is magnetic to the Griffin's blood," Savannah explained. "It's very hard to fall off."

"Still, I'm not sure I can do this."

"Yes, you can. Just take my hand," Savannah held a hand out to him and he reluctantly took it and took a seat. The others all loaded their crossbows and waited for Roy to lead the way.

"Let's just take a spin around the lake for a few minutes, give our crews some maneuvers. Get them used to flying with us. As you both know this is not like flying around the city."

"Yes, sir," Savannah said, immediately sending her Griffin into a steep ascent. Much to Roy's amusement, Alexander could be heard screaming nearly the entire way as they rocketed into the sky. Roy and Jonathan took their Griffins into the sky and caught up to Savannah, who surrendered the lead to Roy. They flew in several tight formations and performed a number of maneuvers that also freaked out Alexander.

"How's Alexander doing?" Roy asked Savannah. His voice was heard clearly through the green sactaline on the front of his uniform.

"He hasn't died of a heart attack yet, so I think he's doing okay," came the reply. "I hope he gets over the screaming though. Can you hear it?"

"Quite clearly," Abby said, close enough to hear the conversation.

"Let's get down to business. Tell Alexander it's time to stop screaming and time to start looking for rocks."

Throughout the course of the afternoon, they circled island after island searching for and shooting at the purple painted rocks. It took them most of the afternoon to hit all their targets as they missed the shots for a while.

"It's harder to hit these when you're moving so fast," Abby exclaimed, firing another arrow and missing. An explosion followed.

"I'm sure you'll get it. Just keep on trying," Roy encouraged. They descended again, whirling past several purple painted rocks. A small cheer when up as one of the other people with Roy hit their target. The cloud of fire was green this time instead of the usual orange flame indicating that it had been hit. With many more approaches and flyby's they were able to get the rest of their targets, having to stop twice because Alexander fell off.

"That's the last one. Let's head back," Roy said. The others followed behind him and everyone slung the crossbows on their backs as they flew the rest of the way in a relaxing formation.

"I'm glad this flight is better than the last one you took me on," Abby told him.

"Me, too. I'll be curious to see what your brother thinks when we get back." They landed in the main area with another regiment showing up as they began unloading. Alexander slid off the Griffin and collapsed to his knees. Savannah helped him up, trying not to laugh.

"That was absolutely terrifying!" Alexander exclaimed. "I don't like this flying thing."

"Just be glad you didn't drown," Savannah encouraged.

Sergeant Parks approached them, smiles on his face. "First, again. You're getting a reputation."

"I'll take that as a compliment," Roy said.

Parks smiled. "As you should. Well done."

* * * *

The next day was much like the first had been, shooting at targets from the air. Within a few days they practiced quick mounts and dismounts, often going from using their swords to firing a crossbow to jumping aboard a Griffin all within a matter of seconds.

As the next couple of weeks passed, they were trained vigorously, for all kinds of scenarios and for all kinds of weather, even traveling to distant mountain ranges to practice in snow and striking targets in the rain.

At the end of their eighth week they were allowed to join the air corps that watched over the city itself. Only Roy, Savannah, and Jonathan participated in those exercises, but it was enjoyable either way.

Roy and Abby continued to spend a good deal of time together and although Alexander made a show about it being just 'weird' that they were dating, secretly Roy thought he didn't mind that much.

Every third day they would get a small break from training, as they were assigned a regular shift on the security roster for the city. Roy enjoyed it, even if he did spend a large amount of his time in the bridge, communicating with everybody. The Dreygar sightings had dwindled for nearly a week and as of yet none had been spotted today.

By the time their shift started, the sun had long disappeared. For the most part Roy didn't mind the night shifts because they were quieter with less likely to happen. Roy and Abby were positioned in the bridge, keeping careful eye on the sactaline, which glowed brightly in the distance.

"You seem quiet tonight," Roy commented.

Abby nodded. "I feel nervous."

"What about?"

"Sometimes the night shifts are too quiet for my liking. I always think something's going to happen."

"Anything I can do for you?"

She shook her head. "It's time to check in," she said.

Roy put the green sactaline into his uniform. It lit up brightly.

"Alexander. Anything to report?"

"Negative. My part of the city is silent as a tomb."

"Savannah and Jonathan, anything of interest in the air?"

"Silent up here, too," came the reply.

"Wiggs, how about your group. Any activity?"

"No, sir," Wiggs replied.

"Sounds good, keep me informed." Roy took the sactaline out. Even though he needed the sactaline in his uniform to speak to people he didn't need it to hear what they were saying through it.

"I feel a little uneasy tonight as well," Roy admitted.

"Why?"

“The Dreygar sightings have stopped. I wish I knew why.”

An hour passed as they talked and observed, speaking with the members of the regiment. Abby sat up and leaned towards the window.

Roy joined her. “See something?”

“We need to check it out. I don't see anything at the moment, but I sure thought I did.”

Roy put the sactaline into his uniform again. “Hey everyone, stand by, we're checking something out. Jonathan and Savannah, keep close to platform 5-2-1. We're heading there now.”

“Roger that.”

Roy followed Abby who had already grabbed her crossbow and moved to the door. They both entered the winding staircase and descended until they reached the long hall that would lead them to the sactaline. They moved through the door and entered into the glowing red light of the sactaline.

Abby began a search of the area, taking the lead, bow at the ready. Roy's hand hovered near his sword.

“Alexander, Wiggs. Make sure stations three and four are secure. Jonathan and and Savannah, anything to report?” Roy asked.

“Dreygar spotted,” Savannah replied.

“Location?” Jonathan asked.

“South side, three o'clock.”

“I'm on my way.”

“Do we need backup?”

“No, I've got the target in sight.”

“Engage?” Savannah asked. Several bowmen were with both Griffins just in case.

“Is there anyone on it?” Roy asked. A moment of silence passed.

“Can't tell,” Savannah said.

"Jonathan?"

"I can't tell for sure either," Jonathan added.

"Stay with it but not to close, see if you can follow it."

"Yes, sir."

Abby and Roy continued to search the area, finally finding a single envelope in the middle of the floor on the far side of the area. Abby scooped it up and unfolded it.

"Do you have a sight on the Dreygar, Savannah?" Jonathan questioned.

"No. It seems to have vanished."

Roy mulled over the situation carefully. Abby hastily handed the paper to Roy who read it aloud for everyone to hear.

*To the recipient of this letter:*

*I have gotten through your defenses. In fact, I have done it five times already. If I had wanted to, I could have destroyed your city, but I assure you that is not my intent.*

*I wish to warn you of coming events. I do not have time to stay and chat tonight. But I will be back. You have the 'War Games' in one day. Three days after that, I will be at platform 981, during the night. I will be in contact. Good luck.*

"What are we supposed to do about that?" Alexander asked.

"I'm not sure," Roy replied. He was lost in his thoughts for several moments.

"I wonder if they have someone on the inside?"

"Good possibility," Roy concluded. "Whoever this is knows our schedule a little too well. Correct me if I'm wrong, but isn't platform 981 unfinished?"

"That's correct," Jonathan replied. "This person could be hiding out there."

"Very considerate of this person to wait until the 'War Games' are over," Abby pointed out.

"What are your orders, Captain? Should we search platform 981?" Wiggs asked.

Roy again considered the options. "No. I'll report the Dreygar sighting, but right now we'll do nothing else," he replied. "Whoever this is knows some stuff. If he's going to this effort to contact us, I feel like we should give this person the benefit of the doubt. Whoever it is clearly doesn't intend to harm us yet, he may change his mind if we tip anyone off." Roy stuffed the note in his pocket and turned to go back inside.

# 19

**THEY ARRIVED AT THE CANYON** earlier than was usual. Right after breakfast they had received word from Sergeant Parks that the recruits were supposed to report to the canyon immediately. It had barely been light when they had left the city, and it was clearly nowhere close to daylight when they arrived at the canyon. Sactalines lit up the main assembly area, where each regiment formed a line and waited to be called on.

"Roy Van Doren! Come forward," a man called. Roy hurried to a man who sat behind a large desk, five others flanked him on either side. Roy assumed they were the leaders of the canyon. "Do you understand what the War Games are."

"Tactical simulations, to see how we, as a regiment, do working together to achieve the goal which is given to us."

"Precisely," the person in the middle said. "You will have one day to carry out these orders. You'll be graded on teamwork and strategy, and of course, overall time will all play a factor into your final score. Your score will tell us what kind of missions you should be considered for. Is this understood?"

"Yes, sir," Roy answered.

"You are currently Team A. You, as captain, may choose a name for your regiment. If you do not choose one, your name will be Team A for the remainer of this test and then be assigned a Regiment number afterwards, for example, Regiment 892 or something like that. Do you wish to choose a different name?"

"I can pick anything?" Roy asked.

"All names are subject to final review, but for the sake of the competition any name can be selected."

Roy thought for a moment. "How about the A-Team? We'd like to be the A-Team. Is that okay?"

"That's highly unoriginal, but I don't foresee any problems getting a boring name like that approved in the end. Very well. Captain Roy Van Doren of the A-Team. Here are your orders and your clock starts ticking now."

Roy graciously accepted the sealed envelope and headed back towards the team. They followed him to the left of the assembly area where finally they came to a stop and he broke the seal on the envelope. Inside was a sheet of paper and then a map of the canyon. He handed the map to Jonathan and Savannah and read the note to everyone.

*'Please find Sergeant Parks for further instruction. His last known location is marked on the map. There were reports of large troop movements in the area.'*

"The spot shouldn't take more than an hour to get to," Savannah said, handing the map back.

"Let's get going then. Time's a-ticking." Roy started towards the Griffins, everyone else following behind.

"What's our regiment name?" Alexander asked.

"The A-Team."

"The A-Team?" Savannah asked.

"That's kind of a stupid name isn't it?" Wiggs asked.

"I kind of like it," Abby said. "Is this an off-worlder reference?"

"Yes, it is."

"So who exactly is the A-Team?"

"A group of criminals—"

"Goodness!" Jonathan exclaimed. "Certainly you're not saying that we're criminals."

"Of course—"

"He's saying we'll have to be sneaking like criminals?" Alexander interjected.

"I just thought it was a cool name!" Roy exclaimed.

"Oh, it's totally a cool name, I've just never heard of any regiment named like that," Savannah replied.

"I guess that means we're special," Alexander said. They laughed as they climbed on the Griffins.

*　　　*　　　*　　　*

An hour later they approached the area on the map. Roy flew in the lead with the others to either side of him in tight formation. They had slowed now to a steady pace.

"We're nearly at the target," Jonathan said.

"Okay. Have everyone load their bows and be ready. Spread out and do a sweep of the area, then check back." Roy ordered.

"It looks empty to me," Abby said. Roy looked over the side, concluding the same thing.

"I'm going to put down, everyone else stay up in the air until I give the okay." Roy swiftly but gently guided Skyquill down to a nice soft landing and they all slid off to the canyon floor. The particular area they were in consisted of densely populated pines with an occasional clearing. "Henderson, stay with Skyquill. Everyone else follow me." They started walking through the trees.

Twenty minutes passed and steadily the trees grew bare and a chill wind began blowing. Any vegetation in the canyon disappeared completely with no trace of life to be found in the trees or on the ground. The ground that had been soft and moist and covered with plant life became, bare and desolate. The path seemed to shift and churn, throwing loose sticks and dirt onto the path, making the ground hard to traverse.

Any sign of the rising sun was rapidly covered by clouds. In a matter of minutes, the temperature had fallen to the freezing point, forcing them to put on their coats. The ground, now frozen, was difficult to walk on. Thick fog mysteriously formed.

"We have no visual of anything on the ground," Jonathan said. "Not even you. Do we land?" Roy gave Abby a look of question.

"Land, but don't shoot anything unless you have to. Keep pressing towards the location on the map and we'll see what happens."

"Roger that," came the reply.

"This is a bit creepy," Abby whispered.

"Tell me about it. They used the word simulations, but I can't say I expected anything like this."

"Is this all a simulation?" Abby asked.

Roy thought for a moment. "That's a question I can't answer."

# ALLIANCE

Five hundred feet later, they finally stepped into a clearing. A fallen tree lay in the middle of the clearing. As they approached, the fallen tree caught fire and burned brightly, sending up pale blue flames. In an instant the fog retreated allowing them to better see their surroundings. Jonathan and Savannah both stepped into the clearing with their groups behind them.

"Looks like a lot of people were here," Abby noted. Roy noticed the large number of footprints.

"There are some ropes and blood over here," Savannah cried out. They all moved towards her and inspected the area.

"I wonder if Parks is captured?" Abby asked. "I thought he was supposed to meet us here."

"The note said find Sergeant Parks." Roy mulled the note over and over in his head. "Something about this doesn't line up."

"What do you mean?" Abby asked. The others waited expectantly.

"I'm not sure the note we were given was for the 'War Games'."

"Why not? What are you talking about?"

"The note on the platform the other night, it's the same writing. It's also in green ink. I've never seen any papers written in green ink. Have you?" Roy searched the regiment but they all shook their heads no. "Whoever left us that note last night is trying to get to us again."

"So is Sergeant Parks captured, or not?" Alexander asked.

"I'm not sure, but right now we need to plan as if he is," Roy said. "Savannah, take your group and follow the path for a half hour and then report back. Jonathan take yours and stake out a perimeter and let us know if anything happens. The rest of us will thoroughly search this area for any signs that might tell us what's going on."

"How about I save you the hassle?" a voice cried out from beyond the fog. They turned to the sound and watched intently. Jonathan and Savannah withdrew their people creating a perimeter just within sight, arrows ready.

Roy and Abby motioned for arrows to be ready, while moving their own hands to hilts of their swords.

"I mean you no harm!" the voice exclaimed.

Roy's heart stirred slightly.

"Promise you won't shoot me?"

"Show yourself Cyrus!" Roy declared. Slowly out of the fog, Cyrus came walking towards them. Abby shifted uncomfortably, while Roy's mind was thinking and analyzing everything.

"Sergeant Parks is currently held hostage and being interrogated far beyond the reaches of this canyon." Cyrus looked to both of them. "And contrary to what you might think, I am happy to see both of you,"

"How do you know about Sergeant Parks?"

"Because I know who captured him, and I know how to get him out," Cyrus replied. "Your own commander Uri was found to be loyal to a different cause, was he not?"

Roy nodded.

"He brought Parks to Sayatta last night. He was paid quite handsomely too."

"Who was paying him?" Roy asked.

"Lucerine," Cyrus answered. "Is Alexander here? There's a lot to talk about. Can we by chance do it without bows pointing at me?" Roy nodded to Abby who tentatively motioned for the bows to be lowered.

"Alexander, come forward. Everyone else will be keeping their bows ready, however."

"That's fine." Alexander came and stood next to Abby. "First things first. I'm sorry I left you guys in such anger and frustration. We've always had a good relationship, and I'm sorry that I might have destroyed that. I hope in the future I can regain your trust and forgiveness."

"I think that will largely depend on how you answer Roy's questions,"

Abby said. She nodded to Roy who stepped forward. Cyrus, as if reading Roy's thoughts dropped his weapons at Roy's feet and sat down on the fallen log, The fire that was burning withdrew a few feet and burned brighter.

"Are you here alone?"

"I am now."

"Were there more of you?"

"I had ten with me when I entered the canyon.

"Where are they now?"

"Dead."

"Did you kill them?"

"Yes."

"Why?"

"I didn't want anyone else knowing about this canyon."

"About that, how did you get here when this is a hidden canyon?"

"You've noticed the Dreygars in the sky, no doubt. We captured a wild Griffin almost five weeks ago. We came in, and no one noticed us."

"What's your purpose in coming here?"

"To seek you out and assist in whatever way I'm able," Cyrus said.

"Why would you seek to assist us?" Roy inquired. "Your sword is of the make and style of a Hentarian Knight."

"It's true. I am a Hentarian Knight, but there are some things that I must do regardless of what the Hentarian code says."

"Are you the one who left the note last night?"

"Yes."

"I thought we were supposed to meet at platform 981? That's what the note, your note, said.

"It was no longer safe to meet you there."

"To the point Cyrus," Roy said sternly.

Cyrus nodded. “Things have gotten sped up a bit.”

Roy gave him a hard expression.

“I know what you're thinking. I'm not the one in charge. Not even close. Lucerine is going to use the Alliance to have an attack tonight on the three key cities. He's already planted bait for some of his un-freindly foes to take to arms against him. These people are going to be dressed in your attire, thanks to commander Uri. He'll bring out Alliance troops to crush the uprising, and therefore start a justified war against the Chrystarians.”

“What are the three key cities you spoke of?”

“The only three that I know of are Sayatta, Avigont, and Darsujes. I'm sure there will be more in the future. I don't know what Lucerine's end game is.”

Roy pondered everything for a moment. “You said that Lucerine has Parks?”

“Yes, he's trying to get the location of the city out of him. This city seems to always be in motion. Even Uri didn't seem to realize that. Parks is a smart man, and I believe he knows the location.”

“He won't give it up,” Alexander said.

“I know. I saw Parks last night. I'd be surprised if he cracks.” Uneasy silence fell over all of them. “Look, I know you're in the middle of your war games, but there's no time to finish them. Mom and Dad are going to be right in the thick of it, and I unfortunately cannot do anything to help them.”

“Why not?” Abby asked.

Cyrus looked at her for a moment. “It's complicated.”

“They're family.”

“I know, but you have to trust me.”

“Why?” Alexander asked.

“Because everything is happening *now.* I need you to do what I can't. I'm stuck! We can debate this all day, but the reality is, war is coming now. Something is going to happen on platform 981 tonight! For all we know, the attacks may be underway now. You have no choice but to rush into action and save people."

Abby and Alexander, though still conflicted, nodded their agreement to what he said. Roy took one step closer to Cyrus, standing nearly nose to nose with him. He stared at him hard and long.

"Alright," Roy agreed. "We'll take the bait, but under one condition. You give yourself into custody and let the courts and Chrystar find the truth in your words."

Cyrus thought long and hard. "I'm sorry, but I can't do that."

"Take him," Roy said. Three men came and bound his hands tightly behind his back. "Everyone wait here until I get back. Abby and Alexander come with me."

They marched Cyrus past the burning tree, until they were under the cover of fog once again. They walked until they abruptly came to a large cliff.

"Any last words?" Roy asked, pulling his bow out and holding it up.

Cyrus shifted nervously. "You're going to kill me?"

Roy quickly shot the bolt at Cyrus's feet, making him flinch and sending up some dust but causing no further damage.

"No." Roy said. Abby and Alexander relaxed. "You're giving me what could be vital information. I should not kill a man for that. Now if this is all a trap and what you say is not true, than I should think I won't be quite so merciful next time. Understood?"

"Thank you, Roy," Cyrus said.

Roy smiled. "Don't mention it." He looked to Alexander and Abby. "A war is no time for a family to be divided against itself. For a single braided cord is easily broken, but a triple braided cord—"

"Is not easily broken," Abby and Alexander said in unison. The three of them stood in silence as Roy slipped to the back.

Alexander finally broke the uneasy silence. "I hope what you say is true. We'll do what we can to get mom and dad out alive."

"Thanks. I wish I could do it myself, but like I said earlier, I'm stuck."

"Is there anything we can do to help you?" Abby asked.

"You kept me alive, so that's good." Cyrus thought for a moment. "but there is one more thing I could use. I almost hate to ask you for this, and if you say no I will completely understand." He paused. "I need a pilot and a couple of bowmen to get in and out of Darsujes before war breaks out."

"You said you have a Griffin," Roy reminded.

"Yes, I do. But I can't fly it very well, if at all. Let alone, if I reach Darsujes too late, the whole city will be engulfed in war. I would never make it in and out alive."

"What's your purpose in going to Darsujes?" Abby asked.

"Retrieval mission. People. Innocent people."

"Innocent by whose standards?" Alexander asked.

"They're civilian people. I need to get them out alive."

An eerie silence fell over them as Roy tried to sort out everything. "Alexander, keep an eye on your brother. Abigail, can I talk to you for a minute?" They started walking away.

"He calls her Abigail now?" Cyrus asked in a whisper. Roy and Abby both smiled as they were now out of earshot.

"What are you thinking?" Abby asked.

"I'm not sure. First, he comes and supposedly tells us the plan the Alliance is making, then he asks us to help him get innocent people out of what will soon be an Alliance 'controlled' city . . . if you believe his story. He claims to be a Hentarian Knight."

"I'd believe that. He always wanted to be one," Abby said. "I was okay believing him until he started with getting innocent people out of a city. Why would the Alliance ever do that?"

"Something's not right with this, and I'm not sure what it is," Roy said. They fell silent, lost in their thoughts.

"I agree something is not lining up," Abby said. "But I think we should believe him. If the Alliance was trying to find and destroy the canyon, then they would have done it by now. If he was lying to us about these things, he could have killed us a hundred times over."

"You're right," Roy admitted. They walked back to the cliff, where Alexander and Cyrus were waiting. "Alright. We'll trust you on this."

They walked back to the group, all of whom were surprised as Cyrus was brought back and then untied.

"What's going on?" Jonathan asked.

"Savannah, along with her company and Alexander, are going to take Cyrus to Darsujes. Help him with whatever he is doing. If it goes sour, you can kill him. The rest of us are headed back to the city at the fastest speed possible and getting to the bottom of Platform 981," Roy said. "We need to send an emergency signal to Gideon and get him to cancel the war games. The games are over. War is here."

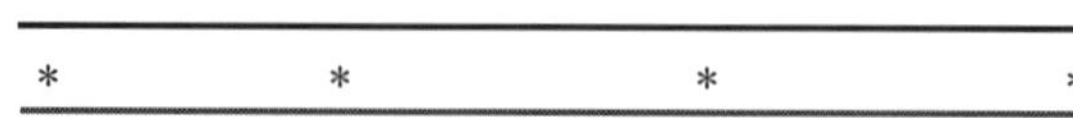

They made it back to the city in record time, and immediately things were being reorganized with the new information they had to provide.

Gideon had sounded the alarm at once, and the 'War Games' had immediately been canceled.

"Don't rush in too fast!" Gideon warned. "It's an unfinished section of the city. Your brother might have said that he killed the people who snuck in with him, but there's no way to prove that as of yet."

Abby and Roy led their group of over the walkway that connected the two platforms. A minute later they stepped foot on the eeriest ghost town that Roy had ever heard of. The buildings were tall and large, but there were no lights, no sounds, or sights of life. Abby pointed to the left where a pile of bodies lay.

"Cyrus was telling the truth. There's the proof."

Roy didn't look any longer than he had to. "We'll perform a sweep up here, but right now I don't see anything of threatening nature. Jonathan?"

"I don't see anything wrong from up here."

"Give it a thorough sweep. I'll see what I can find out and get back with you," Gideon said. "If you need anything while I'm gone, Evelyn will be on the line."

"Copy that," Roy said. Time passed slower than Roy thought was even possible as they searched floor after floor and found each one of them as empty as the one before it. Finally, they reached the top and stood looking out at the city.

"What now?" Roy asked through the sactaline.

A moment passed before Evelyn's voice came on the other line. "I'm not sure what's going on, Roy. Gideon went down to check the sactaline beneath the platform and I haven't heard anything from him since. That was a hour ago. I'm getting nervous."

Roy's mind came alive. "We'll move there and find him. Jonathan, I'm not sure what to advise just yet. Stay near to the underside of the platform, though," Roy said. Together he and Abby led their group back down the platform as quick as they could, locating the spiral staircase that would lead them down to the sactaline. Roy readied himself, ready to throw open the door. He jumped and paused as Abby touched his arm.

"Be careful, okay?"

He nodded, and she threw the door open. Inside the stairwell was dark and empty.

"David and Carl, stand guard." Roy ordered. They began walking down the steps. "Also Jonathan, the sactaline hides the walkways, but a few well placed arrows can dismantle that part of it.

"How many arrows and where?" came the reply.

"Twenty arrows, in unison directly at the sactaline. It won't destroy the sactaline, but if we need help be ready to shoot."

"Copy that," Jonathan said. They continued down the stairs, their anxiety growing more with each step that passed.

"Roy!" Abby called out.

Roy quickened his pace seeing a shadowy figure lying on the stairs. They grabbed one of the torches on the wall. Gideon lay on the stairs, beaten and badly bruised with a couple large gashes on his forehead. "He's still alive!" They all breathed a sigh of relief.

"Arrow, Merk!" two of the other men came forward. "Get him to the medical wing. Everyone else with me!"

Gideon was carried off, and Roy and Abby ran down the rest of the steps, each lost in their own thoughts. They reached the door and looked through the window, seeing one dark, cloaked figure standing in the light of the sactaline.

"Jonathan, are you in position?"

"Yes, ready to fire whenever you say."

"Stand by."

"I don't like this Roy," Abby said. "Whoever this is, is far to comfortable and seems utterly unconcerned that they could be caught."

"What do you think we should do?"

"Go out as innocent guards on patrol. With everyone else ready to rush in if needed," Abby suggested getting nods of approval from the rest of the team.

"Alright," Roy agreed, the two of them put their crossbows on their back and resisted the urge to grab their swords. Abby nodded and they slowly opened the door. They both took one deep breath and walked into the light of the sactaline.

To their surprise their presence did little to startle the cloaked figure. As if they had been expected. They pushed the thought from their minds and continued walking towards the cloaked figure. The figure didn't move or reach for any weapons, and instead held a hand up to motion for them to stop ten feet away.

"I assume the body in the stairwell was your handy work?" Abby asked, casually but to the point.

"Casualty of war," a woman's voice replied. For a moment both of them were taken aback, having not expected it. "He's still alive though."

"We know." Roy studied the mysterious woman. "Thanks for not killing him. He is a friend of ours."

"I figured he was," the woman said, looking at the two of them intently. "Your name is Van Doren, right?" Abby and Roy both froze, unsure of how to respond.

"Who's asking?" Roy asked. The cloaked figured look at him. Somehow even though they couldn't see her eyes, they felt as if they could sense her feelings.

"Tarjinn," the woman replied. "I'm supposed to take this sactaline out from under the city."

"We're here to stop you," Abby said pulling her sword.

Tarjinn didn't move. “If you wish to do something good, get off the platform now!” she exclaimed.

“Make me,” Abby taunted.

As if Tarjinn had no other option she stood and quickly pulled her sword, which had a faint glimmer of red to it. “You're bold,” she replied. “You are no match for a fully trained Hentar.” Without hesitation Tarjinn lunged into a furious attack with her sword, Abby rose to the challenge, blocking every swing with ease. Roy jumped in but still Tarjinn seemed to be holding them off with relative ease.

Their blades clashed for several minutes until at last Tarjinn swung her blade and struck Abby in the thigh. Abby dropped her sword and was swiftly knocked upside the head by Tarjinn. She fell unconscious. Roy rushed to Abby, but stopped when he felt Tarjinn's cool Hentarian blade. Roy tried his best to hide his fear as he followed the point of blade all the way up to the eyes of the person holding it.

“She's good, but how are you off-worlder?” Tarjinn taunted.

“Roy, what do you want us to do?” Jonathan asked. “I'm not liking the sound of this conversation.” Roy hesitated, unsure what he should do. Tarjinn punched him in the face, sending him flailing backwards. As quick as a flash she snatched the sactaline from it's spot and buried it in her cloak. The bright red light vanished.

Roy jumped to his feet, running after the cloaked figure, his eyes struggling to focus on anything due the rapid change in light. As he ran, he heard loud creaking and rumbling from up above him. He stopped, watching as Tarjinn jumped over the edge of a railing and was lost from sight. He heard the sound of a Dreygar calling out in the night and flapping its powerful wings, carrying Tarjinn away.

“What's going on down there?” Evelyn's urgent voice called out.

Roy was snapped out his thoughts. “Jonathan and everyone within earshot, destroy the bridges on Platform 981!" The creaking and rumbling grew louder and now the sickening sound of metal snapping could be heard from the bridges.

"Come again, Roy?" Evelyn asked.

"Destroy the bridges on 981!"

Roy sprinted back to Abby, and slung her limp body over his shoulders. He scooped her sword into his hands and felt his heart race as explosions rang overhead. Flames and debris fell all around them as the bridges were destroyed and the platform began to fall. The walkway in front of them began to crack and splinter.

Roy jumped and stumbled and fell to the other side, covering both of them up as more debris fell down. He sat up and watched in disbelief as the massive platform faded from sight and fell to the ground far below.

"Roy, are you alright?" several voices frantically called through the sactaline.

"Yes, I'm fine, but Abigail's going to need some medical attention." At that moment, the door was pulled open and the rest of their team came out to them. "Jonathan, make sure you congratulate your team. Good shooting on their part."

"I'll do that. What do we do now?"

"Evelyn?" Roy asked.

"Get everyone back to our quarters," she said. "I'm a skilled nurse, I'm sure I can patch up Abby as good here as anywhere. There are lots of meetings going on, and I think Roy will likely have to be dragged to many more before the night's over."

# 20

**ALEXANDER INTENTLY STUDIED** his brother as they streaked through the sky. They were already closing in on Darsujes, and from the looks of things it wasn't going to be an easy trip. Even from a great distance, the smell of smoke and the flashes of great explosions could be seen.

Savannah looked ahead, studying the ground and chatting lightly with Cyrus, who looked even more nervous than Alexander was. The few other bowmen that had come with them shifted anxiously as they approached the city.

"Thank you, Alexander, for helping me," Cyrus said. Alexander remained silent, unsure how to respond. "I owe you one."

"Do you want to tell me what this is all about?" Alexander asked. "Who are we rescuing? Are they actually innocent people?"

"Yes, they are innocent. I'm not going to lie to you, Alexander! You must understand that there are some things I can't tell you right now. I'm sure you have things you can't tell me." Alexander had to concede. "You'll just have to trust me."

"Okay," Alexander asked. "So how have you been? Did you make the rank of Hentarian Warrior? I know you've wanted that for a long time."

"Yes I did," Cyrus answered. "Have a sword to prove it, too." He pulled out his sword and handed it to Alexander, who had to admit it was a beautiful sword.

"Congratulations."

"Thanks," Cyrus said, putting it away. "What have you been up to?"

"You know, training and such stuff."

"Don't forget screaming like a little girl!" Savannah interjected.

Cyrus laughed. "Really?"

"She's exaggerating," Alexander replied.

"No, I'm not. Even Sergeant Parks said you screamed like a little girl."

"In my defense, I always had good reason to be screaming as such, if it must be described in such a manner."

"And these reasons are?" Cyrus asked.

"He set himself on fire, fell off this Griffin during training at least three or four times, and—"

"I think you've really given him enough examples," Alexander said.

"He also showed up for training without shoes on," Savannah continued. "That was a memorable day."

"I wish I could have seen that one," Cyrus replied.

"We're not going to talk about that *ever* again!" Alexander declared. Cyrus and Savannah laughed.

"Where are we headed in this war zone?" Savannah asked.

"Sector ninety-eight, tunnel one hundred and three," Cyrus replied. Savannah's face showed surprise. "Do you know where that is?"

"All too well, I grew up in the same sector, just three tunnels to the east," Savannah answered. "My parents still live there."

"I hope they're okay," Cyrus said. "I don't know what we'll find when we get to the city. I'm not even quite sure where we're going. I've never been to Darsujes before."

Alexander considered everything carefully. “Yet, now we're headed there to help some people. Why?”

“Because it's the right thing to do, even if it's the hard thing to do,” Cyrus answered.

Alexander nodded his agreement.

“If I could be so bold, Savannah,” Cyrus said, “once we're at the city we should get as high up as we can.”

“Why?” Alexander asked.

“Because then we can go into a nosedive and land directly at the right spot. Hopefully, without being shot down and killed,” Savannah replied.

They remained silent for several more minutes, the city slowly getting closer. Soon a great number of Dreygars and Griffins filled the sky, and the number of Tantine arrows was truly impressive and intimidating at the same time. As they got closer Savannah shifted and handed two balls of cotton to Cyrus.

“What are these for?” he asked.

“So you don't have to listen to your brother in about three minutes.”

“My brother?”

“Earplugs! So you still have hearing left when we land.” Savannah gave him a wink and then turned back to the view in front of them. Without warning, as though they had passed an invisible shield, an immense sprawling city was stretched out in front of them.

The city was flat, sprawling on for miles and miles, but between the borders of the city, the entire area was filled with massive holes. Large towers jutted up into the sky, they were covered in armor and hundreds of archers sat atop each one.

“I didn't expect the city to look like this!” Alexander cried. “Where is sector ninety-eight?”

“Each hole is a different sector,” Cyrus explained. “And within each sector there are two hundred tunnels."

Arrows were immediately launched in their direction, taking out a couple of their bowmen within seconds. Alexander and Cyrus drew their swords and tried their best to block some of the arrows before they struck the Griffin's armor. Savannah looked at the scene in front of her, worry inevitably showing on her face.

"Are you okay?" Alexander asked.

"I can see sector ninety-eight from here!" She yelled. "All I see is smoke."

Alexander tried to push the worry from his mind as they looked ahead to the consistent stream of smoke, billowing from the hole.

"We're not stopping!" Alexander encouraged. "We'll do whatever we can to find your family Savannah."

"Cyrus's people first, though," Savannah said. Alexander knew better than to argue. They flew towards the smoke, which was now drifting towards them, against the wind.

"I'm not sure we'll be able to see in the smoke. It's too thick!" Cyrus yelled.

"I think it'll work out. Have a little faith," Savannah said, encouraging her Griffin to speed up. Suddenly and without warning, the Griffin let out a deafening roar. The whole city shook and trembled, and as it did they began to understand that it wasn't the Griffin that had made the great noise, but something greater and far more powerful.

The rest of the people didn't seem to notice, but in an instant the cloud of smoke became a billowing cloud of flames. Then as though it had never been there, it vanished and the veil dissipated, leaving them a crisp clear view of what was actually going on in the city.

They started a sharp descent, the arrows getting thicker with every inch that they traveled. Arrows pummeled the armor on their Griffin, threatening to destroy it. They quickly deployed new armor, but their hearts sank when they realized it was their last.

"Can you see the tunnel yet?" Cyrus asked.

"Yes, but we'll never make it out once we're in," Savannah cried. "There are too many arrows. They'll never get the safe door shut."

"Yes, we will."

"Keep flying, you're doing great!" Alexander encouraged. He looked to Cyrus. "How are we going to live through this?"

"The safe doors are immune to bows, but not swords. We jump off as she flies in, cut the ropes and hopefully we can ride the door down and get in before it closes all the way."

"That's daring," Savannah said.

"Unless you have another idea."

"Carry on, boys, but be careful."

"We will." Alexander and Cyrus stood side by side waiting for the right moment. They sped into the core, lining up now with the tunnel they desired.

"Jump!" Savannah ordered. They did as she said, both of them grasping the top of the safe door. They both pulled themselves to the top of the door and then grabbed extra rope which was hanging on the wall. They drew their swords and swung at the rope holding the gate open. The gate slowly began descending. They quickly sheathed their swords and threw the ropes over the edge, walked down the face and swung themselves into the tunnel, which was now sealed off from the war outside.

"That was awesome!" Cyrus said. He and Alexander celebrated, but then realized their sorrow. In front of them, the tunnel, which spanned one hundred and fifty feet across, was filled with the horrors of war and the remains of those who had been killed. A somber silence came over them as Savannah came walking up to them.

"Looks like we were too late," Savannah said. Cyrus hung his head and then began pacing.

"Did the Alliance really do all of this?" Cyrus asked. They poked around grabbing arrows from some of the bodies, they handed it to Cyrus. He examined it closely.

"It looks like one of ours," Alexander said, pulling one for him to compare.

"So it does, but beneath the surface . . ." He pulled out his Hentarian Sword and touched the hilt to the arrow. In an instant it changed form, seeming to shed the old one as though it was a snake escaping its old skin. "The truth is revealed."

"What good does that do for anybody, though?" Alexander asked. "We're still standing in a tomb, and have failed with our rescue attempt."

"Maybe not," Cyrus said, clearly thinking. "If these arrows are meant to look like yours, hence creating the illusion of war, then I would think that the only logical move would be for the Alliance to send their troops to kill these 'fake' Chrystarian warriors. Furthermore, if that was their only intent —"

"The rest are alive somewhere else," Savannah finished. Cyrus nodded. "Either they took prisoners or the people escaped." Cyrus studied the scene once again.

"They were taken as prisoners," Cyrus assured. "The Alliance has thousands of slaves as it is, and with a war they'll only need more."

"If they took them, where do we find them?"

"I'm not sure," Cyrus said. "But we have a Griffin that can fly fast. Let's see how fast it can go." They clamored on top the Griffin and took off again. They flew for almost five minutes through the winding tunnel until they found that it connected with the other tunnels.

Finally, at Cyrus's signal, they landed and remained quiet and still for some time. Then as their hope began to fade a distant wailing could be herd. Cyrus led the way now as they rushed through the tunnel at breakneck speed.

They ran for several more minutes until they came to a place where they could peer out into the war torn outside world. They could faintly see large metal gates at the end of the tunnel.

"What now?" Savannah asked. They were interrupted by a great chorus of voices behind them. They quickly darted into the shadows as a large group of people came, driven by a hundred men with whips. The company rushed forward. They held their breath as the Griffin, who had been walking behind them, stood in it's place, but somehow wasn't seen by anybody.

"I wonder if they can't see Griffins," Alexander whispered.

Cyrus shrugged. "Might make a handy escape," he suggested.

"My parents!" Savannah exclaimed, as quietly as she could. She pointed them out as the company was rushed by. Before anyone could stop him, Alexander busted out from his hiding spot and ran into the middle of the group. Savannah joined him, the people stopped and great confusion was heard by the soldiers at the rear of the possession. Savannah and Alexander both exchanged looks, wondering who was going to speak first. Finally, Alexander began to speak.

"Citizens of Darsujes! People of this good earth! I ask you what is this all about? Why do I see these citizens torn from their homes? Why do I see a great city paralyzed by fear? You have all been deceived, and I have come to set the record straight.

"Great tales and lore always speak of moments like this. One when the people, aware of the evil that is happening, take action. I could help you, but I am but one man. A single braided cord is easily broken but a rope of three strands is strong and can face the challenge.

"You have been told that the Alliance looks out for you. I only wish to point out that it is the Alliance that is running you out of your homes now! The choice is yours. Do you stand and defend your homeland? Who's with me?"

The great company roared their approval and turned at once and rushed back at the soldiers at the rear of the company. Alexander and Savannah both grabbed her parents arms and pulled them to the side. Alexander smiled as both her parents embraced her, no doubt having so many questions, but having no words for them at the moment.

Alexander searched through the surroundings, seeing the people turning against the Hentar and the Alliance. In the midst of it all, he spotted Cyrus, who had disappeared momentarily. He was now coming up into the tunnel with three young girls in tow. They looked scared and uncertain, the oldest no more than ten and the youngest looked like she was five.

"Unfortunately our rescue was only partially successful," Cyrus announced as they all climbed on the Griffin which still seemed to be unseen by everyone. No one asked any questions or spoke at all as they took off and exited the tunnel, quickly ascending into the sky, leaving the sounds of war behind them.

They flew for a while until Cyrus asked for them to put down in a small clearing the middle of the forest. He slid off and Alexander followed suit. Savannah and everyone else remained aboard the Griffin.

"Thank you for your help, Alexander," Cyrus said. "I'm glad we could be on the same side again."

"Me too," Alexander replied. "What now? Are you just going to walk away?"

"For now, it must be that way," Cyrus replied. "But I hope when next we meet, we can meet as friends."

"Friends," Alexander said, shaking his hand and then embracing him.

Cyrus embraced him back and then they separated. He turned and walked away.

"Cyrus."

Cyrus looked at him. "Who are they?"

"Innocent. Treat them well, and teach them what you've been taught," Cyrus answered. Without another word or response he walked away, while Alexander watched, smiling.

# 21

**IT WAS LATE** in the night when Roy finally walked through the doors of their dwelling space. The lights were off and everyone was in their beds, except for Evelyn. Gideon and Abby were stretched out on the couches fast asleep.

"Meetings are the curse of being a Captain," Roy lamented as he collapsed in a chair.

"You've had a busy day," Evelyn said.

"How's Abigail?"

"See for yourself." Evelyn pulled the sheet back from Abby, exposing her legs. The wound where the blade had struck her was black. It appeared rough and dried out, with cracks branching out from it. "I got her patched up the best anyone could."

"You said you were a nurse?"

"I was a nurse for years. I've healed many injuries," Evelyn said.

"What happened to her?"

"For each level of the Hentar, their swords become more deadly. The sword she was cut by was the sword of a master. If they're not properly treated the wounds will kill their victims. She'll probably be out for a couple days, but it depends on the person. The poison affects some people more than others."

"How's Gideon?"

"Not as bad as he looks. He had some pretty significant blunt force that knocked him out, and it looks like only regular fighting injuries besides that. He'll be out for another day, I think."

"Gideon and Abigail are lucky to have you by their side."

"Thanks," Evelyn replied. Silence followed for several minutes as Roy stared at Abby's face. "Don't worry. She will get better."

"I know," Roy replied. "I would miss her terribly if she died."

"Everyone has that moment when they realize just how much they've grown to love someone," Evelyn said. "It sounds to me like you just had yours."

"I suppose," Roy said, with a chuckle and a smile. "I like the way you put it, *'grown to love'* ."

"It's an expression I heard many years ago by a friend of mine, and I've found it to be a most accurate expression. I certainly didn't love Gideon when I met him, but over time, the little things became more important. You know?"

"Yes, I do." Roy was lost in his thoughts. "Have we had any contact from Alexander and Savannah?"

"Yes we have. Their mission was successful, they acquired three young girls on the rescue mission."

"Who are they?"

"No idea," Evelyn replied.

Roy fell into his thoughts for a moment. Finally he pushed them from his mind and pulled some papers from his pocket. "Everyone who can fight is summoned to the canyon assembly area in three hours."

"That's what I heard. Go and get some sleep, and I'll make sure everyone is ready on time. If I need a hundred cups of coffee than so be it!"

Roy laughed. "Make two hundred. I'll be going on three hours sleep. I need all the caffeine I can get."

*   *   *   *

"It's strange without Abby here," Jonathan whispered to him. They stood in formation waiting to find out what was going on.

"She's not going to be happy that she was left behind."

"Any updates from Savannah and Alexander?"

Roy shook his head. "I'm sure they'll be okay."

"You have more faith than I have," Jonathan admitted. "Cyrus may be Abby and Alexander's brother but he is loyal to the Hentar now."

"Or is he?" Roy asked. Jonathan gave him a look. "The way I see it, he risked his neck by coming to me in order to tell us about an attack on specific cities and the plot to take down our city. And let alone, the part that was taken down was an uninhabited part of the city. The way I see it, I'll trust Cyrus this much and trust that my team can handle themselves if he goes against the character I think he has."

"What about the three girls they picked up? Any news on them?"

"They gave the names Ember, age 10. Henley, age 7 and Bristol, age 5."

"Do we know anything about them?"

"They are scared. Other than that...no. We don't know anything about them."

Jonathan nodded but didn't get time to respond as trumpets blared and Chrystar appeared at the front of the assembly.

"Citizens and people of the Kingdom! Last night there was an invasion of three cities that were under control of the Alliance. Sayatta, Darsujes, and Avigont. We believe these cities to still be controlled by the Alliance as they are using these 'other groups' as a mask to move their own troops in.

"It is confirmed that the groups used in this attack were dressed in a fashion and armor that we once dressed in. So there will be no confusion between us and them. We have new uniforms and weapons for you on the way.

"The main objective at this moment is misdirection. Many of you will experience the heat of battle, while other more specialized units will be carrying out special missions.

"As sure as I stand before you today, the Alliance will fall and the Kingdom will reign forevermore. But first, this war will tempt you. This is the moment of truth. This is when we will find out whose hearts are truly devoted and whose are not. Some will fall away, either out of fear or pressure from those they love. When you die, let it be said of you that you have run the good race, and run it for the love of others!

"File through your normal entrances, get your new armor and weapons, and then Captains can pick up the orders for your team before you get on your Griffins. Many blessings to you, and I look forward to your speedy return."

The lines began moving immediately, and Roy led everyone into the building the way they normally would. Dozens and dozens of lines were created in an instant. They filed through, grabbing dark red sactalines and tapping them. In an instant they were covered in new uniforms, these ones a deep burgundy red, the front bearing the sign of the Kingdom.

They picked up their new swords and crossbows and several large bags of sactalines that had extra bolts stored inside as well as extra armor for both soldiers and the Griffins.

They exited the building, picking up the envelope that had *A-Team* written on it. Roy chuckled to himself as he broke the seal.

"What's our mission?" one of the men asked.

"We're going to retrieve Sergeant Parks." The group cheered.

"Looks like we're heading to Sayatta!" Jonathan exclaimed. Both of their Griffins landed.

"We need to let the attack force strike first, so we can be less noticeable. In which case, I have a mission of my own for us to carry out."

"Breaking orders?" Jonathan asked. "I'm not sure I like the sound of that."

"I have permission from Chrystar himself to carry it out." Roy climbed on Skyquill and everyone else climbed on board.

"What are we doing?"

"You got your sactalines in?" Roy asked. Jonathan put them into his uniform.

"I do now," Jonathan answered as they took off into the sky. "Are you going to tell me what this super secret mission is about?"

"We're retrieving two people from the outskirts of Sayatta."

"Who?"

"Abby and Alexander's parents."

# 22

**BY THE TIME** Roy and Jonathan reached the outskirts of Sayatta, it was already covered in darkness. Roy shifted nervously, searching the ground below them, hoping he could locate the Reno residence.

Finally, in the darkness, he was able to see the clearing and house, horrified to find it looking run down and broken. His mind began reeling, hoping and praying that somehow Norah and Victor were alive, and he wouldn't be forced to have to tell Abby and Alexander that their parents had died.

"Put down in the wooded section. There are a few clearings," Roy instructed.

"Doesn't look good. I wonder if the Alliance is to blame for it," Johnathan said.

"We're going to find out real soon." They both descended and dismounted their Griffins. Checking their weapons and making sure they had enough arrows, Roy and Jonathan moved ahead in silence.

"What's the plan?" Jonathan asked. Everyone else huddled around.

"Two men must stay and watch over the Griffins," Roy explained. "Two more run recon and make sure the area is clean. I want to be the only one approaching the house. If they see anyone else, they may not show themselves."

They nodded their agreement and did as they were ordered. They approached the edge of the clearing and looked out at the house.

“You think anyone's alive?” Jonathan asked in a hoarse whisper.

“Keep me covered. I'm going in.”

Roy stepped out into the clearing, taking slow careful steps as he approached the abandoned house. For just a brief second, Roy's heart surged, thinking he had seen a small amount of light inside the house.

He walked up to the front porch and stepped over the front door which was laying on the ground. Inside offered broken furnishings and glass shards everywhere. Roy's heart sank with each second that passed.

“Hello?” Roy called out. “It's me, Roy!” For a moment no signs of life came to his ears. “Anyone home?” Finally, a quick shuffling could be heard and to Roy's amusement it was coming from right under his feet. He stepped back moments before a small trapdoor opened up right next to where he was standing.

“Is that actually you?” Victor asked as they climbed out of the hole.

“I'm glad to see the two of you,” Roy replied as both of them gave him a hug.

“What are you doing here?” Norah asked. “Where are the other three?”

“Sorry, they're not here. There will be time to talk about that later. What happened here?”

“The Alliance came through, and removed most of the people in the area,” Norah explained. “They claimed it was for safety. But I don't have any idea where they've put everyone. Our house was heavily damaged and caught in the middle of a fire fight last night.”

“At least it's still standing,” Roy said, trying to be positive.

“What happens now?” Victor asked.

“We get you out of here,” Roy said, moving towards the door and looking out. “Jonathan, how are things looking?”

"Not good," came the reply, though in a whisper. "Our landing must have been spotted by the Hentariains, because the area's crawling with them now. It's going to be a fight to get you out of there. How many with you?"

"Two. How many extra sets of armor do we have?"

"Two."

"Good. Armor!" Roy yelled. Victor and Norah both jumped in astonishment as two dark green sactalines flew from their spot on the Griffins and were drawn to Roy's hands. He handed them to Norah and Victor who were stunned.

"I'm not sure what to say, but I do have a few questions," Victor stated.

"We've got time for two questions. Make it quick."

"What is this?"

"It's armor. Tap it." They did as he instructed, amazed at the outcome.

"I had no idea the Hentar Academy taught things like this," Norah exclaimed.

"They don't. We never went to the Hentar Academy. Instead we found a better option, one that now stands against the Alliance, who is the Hentar Academy. We're part of the Kingdom."

"The Kingdom?" Victor asked.

"Hate to cut you short, but if you don't get out now, you never will," Jonathan's reply came.

Roy motioned for Victor and Norah to come to the door. He grasped his crossbow and looked out the window.

"When I say go, run as fast as you can towards that tree on the far side. Got it?" Norah and Victor hesitantly nodded. "Jonathan, we're coming out hot!" He looked to the two of them. "Go!"

All three of them bolted from their spot and ran out into the open. The clearing was lit up with a flurry of Tantine arrows streaking across the opening. Most of the arrows fell harmlessly into the dirt, but the others all struck the house, destroying it the rest of the way. Jonathan and the rest of the men all fired on the Hentarian warriors, taking many of them by surprise but also managing to draw their fire away. The three of them entered the forest, frantically running until they reached the Griffins. Jonathan and everyone else followed close behind, quickly jumping into their positions.

"What is this thing?" Norah exclaimed.

"Get on now and ask later!" Victor cried. They jumped on, instantly showered with arrows. The armor on their uniforms, as well as that on the Griffins, was lit up with explosions. Although Roy had gotten used to explosions happening all around him, he had never quite imagined it being anything like this. They quickly soared into the sky, leaving the skirmish behind them.

"Are you alright?" Roy asked. Victor and Norah both stared at him with a thousand questions plaguing him.

"We're speechless," Victor said for the both of them.

Roy smiled.

"There's a lot we need to catch up on."

"Indeed, and unfortunately we don't have time. I'll be headed on a mission in just a little bit. But right now we need to hook you up with a ride back to Granyon.

"Granyon? Where's that?" Norah asked.

"I'm sorry, I know this is a lot to take in. But you'll be safe there, that's the important thing."

"Roy, there's a transport Griffin collecting refugees a mile from here," Jonathan reported.

"Good, let's stop there."

They quickly covered the distance and landed in the forest where people were slowly boarding a Griffin, far larger than any Roy had ever seen. Roy got off and walked Norah and Victor to the Griffin.

"I'm sorry we have to part so quickly," Roy said.

Norah looked at him, a light shining in her eyes. "I have no idea what exactly is happening, but you are a fine young man and I am very proud of you. Thank you for doing what you have, and we both look forward to learning what you have learned."

Roy smiled, having never gotten a compliment like that before in his life. He embraced them both.

"I have this for you," he said, pulling an envelope out of his pocket. "When you are unloading give this to the guide and he'll take you right to the house of the A-Team, as it's now called. Abby's already there, as well as several more of our team." They embraced again and then without hesitating, climbed on their Griffins and were lost to the sky.

# 23

**THE CITY OF SAYATTA** could be seen from a great distance away. The city was lit with explosions and the sounds of fighting, while the air above the city was filled with Dreygars and Griffins as they battled for control of the airspace.

"Goodness, it looks like something from Star Wars," Roy commented, mostly thinking to himself.

"What's Star Wars?" Jonathan asked.

"Sorry, just an old off-worlder reference."

"Your world must be confusing. You wanted to name your Griffin Skywalker, which doesn't make any sen—"

"And this is coming from a guy who named his Griffin, 'Griff?"

"Fair enough," Jonathan conceded. "What's your play? How do we know where Sergeant Parks is? This is a big city."

"Let's skip the air battle over head. We go in full speed, flying low through the streets. You get behind me. Archers, be ready to shoot anything, but don't shoot a single citizen. Armed thugs only!"

"You still haven't told me how we're going to know where we are or where we're going," Jonathan pointed out.

"The last report I was given was that they think there are a number of hostages held in the senate chambers."

"So we're headed right for the belly of the beast?"

"Yes, we are. Hang on tight, everyone!" In an instant Roy pushed Skyquill into a steep descent. Jonathan followed. Within a few moments they were passing only feet over the walls of the city and into the war torn city streets.

The people were a blur as the Griffin's sped through the city, having to climb or descend at times depending on how close the buildings were. Explosions occasionally came from the ground fighting, but for the most part they were contained to missed shots from the air.

"Do you know where the senate chambers are?" Jonathan asked.

"Kind of."

"Kind of?"

"Well, I've only been there once. How hard can it be?"

"I guess we're going to find out."

They banked hard to the right, both pilots surveying the city as it flew under them.

"There's something about this that I'm not liking," Jonathan said.

"What do you mean?"

"Look on the horizon." Roy looked straight ahead, seeing what Jonathan had. A great structure of rock and metal towered in a dome shape over the Senate chambers. On top a single lone yellow sactaline glowed brightly.

"That's definitely new," Roy concluded.

"We're not going to go unseen by them," Jonathan said. Roy didn't have to ask what he meant. He was able to see hundreds of men, stationed all along the perimeter and at different levels. Arrows flew towards them, a number of them striking the armor on the Griffins.

"Shoot as many as you can!" Roy ordered. "If we take more hits like this, we won't last long." Their men returned fire, their arrows finding their targets. A few of the men shot at the structure, but no damage was inflicted.

"If we can't shoot that thing, how are we going to do anything?"

Roy pondered a million possibilities in a matter of a seconds.

"Pull up and get to a safe place!" Roy ordered. "We're going to ditch our Griffins for the moment and go on foot. I have a crazy idea but it might get us through the door."

"Will this plan also have a way out the door?"

"Still working on that."

"Comforting. I thought you would have a plan."

"I do have a plan . . . don't get killed!" They quickly climbed into the sky and soon found themselves putting down on a rooftop a few blocks away from the formidable complex that loomed in front of them. They grabbed the bags of sactalines from the Griffins, and then sent them away.

"What is this crazy plan?" Jonathan asked, the rest of the group gathered around.

"From our fly over, it looks like the doorways glow with the same color of the sactaline on top of the dome. If I'm right, that means we won't be able to get through the doors as long as the sactaline is still there. My plan is to have someone climb up to the top and take it."

Everyone stirred.

"Just when I think you can't come up with anything crazier . . . I like the plan."

"Volunteers to climb it?" Roy asked.

Three people raised their hands. They descended to the ground in record time and soon found themselves running through the chaotic war zone on the ground. They fired multiple arrows, saving several citizens from death.

They reached the Senate Chambers and the three people who had volunteered quickly and quietly slipped into the shadows and when they had found a part with no guards, began climbing.

The rest of them remained hidden for nearly ten minutes as they waited and watched the men climbing to the top of the dome. A few minutes later, several guards fell and rolled to the ground from atop the dome. In an instant the yellow sactaline vanished and so did the glowing lights around all the doors. The soldiers began looking up towards the top, leaving their post when they spotted the men.

"Three of you give them a hand with defense. Everyone else, this is our chance. Lets go!" Roy led the way, shooting his bow at a soldier who was running towards them. Roy reached for another arrow but realized he didn't have any. "Bolt!" In an instant, another sactaline had rushed to him and supplied him with more arrows.

By the time they reached the doorway in the dome it had been all but deserted, and they were able to walk through and stop to look at their surroundings.

Ominous shadows lurked around every corner and the flashes from explosions everywhere in and above the city lit up the dome in strange and eerie ways.

"Where are we going now?" Jonathan asked. Roy looked around.

"This way!" a voice said. They looked to see Chrystar running up behind them. Though he was dressed for battle, everyone else still stared at him confused. "What? I'm not going to send everyone into battle and not do battle myself? What kind a ruler would I be if I hid behind everyone else like a coward?"

Still none of them spoke.

"Well, why are you standing there like a bunch of statues? We have a Sergeant to rescue!"

"How did you get here?" one of the other men asked. Chrystar gave them a look.

"If you believe in me, then I will always be with you." Without further delay they followed Chrystar through the halls and corridors of the Senate

Chambers.

"He's being held through these doors," Chrystar said. "Intelligence said there are fifty soldiers guarding them. Several Hentarian Knights and Lucerine himself are said to be in the building."

"The gang's all here then?" Jonathan asked.

"Yes, take your team and position them on the balconies surrounding the whole structure," Chrystar ordered. "Roy and I have another thing or two to discuss, and then we'll be along." Jonathan immediately took the men and did as Chrystar had said.

"What's going on?" Roy asked.

"We're getting to a very critical moment."

"How so?"

"I've recently been informed that among all this chaos, there are select people looking for you."

"Me, why?"

"They hope to gain from it."

"Gain what? Money? I don't—"

"They are after you, and you alone."

"What for?"

"I have a few guesses. Three in fact," Chrystar replied.

"They want to get into the other world?"

Chrystar nodded.

"But why?"

"Who knows?"

"Can they even do that?"

"As of yet, they've never succeeded. I say this to remind you that if you needed to hide out for whatever reason, the world where you came from would be a good place to do that."

"Roy!" came Jonathan's voice through the sactaline.

"What is it?"

"I've got a shot on Lucerine. Do I take it?"

Roy hesitated.

"Roy, did you hear me?"

"I heard you. I'm thinking."

"Well think faster, I have about five more seconds before he's out of range." Silence followed. "Roy?"

"Stand down!" Roy exclaimed. He could hear Jonathan sighing on the other end.

"I know you have a reason, but why?" Jonathan asked.

"Because he's unarmed, and if we kill him in such a fashion how are we any different than he is?"

"I see your point, but I'm not sure how that will help us win the war."

"It's not a physical war we're fighting." Roy said. Jonathan and everyone else understood. Roy turned to face Chrystar. "Back to our earlier conversation. I have no desire to leave."

"You may have to."

"Is it even possible to leave?" Roy asked. "Gideon's father never found it."

"It *is* possible to leave. The door in your cabin is unique among the others. It will not reveal itself to a person in this world unless they have learned everything that they were *meant* to learn. You were *meant* to come here, Roy Van Doren, for such a time as this. It did not happen by accident."

"Have you been to my world?"

"I am in your world as I am in this one. Also, I may have been the one who fixed your truck and cabin."

Roy pondered the meaning of everything. "Even if I did go back, it's been months since I was in my cabin. What do I do about money and food and things of those nature?"

"Pay for it with this." Chrystar reached under his coat and grasped an object, setting it in Roy's hand. Roy felt inside and brought the object closer to him, chills running up and down the spine.

It was about a foot long, three inches wide, and a brilliant gold color. There were carvings that ran along the entire thing.

"I found this on the mountain the day I crashed my truck. I threw it away. This is beautiful, but what do I do with it?"

"If you were to sell that in your world, you would have a pretty penny," Chrystar said. "I'm strongly advising you hide out in the other world until it's safe. This is getting more dangerous for you then you know!"

"I'm not sure I could bring myself to leave this world. I love it here. How could I leave?"

"Sometimes drastic steps need to be taken. "

"If I leave, can I come back?"

"It may be a possibility, but I'm not going to answer that question at this time."

"Why not?"

"Because this is a measure of your heart and a matter of trust. Do you trust that I have something great in store for you? Do you trust that I can see where people can't? I do not want to see you destroyed, and it is always your choice to heed my advice or scoff at it. For I know the plans I have for you. They are plans for good and not for disaster, to give you a future and a hope.

"The more you cling to your life the more you will lose it. For you cannot serve two masters. You have your life here, yes, but you also have your life back home."

"I don't have a life back home."

"Not true," Chrystar countered. "You have a life and a family back home, as well as here."

Roy looked away, with fear in his heart. "The choice is yours, as it always is."

Roy pondered the words and followed behind Chrystar as he started briskly down the hall. In the dim lighting Chrystar was hard to see and soon faded from sight altogether. Roy began to grow more afraid. He wanted to call out to Chrystar, but refrained from doing so. His voice would carry much too far in a place like this.

The next thing Roy knew, he was knocked off his feet and landed hard against the wall. Then the whole world spun into blackness as his head touched the floor.

* * * *

Roy's head throbbed as he woke up. He squinted, trying to focus his eyes on the world around him. He was bound and sitting in the middle of the senate chambers. Up above, the battle in the sky could still be seen and the sound of explosions throughout the city reminded him he was still in a war zone.

The sactaline that had been taken by Roy's men had either been replaced or put back as it appeared they were once again protected from the war. He stole a glance at his uniform, still seeing the sactalines within it glowing brightly. Curious that they hadn't been taken from him. He searched his surroundings. What had happened to the rest of his men?

Roy sat in a group of fifteen people who were back to back. Roy strained to try to see, but only able to clearly see the person he was sitting next to.

Sergeant Parks.

He had been beaten badly, but otherwise he seemed okay, and was busy studying everything.

"Nice to see you, Roy," Parks said, sounding strangely comfortable.

"Thanks. I was sent to rescue you. I guess I did a real good job, didn't I?"

"Don't beat yourself up too much. It's war. Things don't always go as you plan."

"I'll have to remember that," Roy said. "So what do they want you for?"

"Because I knew *you*, an off-worlder."

"It seems everyone's after me. I just can't figure out why."

"I've quit trying to figure out why, because most of the time it doesn't make sense to me. Turns out they've been searching for off-worlders and their offspring for the past six months. It's a wonder Gideon wasn't targeted."

"Gideon's injured right now. Perhaps there's a hidden blessing in that."

"It's keeping him alive. I don't know what they are looking for, but when this party started there were fifty of us."

"We don't have much time," Roy said.

"I know, but we're kind of stuck."

"So you say. I say we start working on each other's ropes and wait for an opportune moment," Roy said.

"Are you saying you have a plan to get us out of here?" Parks asked.

"Not really, but we have to try, right?" They lightly talked and sat back to back carefully trying to feel the ropes on the other person and work them loose. The guards who watched them were motionless and stoic, seeming to not care if they talked or not.

A feeling of dread filled the room as two cloaked figures entered. The pair moved swiftly and made directly for Roy. As they approached, Roy identified the second figure as Lucerine who he had met only once; and he hadn't enjoyed it the first time either. The two hushed their conversation as they approached and Lucerine glared down at him.

"Is this Van Doren?" Lucerine asked the other person.

"Yes, my lord," a woman's voice said. Roy's ears perked up, recognizing Tarjinn's voice.

"Tarjinn! So nice to see you again!" Roy greeted. Lucerine glared at him, and Roy was struck across the face.

"Do not speak unless asked to speak!" Lucerine exclaimed. He turned to some guards. "Untie him and bring him at once."

"Am I special or something?" Roy asked, working the rest of his ropes loose. Lucerine and everyone else paused mid-stride as though they hadn't expected him to speak. "What, are you deaf?"

"Roy!" Parks scolded under his breath, while getting the rest of his ropes free. They both held their position.

"You are bold, Van Doren," Lucerine said. "Far too bold. It's only a shame I didn't realize it the first day I met you."

"Sorry to disappoint," Roy replied. Lucerine studied him warily, as though he was a scientific experiment. "So what's your play? We're all tied up and don't know why. Care to enlighten us?"

"No, I don't!" Lucerine exclaimed.

"What are you afraid of? You're in your own mini fortress with more than enough troops to kill us if needed," Roy argued. "I can see the yellow sactaline must be back in place because your force fields are up again."

"Force field?" Tarjinn asked.

"I know, foreign term to you. Not surprised—"

"Silence! Or I will make you silent!" Lucerine thundered. "You are all being examined to see how much you know of the world beyond. I very much wish to get into that world, for it holds a vast amount of things that I desire! Tarjinn is gifted in the arts of reading a person's heart and soul. If you know something and are lying to us . . . she'll know. You'll be tortured and tormented until you have no choice but to cave to our every demand. I can assure you that every moment that you hold out on us will be like living through hell. If you do not know anything then we will save you the trouble of torture and kill you."

"So you want to know?"

"Where the entrance to the other world is," Tarjinn stated calmly.

"No."

Lucerine struck him in the face.

"You will regret your decision!" Lucerine said. "We'll take him with us. Kill everyone else. We leave for Bruden at once." Guards reached for Roy.

"I'll never tell you where the entrance is."

"Oh, but you will. Here's the thing, Van Doren. As many friends as you have, I can take them away. Kill them one at a time. Hurt them, torture them. Especially the whelp you're soft on. Oh yes, I know about her, and she shall be joining us very shortly."

Roy's mind was momentarily overcome with fear and anxiety. Did they actually have Abigail in custody? He looked down to the sactalines still glowing brightly in his uniform. He hoped someone was listening.

"If you have her, then bring her out now!" Roy declared. His last conversation with Chrystar played through his mind repeatedly. He understood now what he had to do.

"I will have her soon, and then I will force you to watch as I torture her, and in turn hurt you. You'll soon become very reasonable. You see, enough hurt and you'll begin to question the motives of Chrystar. Maybe even doubt the words of Chyrstar. Then I can step in."

"You'll never win this war you started."

"Are you a fortune teller now? But, pray tell, why won't I win?"

"Because all you have is hate. When you're full of hate, you can't see beyond it. You can't see the only thing that can change the world is a life filled with love and serving others."

"Your mind has been poisoned, Van Doren," Lucerine said. "Now take a good look at yourself. What good has *serving* others done for you? You are captured and are about to be tortured and perhaps killed. All for what?"

"For something greater than myself. For something greater, that I cannot see. I have come to know this in my heart. My story is part of a greater story, and that greater story . . . that's worth dying for, if it comes to that," Roy said. To this, Lucerine said nothing, but still stared intently at Roy.

As he spoke, Tantine arrows from the perimeter balconies flew towards Lucerine. The yellow sactaline atop the dome once again was extinguished, removing the protection that it provided. What seemed like a hundred Tantine arrows were fired from the sky, striking the dome. It exploded in spectacular fashion, sending all the flames and debris upward and outward.

Lucerine held his hands up and stopped all the arrows coming towards him. They hovered in the air, their light growing stronger as though some force was fighting against him.

In an instant he brought his hands together and the arrows collided and formed a large sphere that glowed blue. Roy guessed it was about the size of a basketball. He hurled it at Roy who quickly jumped out of the way. The building was shaken to the core as an enormous explosion devastated the senate chambers.

Everywhere the blue sphere landed or rolled was decimated. A half circle all around them had been reduced to rubble. Roy drew his sword and frantically searched for Tarjinn and Lucerine but they were nowhere to be seen.

Roy and Parks freed the others and led them across the ruined senate chambers until they were once again outside the great building. Jonathan and the others continued to cover them, firing arrows at anyone who stood in their way.

"Is everyone okay?" Roy asked.

"We lost a few in that explosion, no doubt," Jonathan replied. "But unfortunately, we have to keep moving." Their Griffins dropped out of the sky. Roy's heart surged as Abby was atop of his Griffin.

"What are you doing here?" Roy asked as everyone clamored on, finding enough crossbows and swords for everyone.

"You should know I'm horrible at listening to orders. My leg still hurts like crazy, but I snuck on someone elses Griffin when you left. Then I called to Skyquill and he came. It all worked out quite well I'd say."

"That it did."

Abby moved to the side, letting Roy get down into the pilot position, while she took up his crossbow. They pushed off into the sky, entering into a confusing maze of Tantine arrows. She laid down next to him, carefully aiming. They fought their way out of the city, both Griffins easily maneuvered through the tight and perilous airspace and with much effort escaped the city. For the moment they were alone in the sky.

"Has anyone heard from Savannah and Alexander?" Roy asked.

"Gideon has made contact with them. They are okay and are on their way to us."

"Good, because there's one more mission to carry out before we go back." Roy felt his pocket, feeling for the golden cylinder that Chrystar had given him.

"What is it?"

"I have to leave," Roy said.

Everyone looked at him.

"For whatever reason the Alliance is targeting me specifically. I don't completely understand it. If I stay with you, more of us will get killed. I need you to trust me on this."

Silence followed for a moment.

"Where do we have to go?" Savannah's voice came over the sactaline.

"I'm not exactly sure. But I think Abigail can get us close."

"Lead on, sister." Alexander's voice came over the Sactaline. Abby's eyes were filled with sorrow as she looked out to the horizon. She guided them over the dark landscape until they found a clearing close to where they thought the door would be.

Everyone landed and traipsed through the forest in complete silence. They eventually came to the cave that Abby and Alexander had first blown up on the Roy's first day here. A few minutes later they came to the spot that looked familiar to Roy.

They looked ahead, their breath all taken away as a searing light appeared in front of them. It slowly moved through the air, creating the outline of a great doorway.

"It's real!" Alexander exclaimed. Everyone else was speechless. Roy looked at it, feeling both joy and pain. Their thoughts were derailed by arrows that streaked through the airspace above them. They all ducked for cover as the group of Griffins and Dreygars flew overhead and disappeared.

"I hate to rush things, but we need to be in the sky yesterday!" Jonathan exclaimed. Everyone began following him.

"Can you come back?" Abby asked, her voice faint.

"I don't know. But I need to leave. For a while anyway."

"I understand," she said, falling silent.

Roy's heart wavered, reconsidering for a moment. "Chrystar highly suggested that I should do this." Abby didn't respond. He tapped the green sactaline and it came out of his uniform, for the moment he put it in his pocket.

"Come with me," Roy whispered in her ear.

"What?"

"Chrystar never said I had to go alone."

Abby looked at him again, hope visibly stirring. "What are you saying?"

"Marry me."

"Are you serious?"

"Yes. I am. I don't know if I'll be able to come back right away, and if that happens there's one thing I want to take with me from this world. Abigail Vivian Reno . . . will you marry me?" The smile on her face gave him the answer he had been hoping for as she took his hand in hers. Roy reached into his pocket and put the sactaline back into his uniform.

"Listen up everybody. Mark this location well. But make sure no Hentarian Knights ever step foot here. I have to leave and I hope to return soon. Also, it seems Abigail is coming with me." To this a seemingly endless chorus of exclamations came through the sactaline.

"Does this mean what I think it means?" Alexander asked, finally able to make his voice heard over everyone else.

"Yes, it does!" Abigail exclaimed.

"Good luck, Mrs. Van Doren!" Alexander exclaimed. Though they couldn't see anyone they could tell everyone else was smiling.

"I look forward to hopefully seeing you all soon, but if it's a while, stay strong and keep true to Chrystar. He is a wise and just ruler." They could hear explosions in the distance.

"Sorry to run guys, but we have company here," Jonathan explained.

"We understand. Good luck. And goodbye," Roy tapped the sactaline and he stuffed it again in his pocket.

He reached out to the door in front of them and grasped the fancy golden handle and pushed it open. Only darkness could be seen on the other side. "You ready?" He asked Abigail. Her face beamed, as they stepped through the door.

*    *    *    *

Everyone else watched from the sky as the two of them stepped through the door. Once they had, the door vanished, as though it had never been there.

To Be Continued...